Springtime at Catoctin Creek

Catoctin Creek: Book Three

Natalie Keller Reinert

Natalie Keller Reinert Books

This is a work of fiction. Names, characters, businesses, places, events, locales, and incidents are either the products of the author's imagination or used in a fictitious manner. Any resemblance to actual persons, living or dead, or actual events is purely coincidental.

Copyright © 2021 Natalie Keller Reinert

Cover Photo: Elis.kadl/depositphotos

Cover Designer: Natalie Keller Reinert

Interior Formatting: Natalie Keller Reinert

All rights reserved.

ISBN: 978-1-956575-10-1

Books by Natalie Keller Reinert

The Catoctin Creek Series

The Grabbing Mane Series

The Eventing Series

The Alex & Alexander Series

The Show Barn Blues Series

The Hidden Horses of New York: A Novel

Chapter One

Nadine

A sweet breeze blew across the Maryland countryside, perfumed with blossoms and bearing an appealing message from the sunny south: spring was on its way.

Nadine turned her nose up to the cool air and let it waft over her. That floral scent! The entire morning was saturated with it! She'd never learned much about flowers, their names and all that, so she couldn't guess what bouquets she was sniffing on the steady west wind this morning. She just knew the fragrance was enlivening her senses, making her feel chipper when a full mug of coffee had not, and giving her the energy she needed to get on with this day. She pushed locks of waving black hair back from her cheeks, tucking it behind her small ears, and turned her face full into that fragrant wind.

A thought, unoriginal but nonetheless sincere, ran through her mind: she simply loved springtime.

The idea made her laugh to herself. Loving springtime, what a concept! Who didn't, really?

Maybe Sean Casey. He was so contrary, he probably didn't like sunshine and rainbows, either. But Nadine had decided to not to worry about Sean Casey's opinions anymore. His likes, his dislikes, the women he flirted with. None of it was her concern. Sean was a coworker, and that was as far as things were going between them. She'd already wasted more than enough time on that man. Nadine closed her eyes briefly and put Sean out of her mind.

Of course, she was going to see him shortly, when he came downstairs to get to work, but for the moment, at least, she would live Sean-free. His pretty face could just go—vanish!

Behind her, a symphony of whinnies broke the morning quiet. Nadine opened her eyes and turned around, her hands immediately going to her wild hair as the wind pushed it over her face, and watched the little herd of ponies galloping across the fenced pasture. Beneath their hooves, the rolling landscape shone with green, looking as if someone had laid Easter grass across last year's beige stubble. The nimble ponies flowed across the slopes with all the grace of a flock of migrating birds.

Nadine's heart crept up into her throat and stayed there as she breathed deep, thrilling herself with the sight of those spirited ponies. All that was left of the once-famous Elmwood herd, these six ponies were treasured members of the equestrian center's therapeutic riding and lesson programs. She could name all of them: that was Pumpkin, in front for once, then the gleaming alabaster coat of Ghost—

"Well, that's cute."

Sean's voice made Nadine's pulse jump as well as her feet. She put a hand to her chest, willing her heart to calm itself. Why was he always sneaking around and spooking her like that? Why couldn't he just stay in the barn—or better yet, up in his apartment under the rafters?

Bad enough she had to listen to Sean thumping around at night on the other side of her living room wall, bad enough she had to work with him in the afternoons, when the onslaught of riding lessons descended on the barn. Did he have to come down and bother her before breakfast, too, when hardly anyone was around and she could just soak up the beauty of one of Catoctin Creek's most beautiful farms? She was lucky to live here, lucky to be back in her hometown, lucky to be manager of this gorgeous equestrian center . . . so it would be nice if she could just enjoy a moment of downtime without Sean once in a while.

"What do you want?" she asked, working to keep her impatience from her tone.

"The ponies?" Sean said, looking down at her. "They're very cute."

"The ponies are magnificent," she retorted sharply, because calling Elmwood's priceless pony herd *cute* failed to take into account how majestic, how elegant, how sought-after these ponies were in the upper echelons of the horse show market. For decades, Elmwood ponies had taken pigtailed girls and serious-faced boys to championships, their pricked ears and soft dark eyes emanating professionalism as they jumped around manicured courses, laying their polished hooves into the soft footing just so. Elmwood ponies were many things, cute included, but she wasn't going to let Sean Casey get away with demeaning them with just one word of praise. They deserved dozens. "These ponies are *way* more than cute, Sean. Open up your eyes."

She glanced sidelong at him as she spoke, unable to resist taking in the view through her thick lashes. And it was a good view, as always. Sean was blessed with the looks of a Swedish prince. Or so Nadine had heard. Nikki down at the Blue Plate Diner had once told her Sean looked like a Nordic male model, and that was the source of all his problems in life.

Nadine had found it hard to sympathize. Her pale skin didn't win her any marks in the beauty department, especially paired with her wispy black hair that had to be pounded into submission with a round brush and an elastic band every morning, lest it puff up from her ponytail and get in her eyes while she was leading horses or mucking stalls. She had good green eyes, dark as forest leaves in midsummer, but no one else noticed them enough to remark on them, so she supposed it was probably just a personal preference, her own little vanity. Sean's eyes were a particularly shimmering ice-blue. Not that she ever looked at them, and—

He was grinning at her.

Grinning at her? He ought to be frowning at her. Why couldn't he just wake up and realize when she was insulting him? So frustrating. It was so difficult to throw Sean off his game. He was cheerful, chipper even, through the most challenging days on the farm. Even when their boss, Caitlin was being her usual chaotic self, Sean just carried on as if she wasn't making them crazy at all.

"I know they're good ponies, Nadine," he replied now, his voice amused. "I rode an Elmwood pony when I was a little kid, you know. Elmwood Bowtie. She was a leadline champion at Devon."

She hadn't known that. If she had, she would have hated him a lot more by now—something Nadine didn't even think was possible. Because oh boy, did she *hate* Sean Casey. Even if *hate was a strong word,* as her mother used to chide. Fine, Mom. She couldn't stand him. Did that get across the point?

Such a lying snake. Lying, flirtatious, cheap, lazy, good-for-nothing—just like every other man Nadine had been forced to work with. Ten long years of trying to make a career for herself as a professional horsewoman, and when she finally had the plum spot she'd always wanted, her boss had to go and hire Sean.

"You did not have an Elmwood pony," she huffed, turning her back on him and the landscape behind her. She hated to leave behind the galloping ponies, the flower-soaked breeze, but it was time to head back into the barn. Time to work. Anyway, the first blush of the beautiful morning had passed. There were high, icy clouds taking over the blue sky, and that lushly floral wind was growing a bit stiffer, too. There was a cold note to it which gave her the shivers. "Stop lying about your ponies. I'm going in to work on stalls."

"I'll help you." Sean tripped after her, taking care that his polished black field boots found all the dry spots in the muddy parking lot. "I have nothing else going on this morning. Just a couple horses to ride this afternoon before lessons."

Nadine kept her eyes resolutely forward. The big barn complex, with its double aisles and massive indoor arena attached at one end, loomed in front of them like an airplane hanger. "I have Richie and Rose to help me," she reminded him. "Three people's plenty to get stalls cleaned. Go do something else. Go polish your saddle."

"Three's plenty. Four's even better. Just let me get out of these boots."

She eyed his beautiful riding boots. Nadine was deeply covetous of those boots, which Sean kept in perfect condition even when the rest of his tack could sometimes fall into deplorable condition. She knew it was his best pair, not his everyday boots. "Why are you even wearing your good boots out here?"

"I was going to ride the new horse first thing this morning, and Caitlin was coming to watch with the owner. You know she likes to see me turned out all polished for clients. But it turns out he isn't coming until this afternoon, so there won't be time to ride him. All dressed up for nothing."

"Oh, right. Rosemary's horse. I'd literally forgotten about it." Yesterday, Nadine had prepped the last empty stall in the back aisle for Rosemary Beckett's incoming sales horse. Then a million other things had happened, in the course of a normal barn afternoon, and the new horse was crowded out of her brain. "Caitlin shouldn't have asked you to ride him as soon as he arrived, anyway. He should have time to settle in. I wouldn't ride him before Wednesday, at the earliest." Today was Monday; two days would be plenty of time.

Sean shrugged. "Caitlin said Rosemary wants him sold quickly, so the sooner I know what we're dealing with, the better. He could be very green, y'know? Rosemary gets her horses from auctions, so he doesn't come with any history."

"That's an even better reason not to push the poor horse." Nadine stopped in the barn entrance and peered down the front aisle, wondering if Richie and Rose, the grooms, had started mucking out yet. The big barn took several hours of hard work to clean each morning. They always started on the front aisle—so-called because it was the main barn aisle, lined with stalls housing the boarders, the paying customers. The "back aisle" was a little shorter and less trafficked, home to the farm horses and ponies, and dead-ending into storage below Nadine's apartment, while the front aisle led directly to the indoor arena, the barn offices, and the tack rooms.

She narrowed her eyes at the condition of her barn. The front aisle was a mess this morning. Blankets needed rehanging on their bars—Nadine liked them hung with hospital-like precision in perfect rectangles, their buckles tucked away out of sight—and that lovely spring wind had scattered hay everywhere. A bit of a mess while cleaning stalls was acceptable, but this was beyond normal limits. If Caitlin came down before they'd finished morning chores, she'd have a mini-meltdown. Nadine decided to ask Richie to use the leaf-blower to clear the aisle before they did stalls, while she fixed the blankets.

Assuming Sean went away. Why was he still hovering alongside her? Barn work wasn't his problem. He rode horses and taught riding lessons, and right now he didn't need to do either. Instead, he was still bleating at her about the new horse. The one who wasn't even here yet.

"I'm not going to push the horse, Nadine. Maybe have a little faith in me? Have I been hard on any of the other horses I've trained here?

Maybe he hadn't, but none of those horses had been challenges. Nadine knew tough horses, but she wasn't so sure Sean did. He rode with a stiff, elegant posture which told her he was more about theory than practice—more about looking pretty than riding effectively. Just the opposite of Nadine, as he was in every way imaginable. She sighed and turned back to him. "I'm just saying, you don't even know this horse. He could have been bouncing from barn to barn for months. He might be tired and miserable."

Sean raised a lazy eyebrow at her. "It's touching to see what faith you have in me. Nadine. I promise to be good to this tired, miserable, pathetic horse-tragedy you've built up in your mind. But, I still have to get him going. Sales horses are my responsibility, and I can't just waste time when Caitlin wants me selling, selling, selling—"

"Of course, you're very busy," Nadine agreed tartly. She turned on her heel, heading into the barn.

"I am very busy," Sean countered, chasing after her. "Wait, Nadine. Why are you mad at me now? I wanted to help you guys this morning!"

"Just go change your boots," she snapped. "If you come into a dirty stall in those boots, I'll kill you for boot abuse."

"I'm going to change them, we are literally walking towards my apartment where my other boots are—but listen, Nadine—" His hand rested on her arm, a soft gesture asking her to wait, to give him a chance.

Nadine froze. He'd touched her like this before, and more—giving a leg-up, steadying her while she dealt with a spooky horse, things like that—but they'd been buried under winter coats for most of the time he'd been here. Now, with his fingers pressing through her thin thermal shirt, she could feel those—feelings—again. The same feelings he'd set off with his casual touch when he'd first arrived here, six months ago. When Sean had first come to Elmwood to take on the riding instructor job, and she'd been such a foolish victim of his smile and his charm. She'd let him touch her arm, and felt the warm thrill his fingers gave her skin, and wanted more of it.

That first touch was burned into her brain—as was her reaction. She remembered the silly grin spreading across her face as she'd looked at him, but she didn't remember what she'd said. Or even what he'd asked. Probably something stupid and innocent, like if she knew where he'd left a pony bridle or if she could get a horse's mane pulled. Nothing which matched the magnetic reception she'd felt with his hand on her arm.

And then, after he'd taken those warm fingers away, she'd watched him march right over to Vonnie Gibbons, a middle-aged adult student who drove an Audi and dressed in perfectly matching riding outfits, right down to her thousand-dollar boots, and flash his movie-star smile at her.

Nadine's heart had sunk as she realized their connection was all in her head. The smiles, the charm, the soft touches, the thrills rippling through her at his touch: none of that meant anything. Sean Casey was just a big old flirt.

That's when she decided to hate him, and it had served her well ever since. Except, of course, for the whole working-together thing.

Now she tried to take a step back, flick away those burning fingers, but her feet didn't want to take her away, and her eyes didn't want to jerk from his. So she stood there, seething with a strange mixture of emotions, and let him talk as if anything he said mattered to her.

"Don't you want to stop fighting all the time?" he asked, his low voice charmingly pleading. "Wouldn't it be easier if we got along? I don't know how long I'll be here, but—"

"What does that mean?" Nadine interrupted, momentarily distracted. "You don't know how long you'll be here? Are you looking for another job?"

Sean dropped his hand to his side, his expression rueful. She missed the connection immediately, but at least she had the freedom to take a step back, as if those invisible magnets were slowly giving up their force. "No, I didn't mean to imply I'm looking for a new job, but, you know how it is. If the right thing came along..."

"Wait a minute. How could this not be the right thing?" Nadine was aware she should be encouraging him to apply far and wide to new jobs, preferably in California, or perhaps Germany, but she felt an irrational surge of loyalty to Caitlin and to Elmwood. She'd worked here a year now. She was proud of her work. And this place did things that mattered. Sean did things that mattered. "You have a good job. You're a riding coach with dozens of students, you have sales horses to ride and commission when they sell, you have access to a truck and trailer so you can go to shows, you have an apartment right up there—" she pointed up at the pair of barn apartments, their small windows overlooking the stalls and aisles. "I don't understand what else you could want."

Sean gave her a sideways smile. "I think you mean you don't understand what else *you* could want," he told her. "We're used to different things."

Nadine's lips slammed tight together. That did it. She was done talking to Sean for the morning. Arrogant, entitled, selfish...

She stalked up the aisle, mud flaking from her paddock boots with each step. It didn't matter if she made a mess now. She'd ask Richie to get out the leaf-blower and scour this aisle clean. Then they'd muck out, and he'd blow the aisle again to clear up their mess. By eleven o'clock, this barn would be spotless—just the way she always left it, six days a week.

She was aware of Sean's tread as he climbed the creaking stairs to his apartment, the involuntary slam of his front door as he pulled it tight in the swollen old frame. Then she knew he was on the little linoleum pad just inside his door, unzipping his field boots and tugging them free. She knew where he was, what he was doing, in part because her apartment was a clone of his, in part because when the barn was quiet she could hear his steps on the floorboards, and in part because, for some annoying reason, when Sean Casey was around, Nadine always knew it.

"Well, maybe he'll leave," she muttered, taking down a manure fork and tossing it into a wheelbarrow. "I bet we'd all be a lot happier without lazy Sean Casey in the barn."

Chapter Two

Sean

"They'll miss me when I'm not around," Sean told his mirror.

He'd left his boots in a heap by the front door and gone into the bedroom to change out of his good buff breeches—no reason to dirty them with barn chores when he had some jeans from yesterday which were only moderately dusty. Sean didn't bother cleaning stalls very often; it wasn't his job, technically, and he wasn't particularly good at it. But something about Nadine's attitude over the past few weeks had been needling at him, and he wanted to prove her wrong.

"She's got me cast as some kind of villain," he went on, "and that's just not true. Just because I don't want to live here forever, chasing around these kids and these old ladies who want to learn to ride? This isn't my *life*. And Nadine just doesn't understand."

He sighed at his reflection, who gazed back at him with sympathy. The only sympathetic person in his life. Sean appreciated his mirror with a devotion which he knew was quite sad. It wasn't because he liked his appearance so much. It was because he had no one else to talk to.

"She's so difficult. You shouldn't care what she thinks."

But Sean knew he cared. He'd always cared what Nadine thought—what *everyone* thought.

"You're too dependent on other people, Seany-boy." He gave himself a crooked smile and rubbed his hair back from his forehead. "But dammit, I wish she liked me. Even if I don't like her very much. Ugh. I know that's dumb. But it's who I am."

Sean was not above admitting this to himself; he didn't have to pretend to his reflection that he didn't care what other people thought of him. Why sugarcoat the truth, he often thought—he *was* hyper-aware of what other people thought of him, and he liked to think he was self-aware enough to recognize this fault in his personality. Since Nadine was his closest coworker, a person he saw every day without fail and often worked alongside in the afternoon crush of tacking and untacking lesson horses, it stood to reason that he'd have an unnatural interest in what she thought of him.

Perfectly reasonable state of affairs.

He did need to get over it, though. If Simone could have seen him struggling to get Nadine's attention, hoping to get a shred of approval from his unrelenting colleague, she would have laughed at him, then told him to suck it up. When Simone had been around, he hadn't been so obsessed with his mirror. His old friend, a fellow junior rider on the all-consuming show circuit which they'd devoted their lives to from the age of eight, Simone was the opposite of Nadine—she built him up, told him how great he was.

And when he'd taken the job at Elmwood, she'd told him not to forget who he was. Not to get too comfortable.

"You're better than up-down lessons and commuters looking for cheap board outside the city," she'd informed him, leaning against her bedroom dresser. She'd been wearing a long-tailed dress shirt, her tan legs bare, her honey-colored hair falling to her shoulders in soft waves. Sean had been in the doorway; he'd been crashing on her couch for the past month. Trying to figure out what to do with his life now that everything he'd ever known had come crashing down. "Don't forget that you're Sean Casey, you've got championships behind your name and a big career ahead of you. I want you back on the circuit by next summer. Saugerties, baby!"

"It's going to be pretty hard without my horses," he'd grumbled, and then he'd been ashamed, because Simone's best horses were gone, too. Not his fault, but it sure felt like it. It felt like it had all been his fault. They'd both had to start over, thanks to his family's foibles.

But at least Simone had money backing her up. Simone's grandmother was happy to front her the money for three new horses to take to Florida for the winter. Sean's family wasn't so generous—or so free to spend, according to his mother, who said they weren't spending a dollar in the United States as long as his father's associates were under investigation.

Sean wasn't a dummy. He knew fraud didn't just happen with no one knowing about it. And he knew his parents weren't coming back from their Bahamian beach house in time to save his floundering career. If he wanted to get back into the upper echelons of the horse show world, he'd have to find a way there himself. And that meant finding someone else's money.

It wasn't in a job teaching kids and hopeful re-riders at a western Maryland equestrian center, but there might be someone in that audience who wanted to enjoy the thrill of owning top show horses even if riding at that level wasn't an option for them. Finding that person was Sean's goal, Simone reminded him.

She had crossed the shining hardwood in three quick steps. She looked up at him, lips parted, and patted his cheek like a doting grandmother. "We'll be waiting for you, Sean. Hurry back. Save some money, chat up some investors, and you'll be back in the ring in no time. I'll see you when I come back from Florida."

Simone was still in Florida, spinning out the remainder of the Winter Equestrian Festival in sunny West Palm Beach. She'd head back to Virginia in a few weeks, spending May at the family farm, before the horses shipped to upstate New York for summer showing in Saugerties. Simone, like everyone in their circles, followed the most Eastern Seaboard's most temperate weather: warm days and cool nights were their ideal environment.

Sean had spent the winter shivering under the heaviest snow season in Maryland history. It had felt particularly unfair for his first winter out of Florida since he was twelve years old. His parents, lounging on their island paradise, had not been sympathetic. His friends, riding under the Floridian sun, had not been good at keeping in touch. The winter's chill under these rafters had been more than just meteorological.

Out of sight, out of mind.

Now, Sean looked around his tiny bathroom, an extension of a minuscule bedroom, the natural child of a miniature living room-kitchen combo. This was what he had accomplished on his own, without his dad's credit card.

Not much.

When he'd first arrived here, he'd felt like he couldn't breathe in the dark little apartment. Now, it wasn't home, but he was used to it, and that somehow felt worse. He'd been here six months. How long would Simone really wait for him? The last time they'd talked, she'd promised she'd hold space and stalls in Saugerties for him under her name. But that had been a month ago. What if she changed her mind? Or simply forgot about him?

He had to get out of Elmwood. He needed horses, and money. And that meant jumping on every single opportunity.

Simone had been the one to suggest targeting the older divorcees with money. Sean knew he was naturally good with women, so the premise had seemed simple. Find a woman looking for meaning in her life through horses. Get close to her over the course of her riding lessons. Convince her that while she'd never get back those childhood dreams of stardom, she could still be part of the horse show elite.

All she had to do was invest in him.

It seemed so simple, and Elmwood was always brimming over with rudderless women showing up with a mid-life crisis and a fat wallet. So why did Sean keep striking out? Things always seemed to edge towards the physical. That was why. And he hadn't been willing to take things to that extreme. Not yet, anyway.

Martha Lane was his best shot, but he was running out of time, and he was starting to wonder just what he was capable of doing to get out of Maryland. Out of Catoctin Creek. Out of Elmwood

Equestrian Center, and the endless cycles of up-down riding lessons.

He looked at himself once more in the mirror. On the surface, Sean thought he looked just fine: clean-shaven with cheeks baby-soft, eyes their usual ice blue, and no hint of puff beneath them even though he'd been up half the night, looking at ads for horses which cost more than he'd make in a year. Wondering which ones he could show to Martha that would make her aspirational heart go flippity-flop. He settled on a few different ones every night, mentally spending hundreds of thousands of dollars of someone else's money. But he never made a move.

Well, today, he was going to show them to her.

Martha's riding lesson wasn't until two o'clock; she would be volunteering in the one o'clock volunteer session with the therapeutic riding club, which met at Elmwood three afternoons per week and early on Sunday. The therapy sessions were hosted by Elmwood and used the lesson program's oldest, most reliable horses and ponies, but they were run by the Catoctin Creek Volunteer Women's League and neither Caitlin Tuttle, the owner of Elmwood, nor Sean, nor Nadine, had anything to do with them.

Their attentions were reserved for the for-profit side of things. The therapeutic riding program was ostensibly an exercise in charity and community, but Caitlin used it to recruit new students into the general riding program. Then they became Sean's responsibility: he would teach them, get them hooked, and sell them a horse to board. That was where Martha had come from, and in Caitlin's eyes, that was where Martha was heading: the rank and file of casual amateur rider paying monthly fees to Caitlin to care for her horse.

"This has to work, Sean," he told his reflection. "Because if it only goes halfway and Caitlin finds out, you're a dead man."

His phone buzzed: Caitlin, wondering where he was. Sean grimaced and hopped on the linoleum by his apartment door, tugging on his slightly more serviceable paddock boots. Still beautiful and hand-crafted; a year ago, these boots had never seen the inside of a stall, unless it was to slip a halter over a horse's head when no groom was available to tack up for him. Things had changed, for both Sean and his boots. And they both had new scars to show for those changes: a long diagonal line across the punched toe-cap of his left boot from a dragged hoof; a similar line across the top of his forearm from a dragged pony tooth. Sean had been astonished that an Elmwood pony would bite, but Caitlin had laughed and asked him where he thought the bad ones stayed?

"I don't sell all of them, Seany-boy," she'd told him, pouring lurid red Betadine over the wound while Sean grasped his arm and tried not to howl. "Hold still, you big baby! Is this really the first time you've ever been bit by a horse?"

His boss, ladies and gentlemen.

His phone buzzed again. "Coming, coming," he groused, and pelted down the stairs.

Caitlin was leaning against the wall at the bottom of the stairs, looking at her phone, her lower lip stowed under her gleaming top teeth. Her bobbed hair fell over her face like a golden veil. When she heard his footsteps approaching, she looked up, smiling. "Just the man I want to see," she informed him.

This was rarely good news. Sean glanced up the barn aisle and saw Nadine peeking from a stall door, smiling. Also bad news for Sean. Their eyes met, and she jerked her head back inside.

He managed to force a pleasant expression for Caitlin, who often reminded him she did not like to be thought of as a "boss," but who also demanded sunny dispositions and perfect obedience from her staff. "Good morning, Caitlin. What's up?"

"A couple of good things." Caitlin waved her phone at him as if it displayed all the answers. "The Robinsons are definitely on for tonight to look at Bailey. Make sure the daughter rides him in her lesson. You should get on him this afternoon to tighten him up. Nadine will get him polished before they get here. She's going to pull his mane and bathe him. But that means you need to help tack the first group lesson, because she'll be busy. Don't forget to punch lesson cards. I don't want anyone riding for free. Also: the hunter pace is a go for the second-last weekend in May. That gives us almost eight weeks. I talked to my contractor, and he's going to start on fences this week. So that's good, but I'll need you to start planning outdoor lessons to get kids prepped—everyone needs to put in a good showing or it's not a very good commercial for our services, now, is it? Oh, and the Beckett horse arrives at twelve-thirty, so be ready to ride him right after Rosemary leaves. One o'clock, hopefully."

Sean blinked at this list of events, all of which meant work falling directly upon his shoulders. He sometimes suspected he'd done this very thing to his old staff. He used to stroll into his barn relaxed and happy, content that he had the best employees in the whole world to manage his affairs for him, not quite understanding that every chore he added to their day was a task which required their brains and muscles to put in a full effort on top of everything else they were already facing. When they'd occasionally protested, as he was about to do, he'd just scowled and wondered why they were being so difficult.

He cleared his throat and tried to look apologetic. "One o'clock's tough for me today; I have to teach Martha Lane at two, and Veronica's volunteers have the arena at one, anyway. And if you want me to add Bailey to the day, I have to rearrange my schedule because I'm already riding Chocolate Kiss and Calypso. Any way we can just do the Beckett horse tomorrow?"

Caitlin looked at him as if he'd suggested killing the barn cat. "Sean, I need these things taken care of today. There isn't any way around them. I'm keeping the Beckett horse for free as a favor; every day he's here costs me money. So we start the process immediately. Does that make sense? I know you're not a barn owner, but I'm sure you want to run your own place someday—"

And she was off and running, talking down to him about expenses and employees and rates of return, not knowing that these were the things Sean really knew about, that he'd been lectured about all of this by his father since he was eight years old. Sean understood the dicey economics of using horses to make money. It was the practical stuff he was hazy on. The equine details he was now expected to handle every day, with the assumption that he was an expert. Mostly because he'd said he was an expert.

Luckily, someone else in the barn really was an expert in horse care and keeping, and she was the barn manager. Unluckily, that person was Nadine.

There was no way to be honest with her when he wasn't quite sure of something, like when he'd been asked to handle blanketing on the school horses last week, as Catoctin Creek shivered through a late spring cold snap. When Nadine saw that he hadn't crossed the leg straps, instead of just snapping them to the rings on their corresponding sides, she'd nearly lost her mind.

He hadn't realized something so trivial could matter so much—the leg straps were around the horses' hind legs, and nothing was dangling or dangerous—but he was never quite ready for how seriously some equestrians took their work. Which was why he'd never valued his old team as much as he promised himself he would, when he had some staff working under him again.

Handling things like crossing leg straps.

Nadine really had blown up at him about that. It was funny, considering what a weirdly minor little mess-up he'd made. And it wasn't like there were instructions somewhere on how to blanket horses. Different blankets had different straps, for heaven's sake. There wasn't a universal school of horse blanketing he could have attended, which would have made sure he was on the same page as Nadine in all things leg straps. She was just always after him, dogging him for things which she would excuse in anyone else. Just yesterday she'd totally given Richie a pat on the back after he'd put the wrong saddle on Rainbow, and Richie knew it had been the wrong saddle when he'd done it. He'd just figured it wouldn't make any difference and that it saved time to leave it that way.

Sean had known it made a difference—Rainbow had a wide back, and Richie had chosen a saddle with a narrow tree, which would have pinched the horse—but instead of getting mad, Nadine had simply offered to help him switch out saddles so they'd still be on time before the kids arrived for their lesson. And she'd done it with a smile, besides, and Nadine had a pretty smile, not that Sean should even know, since she never turned it on him without some sort of coercion from Caitlin, like when they were being photographed for a series of candid shots in the new Elmwood Equestrian Center brochure. She'd smiled at him so many times that day, he'd felt like he'd met a new person.

He'd liked her.

"Sean!" Caitlin snapped her fingers at him. "Where's your brain?"

"Oh, uh . . ." He couldn't even answer. What had they been talking about? Sales horses. "The only way I can make it work is if I ride Bailey right now," he told her, hoping she hadn't been saying anything important while he'd been thinking about Nadine.

"Then go and do it," Caitlin sighed as if he was being impossibly slow. "Make sure you get every horse on your list ridden today. And notes in the training journal, please. Not just flatted twenty minutes. I want to know what you worked on and how the horse did. It's the only way to keep track of them all."

With that, his boss pushed away from the wall and went stalking off down the aisle, no doubt to bother Nadine a little more—although Nadine never seemed to mind Caitlin's roughshod mangling of the barn affairs she'd hired Nadine to handle—before she vanished into her office or went off to one of her many appointments and events. Sean looked down at his jeans and paddock boots, and sighed. He'd just changed into work clothes.

He went back upstairs to change back into his breeches and field boots.

He glanced over his shoulder at the barn below before he pushed open his door. He liked this view, even if the landing was narrow and the staircase vertiginous. He could see across the walls of all the stalls and right into some of them—Richie and Rose were visible cleaning stalls, and Nadine was standing in one, looking at Caitlin from across the barrier of a half-filled wheelbarrow. The few horses who stayed inside because of various lameness complaints were tugging at their morning hay or snoozing. Sean tried to look at them, but his gaze kept wrenching back to Nadine and Caitlin, wondering what they were talking about.

Somehow, he always suspected their whispering was about him. And he didn't know if that was because he was as vain as Simone had always told him, or if it was just because the powerhouses energizing both of those women kind of scared him, and it felt smart to keep his eyes on them. After all, he had his own schemes to keep close to his chest. If Caitlin found out he was planning to steal away Martha Lane for his own equestrian dreams, instead of meekly continuing to push her through the lesson mill process, she'd probably fire him. And if Nadine found out, she'd definitely tell Caitlin. He knew where his colleague's loyalties lay, and while he wished it were with him, he also knew it didn't matter. When he left, Nadine would stay, and they'd just hire a replacement. Like he'd never even happened.

Sad, really, to think he'd spent six months of his life here, and would likely spend two more—there would be no reason to leave before Simone opened up her house in Saugerties in June— without doing anything of value, without leaving a mark. The students, Caitlin, Nadine—they'd all forget him.

Caitlin turned away, heading off down the aisle, and suddenly Nadine's glance swept up to Sean. He froze for a minute, a deer in the headlights, and then he shoved his shoulder against his door, pushing it past the sticky jamb, and closed it firmly, feeling as if the cheap metal door was no match for his colleague's piercing green gaze.

Nadine saw right through him, and it scared him.

Chapter Three

Nadine

He was probably thrilled to be getting out of mucking stalls. Nadine glowered at the closed door for a moment, then went back to work. She liked mucking stalls; Sean didn't know what he was missing. This was the best time of her morning—with horses out in the paddocks, no boarders or students running around the barn asking her questions or making messes, and just the gentle babble of the light rock station Richie and Rose preferred in the background. To a seemingly endless loop of Billy Joel and Pink Floyd, Nadine worked her way through stalls each morning with her thoughts running wild and her manure fork working nearly on autopilot.

And after each stall was picked, the shavings left behind as pristinely cream-colored as possible, she had the pleasure of sweeping back the clean bedding from the door and beneath the feed and water buckets that lined the front wall, exposing the black rubber stall mats. It kept shavings from being wasted beneath the buckets or mixing too much with the hay they would toss into the front corner of the stall, so the practice had an efficient purpose.

But this pattern of black and beige also left the stall almost unbearably tidy. Nadine always paused to admire the straight line of shavings, the perfectly clean stall mats.

Afterwards, she could step away from that stall with a sensation of delicious pleasure; it was like leaving behind a perfectly clean hotel room for her favorite guests. She could have left a note that read *Housekeeping was here,* but horses couldn't read, and anyway they didn't care. They just wanted to eat hay and trash the place.

That was job security, right there.

Besides the simple pleasure and reliable routine of cleaning up after horses, every big move of Nadine's life had been premeditated and hashed out in a dirty stall. The decision to leave Catoctin Creek ten years ago had come from an idea hatched while cleaning a stall at Mike and Joe Remsen's barn, the horse traders who had hired her on when she was just a high schooler, desperate to learn about horses. The decision to come back and work for Caitlin had been tussled with, again and again, while she was cleaning around foal-heavy broodmares at Ryce Arabians, just on the other side of the Catoctin Mountains, after she had made a long and painful loop around Maryland and Pennsylvania, working and learning at a dozen different barns. If she hadn't gone to Mike and Joe's all those years ago and gotten a job cleaning stalls, would she have done something very different with her life? Probably, but only because she hadn't been able to give her life the proper meditation it required.

"And Sean doesn't get any stall-cleaning time, so he doesn't get any thinking time," she murmured, sweeping back the shavings from the door. "No wonder he's such an idiot."

She knew the words were unfair. Sean wasn't an idiot. He was just—well, he was just a liar and a flirt and lazy, besides. But a person could be all of those things and still be quite intelligent. In fact, Nadine figured, that was what made him dangerous. Unlike, say, her mother's boyfriend, a man who had been way too influential in Nadine's life. She'd left Catoctin Creek in part to teach her mother a lesson about Reg; she'd come back, in part, because Reg was back, and she wanted to keep an eye on her mom.

Kelly Blackwell was many things—a good painter, a well-meaning if incompetent mother for Nadine, a deeply committed vegetarian—but she was not a good judge of men, and Reg was a liar, a flirt, lazy, *and* an idiot. That last part made him dangerous in a different way than Sean. Dangerous because of the sort of people he could find himself associating with, and the kind of situations he could embroil her hapless mother.

Nadine wished she could wave a magic wand and convince her mother to dispense with Reg altogether, but since Kelly refused to see the worst in him—in anyone, really—the best she could do was live in the same town and take her mother to dinner at the Blue Plate once a week, for a check-in.

"Hey, Nadine, can you help me quick?"

Thoughts scattering to the wind, Nadine cast an annoyed look at Sean. He was leaning around the stall door, looking hopeful. She gave him a sour scowl. "What? I'm in the middle of this."

He glanced at the stall. "You're done."

"I'm not done sweeping," she informed him.

"That doesn't seem time-sensitive. And this is." He gestured to the horse he was holding.

"What's the problem?" Nadine asked coldly, as if she couldn't see it. Bailey was a good horse, but man, he loved a mud puddle. The horse's gray coat was completely splashed over with orangey-brown goop and water. There was a green grass stain on his hindquarters, and there were brambles in his forelock. Nadine raised her brows. "Bailey, where did you find a briar patch in your nice tidy paddock?"

"I'm on a time-crunch here, Nadine. Can you *please* help me clean him up so I can ride him before Rosemary gets here? This horse was just added to my list, and that puts me behind."

She sighed dramatically and put aside her broom. "Look, all you need to do is hose him off right now and get on him. None of the other stuff matters right now. I'll clean him up this afternoon. Caitlin let me know that was a priority. But it's for after your ride."

Sean eyed the dingy horse. "Are you sure? He looks like a disaster."

"I promise. Go ride him like that. Just be sure to get the mud off all of him, legs and everything, first. You can ride him wet, but not muddy." She noticed Sean's quizzical expression. "I can see you thinking about that. Are you wondering why he can't have any mud on him?"

Sean blushed. He actually blushed. Nadine almost liked him when he did normal human things like that. It reminded her of when he'd first come here, and she'd thought he was a nice guy. "I am wondering, actually."

She appreciated his honesty. "It's to keep his body temperature stable. If he has dried mud caking his skin and you end up getting him really hot, he could overheat muscles and tendons anywhere there's mud holding the heat in."

"Gosh." Sean looked astonished. "I never heard that before."

"I worked for a three-day event rider up near Fair Hill for a while." Brett Tatum had been a conscientious horseman, a kind boss, and a dedicated drunk. She missed him often, but when he'd started sleeping through morning rides and gallop sets, his business had started to suffer. She'd packed his suitcase herself when he shipped off to rehab, and as far as she knew, Brett had never come back to Maryland. "Picked up a lot of fitness stuff," she added. "I guess some of it might be outdated, but you can never be *too* safe with a horse. Plus, mud could hide cuts or punctures, so better get it off."

Sean's gaze turned pleading. "If you hose him, I could get out my tack, and we'd have him done in five minutes. What d'ya say?"

The sooner he was riding, the sooner he was out of her hair. "Fine. Hand me the horse."

"Thank you, Nadine. Thank you, thank you, thank you—"

"That's enough. Go and get your tack."

Sean scattered. Nadine sighed and looked at Bailey, who had regarded the entire proceedings without much interest. He put his head down and rubbed his eye against one muddy leg, bringing back a face which was now just as goopy as his lower half. "Great work, genius," she told him. "Let's go and get you cleaned up."

She had just started walking Bailey up the aisle when Richie popped out of a stall to her left. Bailey startled, jumping to her right, nearly pulling the lead-rope out of her hand. Nadine gathered up the slack quickly. "Goodness, Richie, warn a girl first. And her horse. You'll give this doofus a heart attack."

"Sorry about that." Richie was beaming at her, anyway. A towering, seventy-two-year-old Santa Claus lookalike, Richie and his little Mrs. Claus, a white-haired angel named Rose, had started at Elmwood a few weeks before. They had settled down in an RV at the Catoctin Creek Campground for the spring and summer months, but they usually wintered at Florida racetracks, grooming horses and hot walking. Nadine had been ecstatic when they'd started, because racetrack grooms were typically meticulous horsemen, and she hadn't been disappointed. But Richie could be surprisingly stealthy for a man of his height and girth. This wasn't the first horse he'd spooked, and she had to wonder how many racehorses he'd sent through the ceiling with one of his surprise appearances. "I heard ya talking to Sean."

"Well, he works here, so."

"I think you two would be cute together," Richie told her, faded eyes sparkling. "Ever think about it? You'd fight like cats and dogs, of course, but that's alright. I fight with Mother over there."

"Don't call me *Mother,*" a reedy voice retorted from the depths of the neighboring stall. "If I've told you once, I've told you a thousand times."

Richie's smile grew even larger. "She hates when I call her Mother," he whispered, loud enough to be heard through the entire barn aisle. "That's why I do it. Add a little spice to the morning, so to speak."

"Richie, you're going to be locked out of the RV tonight if you carry on like that." Rose's sweet face appeared from around the corner of the stall door. She looked like a cartoon grandmother, but when Richie annoyed her, she had the temper of a cartoon motorcycle gang member. All of which just made Richie happier, somehow. "Nadine, don't let him hold you up. He'd just talking nonsense as usual." She cast an adoring smile on Richie, who beamed back at her.

Nadine shook her head at them both and tugged at the lead-rope, pulling Bailey along to the wash-racks in the middle of the barn. Richie and Rose were like a comic duo from the black-and-white era, and if she stood there, they'd just keep running through their routines regardless of whether anyone was laughing or not.

"I admit they're cute," she murmured to Bailey, snapping the ties on either side of his halter. "But I don't have time for it right now. Not when we have to get Sean on your back, right?"

Bailey shook his head, sending mud flying all over the wash-rack —and Nadine. She stood still for a minute, dealing with the shock of cold droplets on her face and splatter over her shirt. Just as she was regaining the power of movement, Sean came around the corner, his arms full of saddle, pad, girth, and bridle.

"Oh, no." He stopped short when he saw her. "He got you, huh?"

Nadine turned to him slowly. She shook dirty water from her hands, trying to aim at him. "This is your fault."

"It is my fault." Sean seemed to be going for an *approach with caution* tactic here. It worked; Nadine felt her temper, which had bubbled up quickly, simmering back down to acceptable levels. Sometimes horses got you muddy. That was part of barn life. Why was she being so uptight about it?

Sean set his tack on a saddle stand. "Let me just hose him off. I'm sorry I bothered you."

"No, it's fine." Nadine clipped the cross-ties to Bailey's halter. "But grab a towel to get the mud off his face and neck, okay? I'm not going to get him wet all over. It's chillier than I thought."

Sometimes you had to get wet yourself to find out just how much bite was in the air.

Working in tandem, they made quick work of tacking up Bailey. "Well, he doesn't look clean, but he isn't a pigpen anymore, either," Sean observed at last. "Thanks for your help."

"Don't worry about it." Nadine hung up the hose again, arranging the loops just so. She stood back and admired it for a moment. So tidy, so symmetrical!

When she turned around, she found Sean watching her, his expression amused. She felt a surge of irritation. Why was he always laughing at her? "What?" she snapped. "You see something you could do better?"

"No! I wasn't—you're just a little obsessive about the barn, that's all. It's cute."

She'd *cute* him. "I am not obsessive. I just like things neat. You could learn a thing or two about that, Mr. Leaving Out Your Dirty Bridles All The Time."

"Come on, Nadine. You're very obsessive. Watch this." Bailey had been wearing his halter over his bridle, still clipped into the cross-ties. Now, Nadine watched Sean unsnap one of the cross-ties, slip the halter from over Bailey's ears, and let the halter swing to the wall, dangling from the remaining cross-tie. The brass buckles and leather straps banged against the wooden planks.

Nadine took a deep breath and folded her hands behind her back. She would *not* swoop in and fix this. She'd make him do it. "Sean, you unclip that halter and hang it up nicely!"

Sean grinned at her, that damn shiny pearly-white grin of his. "If you can leave it there while I ride, I'll take back saying you're obsessive. You have to leave it there the whole time, though."

"No. You just fix it. There's a way we do things, and we hang up our halters. And," she added, grabbing the free cross-tie, "we snap up our cross-ties so they don't get wet and rust!" She clipped the cross-tie snap to the o-ring mounted on the wall above her head. "We have standards in this barn!"

"But what if we don't?" Sean asked. "Then what happens?" He walked Bailey out of the wash-rack and turned down the aisle, heading for the indoor arena.

Nadine watched him disappear around the corner, her fists balled at her sides. Then she looked at the halter hanging against the wall. She knew she should let it hang there. But it was so upsetting. Like a dead animal or something. She couldn't stand it.

Nadine grabbed the halter, unclipped it from the cross-tie, and hung it up neatly by the side noseband rings, the way she had learned at the Thoroughbred breeding farm where she'd worked a few years ago. And then she snapped up the cross-tie, the way she had learned at Brett Tatum's barn, so the snaps wouldn't dangle against the wet walls or floor and get rusty.

And *then* she went back to the stalls she'd been mucking and got back to work.

She was not obsessive. But she still picked up her broom and brushed back a few stray curls of wood shavings from the stall mat before she moved her wheelbarrow down to the next stall in the line.

Sean was just trying to get her all riled up.

Caitlin came down to talk to her while she was picking out the next stall. Spending a half hour in her office had evidently given her a laundry list of new topics and tasks, from boarders she wanted Nadine to talk to about various issues, to the horse list for the next farrier visit. "What day is Gus coming this week?" she asked, consulting her clipboard of notes. "I want him to put shoes on this new horse coming in, too."

"Gus and Kevin are here on Thursdays for the rest of April, and I think May, too," Nadine replied, her eyes on her work.

"Kevin still doing a good job?" Caitlin's voice was absent now, her mind already moving on to the next problem. Caitlin never dwelled on one thing for very long.

"Yeah, he's very good. Gus keeps him on the easy horses, so there's nothing to worry about. But he's not driving with Gus every day right now, because he's working on the house with Nikki."

"That's going to be a really good bakery when she gets it open," Caitlin mused. "I'm glad I decided to help them out with the Schubert house."

"We all are," Nadine assured her. "Catoctin Creek will be so much better off with a bakery. We might have to designate someone to go pick up muffins every morning."

"Well, you work hard enough. A few extra pastries won't hurt anyone. And Nikki's muffins are legendary. Okay, so be sure to have Gus shoe this new horse. I'm sure he won't ask Kevin to do it, but just in case, we don't want our little farrier apprentice getting hurt under Rosemary's horse. Lord, Rosemary would kill me."

"So would Nikki," Nadine reminded her. "A double-slaying."

"Good point. Nikki's temper is something scary. You should have seen her back in high school. To see her now, running the diner and starting up a bakery besides, is wild to me. I used to think she'd become an assassin or something. The way she acted as bodyguard for Rosemary . . ." Caitlin shook her head, remembering. "Anyway. I think that's it. Keep Sean on the straight and narrow, will you? He has a lot of horses to get through before lessons, and I know he's going to try to get out of scheduling the kids for outdoor lessons. But he's got to get them out of the indoor."

"For the hunter pace, right?" Nadine eyed her wheelbarrow; it needed to be emptied, but she couldn't go anywhere until Caitlin was finished with her. She propped her manure fork against the wall and waited. "They just have to be able to pair up and take a cross-country course at a moderate speed, trotting and cantering, is that right?"

"Yes, it's a piece of cake—*if* they're used to riding in the field, and you know Sean is attached to that indoor. I don't know what he thinks is going to happen if he goes to, heaven forbid, the outdoor arena." Caitlin gestured at the wall behind them, on the other side of which was a forlorn, rarely used outdoor ring with premium footing and a beautiful course of jumps. "I get using the indoor exclusively all winter, but it's April. The weather is gorgeous. Well, not today, it's getting freezing out there. I guess we're getting a winter rewind today."

"I'll go over the lesson book with him later and we'll make some adjustments," Nadine promised. Maybe she didn't love working side-by-side with Sean, but she *did* enjoy making him do things he didn't want to do.

"Thanks," Caitlin replied. "Stay on top of him, will you? He's not very ambitious with the students. I feel like no one has improved very much this winter, and it annoys me."

Nadine nodded. She could relate to this emotion. And then some.

"And this hunter pace is really important, you know." Caitlin lowered her voice, and Nadine took the hint, moving closer. "I'm running it to benefit the Elmwood Foundation, you know, to cover the therapy program costs. But between you and me, if the therapy program doesn't fund itself this year, I'm going to have to cut it. Money's getting tight around here."

Nadine's cleaning suddenly stopped itself. She looked up at Caitlin in shock. When she'd started working here, the new therapeutic riding program was all her boss could talk about. They'd spent countless hours building it up, gaining dozens of riders from all over the region. The volunteers who poured in to help frequently started riding lessons on their own, which led to selling horses and boarding them. Some of the more cynical residents of Catoctin Creek thought boosting lessons and boarding was why Caitlin had brought therapeutic riding to the farm in the first place, and Nadine suspected they weren't entirely mistaken.

But even if that had been Caitlin's end goal, this still wasn't bad in her eyes, because the therapeutic riding sessions did a lot of good for a lot of people, both children and adults. Losing the program would be a huge blow for the riders who relied on it, to say nothing of the pipeline of students it provided. "I don't understand," Nadine said slowly. "It does so much for us. Why cut it?"

"It's not funding itself," Caitlin repeated. "Money is finite, Nadine. I do what I can. Meanwhile, I've kept ponies for use in the program which I would have sold otherwise. When I ended the breeding program and sold all the breeding stock, I kept some ponies who would be worth a lot as broodmares now. People still want Elmwood ponies, and I get offers on those mares all the time."

Nadine knew Caitlin hadn't given up her mother's breeding program lightly. The homebred ponies which remained were all exquisite. And rich kids—like Sean had once been—still needed beautiful, twinkle-toed ponies for their trips to Devon Horse Show and the Hampton Classic and Wellington. With that in mind, other breeders had been quick to snap up the Elmwood breeding herd when Caitlin put them on the market. "So you'd sell those ponies, too? All the other Elmwood ponies?"

"Understand my position: I was feeding them out of the Elmwood Foundation money," Caitlin reminded her. "That account is bone-dry. Feed prices are up, donations are down. I need more paying horses in my stalls."

"So the hunter pace has to fill up," Nadine said, "Or . . ."

"Or I close the program and start selling ponies." At least Caitlin looked sorry about it when she said, "That's just business."

Nadine didn't know what to say. Well, she did. She just wasn't sure she was willing to take the risk.

Caitlin glanced at her, her gaze knowing. "You're worried about the rest of the farm's business, too, aren't you?"

She shrugged. "Well . . . yeah. When you start talking about selling the therapy ponies, I guess I naturally wonder what else is going to get cut. That's where the business model begins."

"Let's just say we need a really good spring," Caitlin told her. "Or we're going to have to start cutting some fat. The lesson program needs to buck up, for one thing. See if you can light a fire under Sean's ass, will ya? I want more progress, more kids buying horses, more demand. He can't just keep coasting with the work he's doing. If Sean can't hack it at this game, I'm going to cut him, next."

Chapter Four

Sean

By the time Sean led Bailey back into the barn, the gray horse huffing a little from his schooling session but still bright-eyed and chipper, Caitlin's office window was dark and he figured she was gone for the day.

Weird that she wouldn't stick around to welcome Rosemary Beckett and see the new horse, but Caitlin was kind of weird. She spent a lot of time thinking about how to make money from horses, but not a lot of time actually with horses. Nadine said it was because of some local legend that Caitlin had always been the worst rider in town, even though her mother had been a beloved riding instructor who taught every horse-crazy kid in Catoctin Creek how to ride. Caitlin inherited the business, but not the horse gene.

Funny, the way that worked. Sean had inherited the horse gene, but not the business. And you really needed both.

Sometimes he followed this train of thought a little too far and considered Caitlin as a potential investor. But Caitlin didn't seem really high on him these days, for reasons he didn't want to explore since he was determined to leave soon. Anyway, Martha Lane really seemed like a sure thing. He was going to keep his eye on the prize.

"Good boy, Bailey," he told the horse, leading him back into the wash-rack. He noticed the halter had been picked up and hung in that peculiar way, by the rings on the noseband, which Nadine favored. No one else he'd ever met hung halters that way—everyone else used the crown piece, hanging up a halter like a bridle. She had picked this trick up somewhere and wouldn't give up on it, even when no one else followed her lead. Nadine was obsessive, alright, even if she refused to admit it. Sean grinned, unhooking the cross-ties that she'd snapped up, and got to work untacking and cleaning off Bailey.

When the gray horse had been swathed in an Irish knit cooler and put back into his stall to eat hay and dry off, Sean got busy with the next horse. He had to ride Calypso, a dark bay Thoroughbred who was going to enter the lesson program, and then Chocolate Kiss, who was already a lesson horse but needed regular tune-ups to keep him from getting too lazy and stubborn. Both were officially for sale, and he was supposed to be selling them to students who would keep boarding them here, turning them into a long-term revenue stream for Caitlin. She seemed to have everything figured out.

Personally, Sean didn't think she had the best system. For example, he thought Chocolate Kiss would make a nice equitation horse on the circuit, but Elmwood students didn't go to top-level shows. Everyone here had been content to show on the 4-H and schooling show circuit for years, and Caitlin wasn't convinced their parents had the financial fortitude to take on the thousand-dollar weekends common at top hunter and jumper horse shows.

When he first interviewed, she'd told him that she was looking for competent coaching for amateur riders. "If we level up over a few years of training, I'm not opposed to reaching for a higher-dollar client," she'd explained. "I know you come from the A-circuit. But my clientele isn't there yet."

Privately, Sean thought this was a mistake. The *real* money was riding on the A-circuit, at the big shows he came from. If Caitlin wanted to play financial roulette with horse sales, she could at least add a few zeros to the price of each horse who brought home some ribbons in the glitzy rings. Not all of them would pan out, of course, but some would. Sean had ridden dozens of sales horses for owners who didn't have any interest or aptitude for showing their investments themselves, and he'd gotten enough fat commission checks to fuel his own passion for the game. Sure, his family had financed all of his personal horses, but what difference did it make where the horses came from? All that mattered was how much they went for.

"You get, it, right Calypso? Ex-racehorses know how big money works." He saddled the horse quickly, giving him a rub on his star, which left a drifting wave of white hairs across his face. "Ugh. Shedding season is here, apparently."

Sean dusted off his breeches as best he could, but spring had evidently sprung for Calypso, who was leaving his winter coat all over the place. "I'm going to have to change before afternoon lessons," he told the horse, and led him to the indoor arena for their ride.

He was halfway through schooling Calypso when he heard a few high-pitched whinnies, and the sound of hooves rolling across the fields outside. Calypso nearly jumped out of his skin, certain whatever was happening beyond the metal walls of the indoor arena needed his immediate attention. Sean heard the rattling of a horse trailer coming up the drive and pulling into the parking lot, and he tried to settle Calypso so that he could cool the horse out and get back into the barn before Rosemary left. He had to ask about the horse's background, or Caitlin would expect him to just get on the beast without knowing a thing about it.

Leaving Calypso in the wash-rack, pawing with irritation, he ran down the aisle. Rosemary Beckett was standing in the barn entrance, talking with Nadine. She had her truck keys in one hand, ready to leave.

Sean barely glanced at the new horse in the end stall, his brain only vaguely recognizing something of impressive size was skulking within. "Rosemary, hey! Wait up." He skidded to a halt in front of them, panting a little. Running on his own two feet wasn't a normal Sean occupation.

Nadine fixed him with an amused expression. "You okay there, buddy? Need some water?"

"Fine," Sean wheezed. "I just wanted to catch Rosemary before she left, get the details on this horse of hers."

Rosemary, always so soft-spoken and soft-eyed, gave Sean one of her shy smiles. "There's not a lot to tell, unfortunately. I picked him up from Willowdale auction two weeks ago. They had a little kid ride him in the ring, but you know how tiny those auction rings are. He couldn't have done anything dangerous if he tried. I got on him in the barnyard at home, but I don't have an arena, and it slopes so much . . . all I can tell you is he seems really nice and like he's been well-ridden in the past."

Sean fought a feeling of disappointment. What had he been hoping for? A grand prix jumper? "I see. So he could be just a trail horse, for all we know?"

"Well, if he was just a trail horse, he couldn't go under any low trees, I'll tell you that much." She nodded at the horse in the stall behind him.

Sean turned around and got a good look.

For a moment, he couldn't even think of what to say. He just stared.

"Big, right?" Rosemary's voice was amused.

"He's . . . yes. Big." Not that the word was good enough. Sean was astonished.

The horse looking at them from over the stall door was truly massive. And stunningly beautiful, from what Sean could see of him. Black—true black, not dark brown—with a thin strip of white reaching from beneath his thick forelock to the tip of his wide nose, and a bush of black mane which was going to take some serious effort to civilize. The horse would have been a knockout based on his front end alone. But it was behind the withers where things really got next-level. The horse had a blanket of white covering his hindquarters, bordered all along the edges with wide white dapples. Sean had never seen anything like it before. Size, color, build: this horse was a wonder of nature.

"So . . . um . . . is he an Appaloosa cross?" Sean asked haltingly. "Crossed with, I don't know, an elephant?"

Rosemary laughed. "Who knows? Percheron-App, most likely. Emphasis on the Perch. But as soon as I saw that coloring, I knew he was a gold mine as long as he didn't have any murderous tendencies."

"Here's hoping," Sean agreed. "Because he's also what, seventeen hands? I'd hate for him to decide I'm not allowed on his back anymore."

"That's a concern," Rosemary sighed. "Stephen didn't even want me to get on him. I hope you'll be very careful getting used to him."

Sean was suddenly feeling less than thrilled about his new project horse. It wasn't the size that worried him—he was used to tall horses. It was more about the unknown.

Up until this point, every horse Caitlin had asked him to school and sell had been a horse with all the basics intact—all he had to do was polish them up, make them *better* riding horses, make sure their buttons were easy to find and responsive for amateur riders. It was what he knew. In his past life, people had handed him nice horses who needed a little tune-up to show and sell all the time. Making good horses look great was Sean's specialty.

Starting from scratch with a grass-green horse? That wasn't in Sean's wheelhouse at all. Maybe it was a reasonable assumption that a horseman in his late twenties with a resume as long as Sean's should be able to school a know-nothing novice horse without too much trouble, but . . . well, he'd had people for that sort of thing. He hadn't had to do it himself.

"I'll be careful," he said at last, because Rosemary seemed to be waiting for him to say something. "What's your timeline? How long do you want to take before we put him up for sale?"

"It can't be that long," Rosemary admitted. "Not the best answer, I know. But Caitlin is taking him on without charging me board, because my farm is a non-profit, and I know she'll want to get him out of here quick. He eats enough, believe me. And my farm needs the money, too. That's what led me to buying him in the first place. All my other horses needed sanctuary, a place for life, but they eat, too. I have to be able to pay the feed store every month."

Great. The horse wasn't just an unknown. He was also a lifesaver for Notch Gap Equine Sanctuary. That was a fun extra bit of pressure on his shoulders. "I'll do my best," Sean told her, but he wasn't sure his best was going to be good enough.

"Thank you," Rosemary told him, sharing another of her shy smiles. "I better get going. Call me if you need anything."

With Rosemary gone, her truck seeming to sigh with relief now that the trailer behind wasn't filled with a half-ton of giant black and white horse, Sean turned to Nadine. "You've been awful quiet," he said. "Anything to share about this horse?"

She shrugged, her eyes on the horse's dark head. "I know as much as you."

Sean noticed her face seemed—different, somehow. Lit up, almost. "Everything okay?"

"He's just really beautiful," she confessed. "Have you ever seen anything like him? I feel like I can't look away. Like I'm just mesmerized."

Sean looked over the horse again. "He's pretty nice, I'll give you that. But I don't think he's going to change my life." *Might end it though.*

"I can't wait to see him move under saddle. Are you going to ride him now?" Nadine glanced over her shoulder. "Rosemary said she wanted him to have a couple days to settle in, so I kind of diverted her from the subject. I know Caitlin wants you on him today. Even if I disagree, she's still in charge."

Sean considered the time. If he didn't ride this horse in the next hour, he wouldn't have time to get on him until after lessons were over tonight. And riding horses at seven o'clock at night, after spending hours on his feet in the center of the arena, was not his top choice. He looked back at the horse, weighing his options.

The horse did a quick circuit of the stall, throwing shavings against the walls, then pushed his head over his door and whinnied. The sound carried through the barn and out to the fields. Every horse on the property seemed to reply all at once, which excited him further. He did another spin around the stall, then reared, his front hooves leaving the ground. Sean didn't need this horse to get any taller than he already was.

He shook his head. "I don't think now is the right time at all."

He glanced at Nadine, expecting her to be looking at him rather scathingly, but instead, he saw approval in her dark green eyes. The expression was so unusual, he was actually startled. He let his eyes linger on her for a moment, wondering what it would be like to have Nadine on his team again. Obsessive, over-the-top Nadine. He wondered what *she* knew about training horses.

And if she'd be willing to share any of that know-how with him.

"What?" she asked, tilting her head. "Is there something on my face?"

"No, sorry. I just thought you'd make fun of me for not wanting to ride him," he answered honestly.

She shook her head. "Not this time! You're making the right decision. You go finish up with Calypso—I can hear him pawing from here. I'll give this guy some carrots and see if we can get him to cool off this afternoon. And if Caitlin asks, tell her I said not to ride him."

Sean raised his eyebrows. "Do you have that power?"

"To tell you what you can and can't do with a horse?" Nadine gave him a smug smile. "Yes, actually. Didn't you know that?"

"I knew you *thought* that." His grin was teasing, but she still narrowed her eyes at him.

"Trust me," she told him, with a little shake of her black hair. "I'm in charge around here. Technically, you work for me."

"Well, yes, ma'am." Sean was enjoying this little show of power. Was Nadine always this funny? Had he just missed it because he'd been too busy being annoyed by her obsessive attention to detail? "I'll be sure to check with you before I touch *any* of the horses, ma'am."

Nadine rolled her eyes. "Go deal with Calypso, you nerd. I'll handle this guy."

She turned her full attention back to the black horse, who was still trembling with anxiety.

One more thing occurred to Sean. "Wait a second. Does he have a name?"

"It's Finn," Nadine said, not bothering to turn around. "Short for Finnegan."

"Finnegan Begin Again," Sean said, apropos of nothing.

She glanced over her shoulder. "Isn't that a nursery rhyme? I feel like my mother used to say that to me."

"I don't remember." Sean searched his memory. "I think I thought it was a pony's name, back on the circuit. It just came into my head."

"Huh." She turned back to the horse. "Funny, the way that happens." And she tickled Finn on the nose.

Sean lingered a moment, watching her play with the black horse, trying to get his attention on her instead of the strange new barn he found himself in. She was so gentle and small; it was amazing to see her work her magic on such a massive animal. In short order, Nadine had Finn lipping at her fingers, his ears pricked at her instead of swiveling to listen for other horses. That was how it was done, he thought, that was how a master horsewoman calmed a wild horse. Some people would have called it whispering, but Sean just called it love.

He walked slowly back to Calypso, who eyed him with a disdain bordering on rage for having been abandoned in the wash-rack for so long. "Sorry, buddy," Sean said, slipping under the cross-ties and unbuckling the saddle girth. "You know how it is when new horses come into the barn. Everyone else is chopped liver for a little while."

Calypso shook his head and reached out a foreleg again, scraping his toe along the concrete with a grating noise. Sean let the horse fret on his own terms. He ought to stop him—Calypso had a bad habit of pawing and he wore down his shoes at the toes—but right now, Sean didn't feel like being a taskmaster of a trainer. He just wanted to get through this day in one piece, and hope Nadine managed to gentle Finn before his ride.

He glanced at his watch. Martha and the other volunteers would soon be arriving for the afternoon therapy session. Once he was done with Calypso, Sean figured he'd better go and clean himself up. He needed to look his best before he presented Martha with the horses he'd been ogling online. "Warm enough for a hot-water bath and a cooler," he told the horse, and turned on the hose.

He was scraping excess water off a dripping-wet Calypso when Richie ambled by. "What did you think of the new guy?" Richie asked, pausing in front of Calypso. He put his hand up to let Calypso lip his palm. "Pretty snazzy, huh?"

"Really snazzy," Sean agreed absently. He'd been trying not to think of 'the new guy.' But the big horse dominated his thoughts even while he was riding Calypso.

"Nadine's got a thing for him."

"Huh?" Sean picked up a cooler from a nearby chair and flung it over Calypso's back. "Yeah, you might be right." He didn't want to talk about it. Maybe Richie would just go away if he acted disinterested.

"I bet she'd help you with him."

Sean looked at Richie.

Richie looked back at him and laid one finger alongside his nose.

"I don't understand."

Richie shrugged, good-natured as always. "Just making conversation," he said, and wandered off.

Sean clipped the cooler's belly band in place and put his hand on Calypso's damp neck. "Why does he act like he knows all my secrets?" he murmured to the Thoroughbred. "That guy's a pain."

He led Calypso back to his stall, trying to put Richie's odd little intimation out of his head.

But there was one thing Richie had gotten right: Nadine probably *would* help him with the horse. And from what little he knew of her past, she probably had more experience with green horses than he did.

The only problem would be getting her help without giving away to Caitlin that he didn't feel like he could ride the horse. This job might not be his dream job, but it was the only one he had until something better came along.

Like Martha Lane.

"Time to get cleaned up," he murmured, and headed for the stairs. The ladies would be here any minute.

Chapter Five

Nadine

"No, Mom, this is my job and I'm happy with it," Nadine said patiently into her phone. "I do not want to meet your friend Rochelle and talk about the restaurant where she works. Why don't you do it? A job would be nice for you. You could talk to people all day instead of calling me while I'm working."

Kelly Blackwell laughed, as Nadine had known she would. Her mother didn't work. That was how a guy like Reg ended up in Nadine's childhood house, the faded blue townhouse on a street stupidly named Wonder Avenue. Guys with big promises and shady connections. Guys who could get her mother into trouble if she wasn't careful.

Nadine had kept her mother out of several stunts of Reg's over the years, including the car-theft ring which had eventually landed him in jail.

A sentence which had ended far too soon, in Nadine's opinion.

"Oh, Nadine, you're always fussing me about work, but you're the one I worry about. Are you really going to keep cleaning up after horses forever?"

"No," Nadine replied. She tipped the wheelbarrow she'd been pushing, one-handed, up against a wall. In the shadows beneath her apartment's staircase, far down the back aisle where the boarders and students never roamed, Nadine kept a tidy collection of farm tools, from pitchforks to snow shovels. And all the wheelbarrows, hosed clean after a morning of mucking out. "I'm a barn manager, Mom. I'm not just cleaning up after horses. And I have to go sit down with the riding instructor and do horse assignments for lessons now, so, was there anything else you wanted to talk about before I go?"

"I want you to come have dinner tonight," Kelly said promptly. "That's the real reason I called. Reg got us steaks, and he said he's going to get propane for the grill. Come over and we'll have a real good dinner."

With Reg? Nadine wanted to scream. She schooled her face into patient lines, knowing it would help her voice remain steady. "I can't tonight, Mom. Plans with Caitlin," she lied. "We have a lot to go over for the hunter pace coming up."

"You spend more time with Caitlin than you do with your own mother." A dangerous pout had entered Kelly's voice. Tears were almost certainly next.

Nadine couldn't stand it when her mother cried.

"We'll go get dinner at the Blue Plate on Wednesday," Nadine offered. "Just you and me. Fried chicken night!"

"That's nice." Kelly considered the offer. "You sure you can't make it tonight? Reg wanted you to come over."

I'm sure he did, Nadine thought grimly. *Just to prove to me he's back.* "I definitely can't. This is an important job, Mom!

Sometimes we have to work late."

"Well, okay. I guess if Caitlin needs you."

"She does. And whoops—someone else needs me—I gotta go! Bye, Mom!"

Nadine had the phone shoved back into her pocket before she'd even heard her mother's watery goodbye. Sean had come around the corner, looking annoyingly tidy in yet another clean pair of breeches. She wondered why he'd cleaned up again. "Fall off someone, Sean?"

He held out his hands in an innocent gesture. "Why would you say that to me?"

"The clean breeches. I just assumed there was a reason you'd have changed clothes again this morning. Three times is excessive, even for you."

"There is a reason. Calypso was shedding like he saw a heat wave in the forecast. Anyway, I like these breeches for teaching in, and I teach Martha next." A sudden squawk of chatter in the main aisle punctuated his words. "After the therapy session."

"It's that late already? I meant to send Richie to get food for everyone. Rosemary's horse threw me off schedule."

"I think he and Rose already went back to their RV for lunch."

"Ugh." Nadine considered her lunch prospects upstairs. There was . . . cereal. But if she ate that, she'd be so starving by dinner, Reg's steaks would be impossible to pass up. Nadine didn't want to put her stomach into that kind of dilemma. "My pantry is *bare*. And I still have to do horse assignments for this afternoon, and there is a pile of social media posts to get up for the hunter pace. Welp, I guess lunch is peanut butter crackers from the vending machine." She'd had worse.

"Forget that," Sean said gallantly. "I'll go pick up lunch from Trout's Market. How about that? You want a hoagie? A ham and cheese, little oil and vinegar, right?"

Sean had picked up lunch for the barn crew before, so it wasn't astonishing that he'd offered, or even that he knew her regular order. But she still found herself staring at him like he was an angel descended to earth.

She must be *really* hungry. Usually, she'd suspect Sean was just trying to get out of some chore Caitlin had assigned him.

"Yes, please. And a cherry Coke?"

"And a bag of salt and vinegar chips." Sean touched an imaginary cap. "I'll be right back, princess."

He took off down the back aisle, scrupulously avoiding the buzz of activity in the main aisle. Nadine watched him go, waiting until he'd disappeared into the bright sunlight outside the barn. They *were* nice breeches, she'd give him that. Sculpted his athletic legs and—other regions—quite well.

She rolled her eyes at herself. "Stop ogling the riding instructor," she muttered. "He's still a lazy daisy. And judging by what Caitlin said this morning, he's already halfway out the door."

Then she turned her own boots towards her office by the indoor arena entrance. Tucked under Sean's apartment, her office and Caitlin's were nestled side-by-side, although Caitlin's barn office was seldom used these days. Increasingly, Caitlin worked from her house or was out on the road, networking, making deals, looking at real estate. Her interests were moving outside of solely running the farm, something which both excited and worried Nadine, who had to pick up the slack. She liked the challenge, but she worried that if Elmwood didn't keep turning over profits, Caitlin might decide to sell. This morning's meeting had her even more on edge than usual.

Nadine didn't even want to think about finding another job as good as this one. Chances were, she wouldn't. Not for years. She was still young to be running a big equestrian center like this, and she didn't have any certifications or one of those degrees in equine business. She kept Elmwood pristine and worked overtime to make sure everything clicked like clockwork, but that was still no guarantee of another management position if she lost this one.

To say nothing of losing sight of her dream of staying in Catoctin Creek for good. Where she could keep an eye on her mother, and try to feel a semblance of the hometown pride that people like Rosemary, Nikki, and Caitlin seemed to show so effortlessly. It hadn't been easy to grow up on the outskirts of Catoctin Creek, in the unwanted suburb of Wonder Avenue, but Nadine had still felt the pull of home during all the years she'd been away.

She flicked on the light as she entered her office, a sense of peace overtaking her as she looked around the small, wood-paneled room, with its scarred old furniture and battered books. This was her first office, and she didn't mind that the desk and chairs were from the early eighties, or that the overhead light hummed through a panel slowly going golden with age. She opened the blinds, giving her a view over any activity heading in or out of the indoor arena, and settled behind her desk.

The lesson book was a big, hard binder, and both the covers and the pages inside were a special size of paper she hadn't even realized existed before she came to Elmwood and took over scheduling and horse assignments. Each day got two pages: morning and afternoon. Each hour of the day was accounted for with its own line, segmented into six: room enough for even their largest lessons to fit inside with a box for each horse-rider combination.

Horse assignment was an art; Sean wasn't good at it, so even though Caitlin constantly asked that Nadine turn the task over to him, she had thus far only allowed Sean to sit in and watch her. He was allowed to make suggestions, but she wasn't under any compulsion to listen to them. If Sean had gotten his way last Thursday, he would have put little Kylie Myrtle on Chunky Monkey, who was the largest and youngest pony in the lesson program. Kylie wouldn't have made it through her entire lesson without getting taken for a spin around the ring she hadn't asked for. Nadine put Kylie on Harley instead, a medium pony with a pretty chestnut coat and flaxen mane, and the ride had been so successful, Kylie was heard begging her mom to buy Harley as they left the barn that night.

Nadine had turned to Sean with an arch look after they'd heard that, but Sean had just shaken his head and asked her not to be so smug every time she was right.

"I'm not smug," Nadine said to her empty office now, as she uncapped her pen and opened the binder to Monday. "I'm just very good at my job."

She did find it odd that Sean wasn't good at horse assignments. Sometimes he seemed to have absolutely no judgment about the way horse and rider personalities needed to mesh. More than once, Nadine had wondered just what Sean's last job had been like. Although the students liked him, he seemed low on practical knowledge. She had heard him stammer through explanations for simple questions, sometimes getting things completely wrong.

In fact, when he'd first gotten here, she had strongly suspected he didn't even know how to clean stalls. For the first few months, watching him struggle through everyday barn chores, Nadine had wondered if Sean Casey had a secret past. Sure, he'd given Caitlin references. But friends could be prompted to lie. "Sean Casey? Great riding coach! We miss him here!" was an easy script to follow. And his show results were real enough: she'd done enough searches on his name to see his record from junior years all the way up until last summer. It was odd that an A-circuit rider would suddenly quit showing to take up a job teaching at a local barn. Very odd.

Still, Nadine believed that if a person had a secret, that was their business. She had a few secrets of her own. And eventually, Sean had figured out things... for the most part. He didn't take forever to tack up horses anymore, he could do a decent job on a dirty stall, and they hadn't had to call an ambulance for a student in all six months he'd been teaching here.

Those were wins. Even if Nadine thought everything else about Sean was a fail, those were wins.

So she didn't pry. Anyway, her initial curiosity about Sean Casey had been spent the minute he'd started flirting with every over-fifty student in the barn, and she'd realized his real interest in life was finding a sugar mama to make everything all better.

Gross. How could he think that was okay?

Nadine glanced at the clock and realized she had spent five solid minutes sitting here, thinking about Sean. *Well, that's not great.*

"Back to work, Nadine," she told herself.

She worked her way through the afternoon lessons, checking notes to see which combinations had been successful in the past, and which ones had seen some problems. Sean wasn't the best at making notes, but at least when there was triumph or a failure—a fall, most of the time—he jotted it down, or asked Nadine to do it. The four o'clock lesson was easiest: five brave tweens took this lesson together, and two of them now owned their own horses (thanks to great horse assignment work by Nadine). The other three were very attached to the lesson horses they rode, so she penned in their usual mounts.

Five o'clock gave her a moment's pause; one of the girls had fallen off the week before, but she really liked the horse, and Sean seemed to think she was brave enough to ride him again. After chewing her pen, considering the pros and cons—there was always a possibility that two falls would break the riding lesson habit; kids today did not seem as amiable to getting chucked onto the ground as they had when Nadine was learning to ride—she went ahead and gave the girl the same horse.

"So far, so easy," she muttered. The six o'clock posed a similar problem, but she assigned new horses in that lesson; both students had been riding for six months and were no closer to buying horses now than they had been on day one, which meant some matchmaking expertise was needed.

"There." Nadine put down her pen and surveyed the evening's work ahead. Thirteen horses and ponies would be ridden between four and seven o'clock; ten of those would require her assistance or at least presence to groom, tack up, untack, and bathe; three of those ten would have to be supervised by Sean while she was still bathing Bailey. After each lesson, while she was busy overseeing prep and return of horses, Sean would still be in the ring, teaching until his voice gave out, while Richie and Rose handled evening feeding. It would be a busy, tiring night's work, but she didn't mind.

Especially if there was a hoagie on the way for lunch. Nadine closed the book, checked the time, and decided she could get started on the social media posts before Sean got back with lunch.

While she was typing away at her laptop, the volunteers went trooping past her window: Veronica leading the charge, then four ponies and one horse, each with a rider and three ground-people attached: a person on the lead-rope, two on either side of the rider. Nadine watched them shuffle by, thinking as usual that the sidewalkers had the toughest job. Some riders needed to be propped up in the saddle; some just needed a steady hand ready in case they lost their balance. Either way, walking alongside a horse was much harder than leading one—especially in arenas, because horses were very insistent about walking in the flattened path of the horse ahead of them, leaving deeper footing on either side for the volunteers to flounder through.

Martha Lane was the sidewalker on the last horse, which surprised Nadine. Martha had never struck her as particularly giving person. She showed up in expensive riding boots and tailored clothes, took charge whenever possible, and came dangerously close to bullying some of the other well-intentioned volunteers, mostly middle-aged women, who came to help with the Elmwood therapeutic riding lessons.

And once she'd started taking riding lessons herself, her attitude had gotten even worse. Veronica was a good-natured woman who had clearly seen and done a lot in her thirty years of therapeutic riding work, but even she sometimes looked fed up with Martha's domineering attitude, her way of crowding her way to the front whenever there was a plum assignment or an opportunity to look good in front of everyone else.

Now, seeing her as a sidewalker instead of a leader, Nadine figured the rider was a particularly difficult case, one who needed serious vigilance to stay safe in the saddle. One thing she *would* say for Martha, however grudgingly: the woman wasn't afraid of hard work... as long as it made her look good.

Nadine glanced back at the lesson binder. Martha usually rode Tiny, a Belgian-Quarter Horse cross who was built like a tank and was exceedingly comfortable. Adult beginners and mid-level riders loved him—Tiny was not a challenge, and most of the late starters or re-riders weren't looking for a challenge. They were looking for an experience which wouldn't kill or maim them. Challenging horses were for their brave and ambitious teenage daughters.

But Nadine wondered if Martha wouldn't actually appreciate a slightly more challenging ride. Would she like to show off in front of Sean in her private lesson, prove what a fabulous rider she was? Nadine considered the names in the book for a minute. She could put Martha on Chocolate Kiss and save Sean the trouble of riding him after her lesson. Then he could ride Finn this afternoon instead, rather than having to get on him late tonight after lessons were over.

The whole thing would make Sean's day, and her's, a little easier. Plus, there was always a chance Martha would mesh well with Chocolate. Caitlin's concern over farm income came back to Nadine. If Sean wasn't going to push the students into horse ownership, Nadine might have to take it on.

She went for it, drawing a line through Tiny's name and writing Chocolate's next to it. She'd have to explain the change to Sean, but they were going to eat lunch together in . . . she smiled. Here he was.

And her stomach, at least, was thrilled to see him.

Chapter Six

Sean

Sean was pleasantly surprised when Nadine invited him to stay and eat his lunch in the office. He'd expected her to take her sandwich and show him the door, but she moved jerkily and her cheeks were flushed, as if she were anxious about something. He supposed she wanted the company. The thought was charming, somehow. Nadine never wanted him around. Did he have something she wanted? That would be a change.

"Chilly out there now," he said, unwrapping his hoagie and leaning back in the creaking chair across from her desk. "Guess this little cold front is going to make the daffodils regret opening up so early."

"And yet it's supposed to be seventy-five by Friday." Nadine shook her head. "Springtime is crazy."

"It's beautiful out there, anyway. Buds on the trees, green leaves starting—you ought to go out for a drive. The cherry trees on Main Street are getting ready to bloom."

"I'm going into town on Wednesday for dinner with my mom." She didn't seem enthused about the prospect, but Sean got that—

moms could be pretty difficult. "Maybe a few will be open then."

"Maybe," he agreed, taking a bite. They could make small talk about flowers through their entire lunch break, as far as Sean was concerned. Anything was better than the usual, which was Nadine constantly picking at him. He didn't even think she realized she did it.

Midway through their quiet lunch, Sean turned around the lesson book and looked over the horse assignments. From time to time, he'd been known to make a change, just to annoy Nadine, or to test one of his own theories. The afternoon lessons all looked fine, but his finger landed underneath Martha's name and stayed there. He glanced up at her.

Nadine chewed elaborately. She lifted her eyebrows, as if to say, *problem?*

"Why did you take Martha off Tiny?"

"It's time for her to ride a horse with a little more go," she replied. She took a few chips from the bag between them. "Congrats, you've got her too advanced for Tiny. It only took you four months."

"She likes Tiny." Sean put down the remains of his lunch, annoyed. "I don't think she's going to appreciate a change."

"Martha likes a challenge. She's out there sidewalking today. She could lead if she wanted to and no one would ever tell her no, she leads too much, but instead she took the hard job."

That meant nothing to Sean. He scowled at Nadine, who made a face right back at him. "Riding and walking beside a horse are far from the same thing," he insisted.

"It's not *about* the horse, Sean. It's about the grit required. Honestly, do you have any idea what you're doing out there? I feel for your students sometimes."

If pressed, Sean would have to say the dripping *you're a dimwit* disdain which Nadine loved to infuse into her voice was her most irritating trait, hands-down. But second-most was probably the way she saw right through him.

"You always think you know best," he snapped back. "But I'm telling you, Tiny's the better choice here."

"Well, *Tiny* isn't the horse for sale, Sean. He's a lifer in the lesson program. Horses like him don't grow on trees."

"What does that have to do with anything?"

"Do the math," she said cooly. "Generally, when a horse sells, it's good for the farm and the farm employees."

"Wait, so you have Martha getting on Chocolate Kiss because you think she oughta buy him?" Martha! His Martha! Buying a Quarter Horse cross like Chocolate Kiss when he was plotting to show her two imported Westphalians and a Hanoverian out of an Elite-standard German mare. The idea was laughable.

So Sean laughed.

Big mistake, if he was looking for any reconciliation here. Nadine's eyes narrowed so tightly, he felt like he was looking at a snake about to strike. It was all he could do not to slide his chair back to the wall.

"Do you have a better horse in mind for her?" Nadine's voice had gone from cool to icy, much like the spring day outside was busily doing. "Because it's time to get her on her own horse and boarding. So if you have a suggestion for the perfect horse for Martha, one who is better than nice, quiet Chocolate for a hobby-rider in her fifties, I am all ears."

Sean couldn't answer her. Not without giving himself away. So he settled for being firm. He'd just put on his riding instructor cap and make sure Nadine could see it.

"She rides Tiny," he declared. "That's my decision. *I'm* the riding instructor, here."

Hat straightened!

Nadine glared at him with those emerald eyes, and he had the distinct impression he'd played this situation all wrong. This girl wasn't looking for a masterful man to respect. She'd just as soon push him under the hooves of a rampaging Calypso than take orders from him.

"I'm sorry if that sounded pushy," he added, suddenly feeling sheepish about the whole situation. Her death-glares had a way of doing that. "I just really think she needs to stay on Tiny for a while longer."

Nadine rolled her eyes. Then she dropped her focus back to her half-eaten hoagie. "Whatever, weirdo. If you care that much, fine. But Caitlin's going to be down your throat in two months, wanting to know why Martha isn't a boarder yet. I was just trying to help save you some grief." She took a big bite, filling her mouth so that she couldn't answer him even if he had a comeback. A position of confidence, to give up the chance at the last word.

Or she just knew she'd gotten the last word.

I won't be here in two months, Sean thought. *And neither will Martha.*

The idea was both comforting and disappointing. As if he'd be giving up something besides a job he wasn't particularly good at.

"Thanks," he said, just to try to bring the pressure down.

It didn't really work. They finished their sandwiches in a simmering silence, a quiet much less companionable than before. Sean glanced at his phone, skimming through some pictures Simone had sent him from their latest horse show weekend, while Nadine went back to her work, typing away at her laptop while she picked at the remaining potato chips.

He studied her occasionally from beneath lowered eyelids, wondering, as he so often did, what Nadine's story was. She was awfully young for a barn manager job, probably not much more than twenty-five, but she was experienced with horses, and confident in her decisions. He'd never seen her ride with any purpose in the arena, but he knew she occasionally got on a lesson horse and took them out for rides in the sprawling north pasture, an empty expanse of rolling land where Caitlin had once kept a herd of Black Angus cattle. Since Sean never took horses out of the arena, he hadn't been back there himself, but it was where the hunter pace was being held, so he supposed he'd have to experience it pretty soon.

"Maybe you could take me riding on the north pasture sometime," he said now, feeling like it was time to break the silence.

Nadine didn't look up from her work. "I suppose I'll have to," she agreed.

"Well, not if I'm a chore."

She gave him a proper look now, one which said: *You are very annoying, Sean Casey.* Simone used to give him that look all the time, but she meant it with love. "It's not a chore," she said, somehow infusing into every syllable what a chore it would be.

The silence fell again. Sean considered going outside, but the therapy session had another fifteen minutes on the clock and it was cold out there. He considered the rest of his afternoon. Teaching Martha, riding Chocolate Kiss—Nadine had probably been doing him a favor by trying to put Martha on the horse, go figure—evening lessons . . . and then there was something else, some reason he had to work late.

Ah yes, *Finn.* The mystery horse from Notch Gap Farm. Sean felt a flutter of unease as he remembered the new horse's size and completely unknown riding history.

He sighed. Maybe tonight everything would go down in flames.

"Problem?" she asked brightly, not looking up from her typing.

"I just remembered I still have to ride that new horse after lessons tonight."

"Should be interesting."

He hoped not. He hoped for boring. Very boring. "How green do you think he is? Seriously?"

Nadine looked over her laptop, considering him. Her eyelashes were very long and dark, or maybe her skin was just very pale. Either way, Sean liked the effect. He liked to watch her think. Nadine would be beautiful, he thought, if she was just a little nicer.

She narrowed her eyes again. "What are you thinking?"

"Nothing," Sean lied hastily. "I mean, Finn. Will he be trouble?"

"Well, I imagine he's *pretty* green," she replied cruelly, closing her laptop lid and fixing him with a satisfied smile. "Might even have some pretty bad habits. What are the chances a perfectly nice horse with no vices went through the auction ring cheap enough for Rosemary to buy?"

"Not good," he admitted. "That's what's worrying me, quite frankly."

Nadine tilted her head at him.

"What?"

"I just don't know if you've ever said you're worried about something before," Nadine replied. "I don't know how to take it. I'm actually concerned for you."

"Don't be," Sean huffed, crossing his arms over his chest. "I'll be fine up there. On Mount Finn, the world's biggest horse."

Nadine's face took on that faraway look again, as if he wasn't in the room to annoy her. "He's really cool, isn't he? I love a big horse. Maybe you'll let me ride him sometime."

"Ride him tonight," Sean suggested with a grin. A big, mocking grin to show he was embracing a funny haha moment—even though he was aware he was only half-joking. Or not joking at all. Who was to judge? "Instead of me."

She considered him. For the second time in as many minutes. Sean was beginning to think she liked his face.

Or she just thought he was a puzzle she could solve and discard.

"You don't want to ride him," she said after a moment. "You're *really* worried about him."

"I just don't like the idea of a horse with no history." Sean was defensive. "That's not really our deal, here. If I wanted to work with surprises, I'd go work for a horse trader."

"That's how I got my start. You learn quite a bit riding sales-lot horses. Fast." She paused for effect. "Or you get killed."

"See? That's my point. *You* should be riding him. You're more qualified for the job."

Nadine sat up a little straighter in her chair, and Sean suddenly realized his joke was on its way to becoming a reality. Maybe he really could foist Finn off on Nadine. At least for the first few rides, to see what the horse was like. If Finn was a bucker, a bolter, a lay-down-in-the-dirt balker, or any other sort of problem horse, at least Sean could figure out his plan of attack before he started riding him. Do a little research, call a few friends for advice, that kind of thing.

And if she gets hurt, it's on you, the little warning voice in his head reminded him. He supposed it was his conscience. Which could be a very uncomfortable thing to have, especially when he was trying to save his own skin. "Forget I said anything," Sean sighed, standing up. "I better go out there. Martha will be coming back in any second now."

"Wait." Nadine stood as well. She rested her hands on the desk, making herself a small but commanding presence in her tidy office. "Yeah, I'll ride him. Tonight. Caitlin won't be here, so we can just work this out between the two of us. There's no reason for you to get on a horse you're not sure of, and I really like him. I have a good feeling about him."

Good feelings didn't count for anything in the saddle, but Sean was hardly in a position to tell her no. He wanted her help. And Nadine had never offered to help him with anything before. If she was doing the asking now, then she really wanted to ride Finn.

He hoped she wasn't already attached to the horse. Caitlin and Rosemary had made it pretty clear they wanted the horse sold quickly.

But if she was foolish enough to fall for a sales horse, that was on her. "It's a deal," he agreed. "After lessons tonight?"

"Once the barn empties out," Nadine stipulated. "We don't need anyone hanging around watching us."

He didn't know if it was because they were exchanging roles, or because she didn't want anyone else to see Finn move—another warning sign she might be overly attached already. But either way, he was bound to agree with her. This was the best deal he'd gotten since he'd come to Elmwood.

"I'll see you then," Sean said.

Behind him, he heard hooves clopping on concrete, the buzz of women chatting. The therapy session was over; Veronica and a few volunteers would handle untacking the ponies and turning them out, but he would be meeting Martha in the back aisle to work on prepping Tiny for their lesson. He knew he had to go, and yet he hesitated, his eyes still fixed on Nadine's. She really *was* beautiful, he realized suddenly—it was as if the moment she'd let go of her constant animosity towards him, a new light had suffused her face, and he was drawn to its glow.

For a strange moment, words seemed to fail him, and he just wanted to gaze at her. When he'd first come to Catoctin Creek, he remembered, he'd been drawn to her, this pretty and quiet woman who handled horses with such ease and aplomb. Then she'd proven hard to work with—demanding and judgmental, perhaps rightfully so—and Sean pulled back from her. And as he'd lost himself in the hard work of charming potential investors, she seemed to lose her taste for him, even as a work friend. The split between them went from gap, to rift, to chasm, pretty quickly. Sean got caught up in the world of interesting, enterprising women who lived, worked, and volunteered in Catoctin Creek. And when he was away from the farm, it was easy to forget Nadine.

He'd even had a crush on Nikki down at the Blue Plate for a while. But Nikki was with Kevin, and anyway, she wasn't part of his plan.

Of course, neither was Nadine. But now, he almost regretted it. Almost wondered, for just a single weak moment, what life would be like if he stopped fighting so hard against his life in Catoctin Creek, and simply embraced it instead.

Nadine's long lashes swept over her cheeks, and he wondered if she was thinking the same thing.

Then, there was a knock on the window. Sean jumped and turned. He found Martha waving at him. "See you at Tiny's stall!" she called, smiling broadly. She smoothed her carefully tended hair, its gold highlights shining under the sunlight streaming through the roof's translucent panels, and headed back down the aisle.

He turned around again and saw Nadine smirking at him. "Really, Sean? She was wearing fresh lipstick, for heaven's sake."

He felt a swell of irritation and, worse than that, shame. "You're *really* judgmental, Nadine, did anyone ever tell you that?"

His hand was on the doorknob when she replied, softly, "Yeah, Sean, but I only judge the people who are worth my time."

Chapter Seven

Nadine

She wasn't sure what had made her say that. It was almost like some strange little devil had taken over her brain for a moment—like the tiny ones who sat on Bugs Bunny's shoulder and convinced him to do bad things. Because she'd probably just said it to mess with Sean, right? And that was a bad thing. She should behave better.

Whatever. Nadine resolved not to worry about it. A quick, throwaway line to her colleague, which might make him think a little harder about his work choices, which might make her job easier—who knew? Stranger things had happened. In the meantime, she'd get back to work. The one thing Nadine could always rely on was work. In a lot of ways, she reflected, work was better than people. At least when you had a barn full of horses to take care of, the chores would never, ever let you down.

Nadine locked her office door behind her and crossed the aisle to the feed room. She needed to do a count of inventory, and prepare the farm's weekly order with the feed store. Counting bags of sweet feed was a better use of her time than fussing over Sean Casey.

By the time she had her order phoned in and had collected a week's worth of local gossip from Ronna Routzahn, who was manning the counter that afternoon, school let out and the barn started to fill up with students and boarders. The afternoon began to blur after that. Helping students get tacked and mounted, holding horses when they ran out of cross-ties and wash-racks, taking payment from parents and printing receipts, answering questions on everything from how much it would cost to enter the upcoming hunter pace to whether horses should be fed carrots as treats, or if they required the newest, cutest "horse cupcakes" someone's daughter had seen at the tack shop.

"I'd suggest carrots for every day, cupcakes for a special occasion." Nadine answered the treat question briskly and efficiently, as she tried to do everything when dealing with the customers, even though she thought it was ludicrous. Politeness won her a lot of battles in this barn, where there was often more money than sense. "Cupcakes make for cute pics, but most horses aren't going to prefer one sweet over another. And carrots have way less sugar, obviously."

"Oh my God. Do horses get cavities?" The mother of the cupcake-requesting student looked suddenly anxious, her gaze flicking nervously to the ten-thousand-dollar horse she'd recently written a check for, and Nadine had to think on her feet. Why had she never heard of cavities in a horse's mouth?

Oh, right. She had it.

"Probably not, since horse's teeth never stopped growing."

This was met with more concern. "They *do*? Why don't they get too long?"

"Oh my God, Mom. I've got this, Nadine." The teenage student flicked back her hair, having returned from the bathroom just in time to overhear the last question. She reached to retrieve her horse's reins, and Nadine relinquished the horse gratefully, retreating before the kid reminded her mother of the twice-yearly dental bills she had evidently glossed over when reading the printout "What to Expect As a Horse Owner," which Nadine provided to all purchasers.

"They scrape their *teeth* with a *file?*" she heard the mother squeak, and smiled grimly. Teenagers were great communicators, truly remarkable.

"All right, Nadine?" She turned at the sound of her name, and spotted Rosemary in the aisle, standing amidst a group of parents and looking uncomfortable with the crowd. She smiled apologetically and shrugged. "I came back to check on Finn."

"Rosemary, hi! Yeah, it's just the busy time of night."

"I see that." Rosemary flicked nervous eyes around the aisle, reminding Nadine that the other woman was extremely introverted. "Is it always this crowded at night?"

"Generally. But I know a quiet spot, if you need a break." She took Rosemary's arm and gently guided her past the throngs of bored horses and chattering people milling in the aisle. Unlocking her office door, she escorted Rosemary inside. "Here we go. I shut the door and boom, we're alone."

"That's nice, thank you." Without the buzz of conversation and hive of bodies, Rosemary looked much more at ease. She looked around the office with interest. "Your own space, huh? Must be nice."

"Yes. I love having an office," Nadine confessed. "It does come in handy on nights like this, when no one will leave me alone. This isn't the first time I've sneaked in here!"

"Oh, but I didn't mean to take up your time." Rosemary had settled into a chair, but now she made to stand up. "I was really just looking at Finn, and he seems like he's settled in just fine."

"You're fine! Please don't go." Nadine held out a hand, and Rosemary settled into the chair again. "If you give them a few minutes, it will clear out a little. You got here just as the five o'clock lesson was ending and it's really big. Most people are gone by six-thirty, though."

They chit-chatted about horses for a few moments, while the aisle outside continued to heave with activity. Finally, horses stopped clopping past, and Nadine knew the last of the five o'clock riders were heading home. "All clear," she said kindly. "Unless you need to stick around for a few minutes?"

"No, I'm fine. Actually, Nadine before you go—I just wanted to ask you something." Rosemary put her hands together, looking as if she might actually wring them with anxiety.

"Ask away," Nadine replied, feeling a little concerned by Rosemary's clear discomfort. They didn't know each other well, but she had an affection for Rosemary—as did nearly everyone in Catoctin Creek. She'd long been regarded as the village's kindly spinster, living alone on the family farm after her parents died in an accident. Even though Stephen Beckett had married her, there was still a general feeling of protectiveness where Rosemary was concerned.

"What do you think of Sean as a trainer?"

Nadine lifted her eyebrows. She hadn't expected a question like *that*. And she didn't have an answer ready, either. Was Sean a trainer? Or was he just a pretty rider? She'd asked herself that dozens of times over the past few months. Now, she tried to put together an answer which wouldn't get anyone in trouble. "I—uh—his students all like him, I guess, and—he hasn't got anyone hurt."

"No, not as a riding instructor. I know those words are usually interchangeable. But I mean, *just* as a rider, as a horseman. Is he the right choice to ride Finn? I just want to know he's getting the best possible start—Finn, you know. I worry about him. I've never sent a horse out to sell before . . . I keep all of them for life." Rosemary's sweet face twisted with worry. "I'm afraid I made a mistake."

"There's no way you made a mistake." Nadine spoke confidently; she was on firm ground now. "Between you and me? I'm going to be riding Finn, and I am a very good trainer. So take it from me: Finn is my responsibility, and I won't let anything happen to him."

Rosemary's troubled expression cleared. "That means a lot to me, Nadine. Thank you. And as for Sean, well . . . I don't mean to be suspicious of him. He's a nice guy. But I've never seen him ride. That makes him, I don't know, a little bit of an unknown entity for me, when it comes to training."

"Of course it does. And he's very kind and patient with horses," Nadine assured her. She knew that much was true. What she didn't know, because it had never been tested, was how *capable* Sean was with a green horse. Calypso, Chocolate Kiss, and the horses he'd tuned-up and sold for Caitlin just weren't in the same category as a mystery horse like Finn. "But we agreed I can start him out, see what he knows. I have the background."

Rosemary leaned forward, suddenly interested. "Where did you start riding, Nadine? I know you're younger than I am, but I still think I would've known if you rode at Elmwood."

Nadine hesitated. She didn't tell people about the Remsen barn—not even Caitlin knew she'd worked there. If she could have, she would have worn that experience like a badge of honor. But the horsepeople of Catoctin Creek didn't look at the Remsen sales lot as an acceptable place for their youngsters to learn to ride. And honestly, it was hard to blame them.

But she trusted Rosemary's discretion. "I started riding with Mike and Joe Remsen, you must know them."

"Up near the PA border? *That* Mike and Joe?" Rosemary seemed a little dismayed. "That place is—well, it's a dump, if I'm being honest. And their horses are . . ."

"Dangerous?" Nadine suggested. "I know. That's where I learned to ride. And how to be very quiet in the saddle. When you're riding a ticking time-bomb, you learn to ride pretty softly." Well, smart people did. The ones who didn't want to get bucked off constantly.

"I had no idea you worked there. When was this?"

"Ten years ago," Nadine said. "When I first got a car and could get a job. No one else would hire me at sixteen. So I didn't have the option of being choosey. But I learned a lot, really quickly."

"You're lucky you didn't get killed."

"I know."

They looked at one another for a minute. Then Rosemary glanced out the window behind her. "You said you were needed out there, and I kept you anyway," she said apologetically. "I appreciate your taking on Finn, though. If you rode those horses at sixteen . . ." She shook her head. "You can ride him, no matter what he brings."

"Just one thing," Nadine said, standing up. "This is between Sean and me. We didn't clear it with Caitlin. So if you could keep it to yourself . . ."

Rosemary's smile was sympathetic. "I won't tell our friend the steamroller anything. You two do what's best for you. And for Finn. Keep me posted, okay?"

"Absolutely," Nadine promised. "I'm really looking forward to riding him."

Rosemary's hand was on the doorknob, but she paused before pushing the door open, her eyes studying Nadine's face. Nadine waited, wondering what the pronouncement would be. Finally, Rosemary nodded. "I'm glad you're here, Nadine," she said. "Be safe."

Nadine gave her a few moments to walk down the aisle alone before she followed, figuring it would be easier for Rosemary to leave without feeling any pressure to keep talking. It gave her a little extra time to collect herself, too, reflecting on the things she'd said tonight. Admitting she'd worked at the Remsen farm, for the notorious horse-trading duo of Mike and Joe, was a secret she'd held close for years. The one favor she'd knowingly accepted from Reg, as distasteful as it had been, was an introduction to his buddies who bought and sold horses for a living. She'd traded up over the years, working at increasingly better facilities until she'd ended up at Elmwood, but getting her start working for a pair who frequented notorious auctions, accepted stolen stock, and weren't choosey about where their horses went or what drugs they might be on? Not something she was willing to publicize.

"Well, Rosemary can keep a secret," she told herself, heading out. She looked around her office one more time before locking up. She wouldn't be back tonight. After she helped put away the last lesson, she was going to ride Finn.

The big horse shifted nervously, ducking his head against the bit. Sean jiggled the reins. "I don't think he knows what a mounting block is."

Nadine stood on the top step of the plastic mounting block, wishing it was a three-step instead of a two-step, and tried to gauge whether Finn was too far away for a safe swing into the saddle. If he jumped when she mounted, then yes, she was too far away. If he stood still, then they were golden. But she had no way of knowing which response she'd get.

"A horse this big has to know about mounting blocks," she sighed, gesturing for Sean to circle him around again. "There's no way anyone has been mounting from the ground."

"A tall person with a western saddle could."

That was true. But there were neither of those things at Elmwood Equestrian Center. There was just short Nadine, average-height Sean, and an English saddle from the lesson tack room. "Hold him there," Nadine said, getting down to business. "Perfect. Hands loose, but ready to tell him whoa—perfect." She took a breath, held the stirrup for her boot, and then went for it.

Finn bulled forward, nearly rolling Sean under his hooves. But Nadine was in the saddle and both feet were in the stirrups, and she felt ready for anything. Just about anything. "You can let go," she called, pressing her hands close to Finn's mane, the reins gripped gently between her fingers. "I've got him now."

"I'll walk alongside you," Sean insisted, and she let him, but there was no need. Finn was walking forward with his ears flicking gently between the two of them, his step light and even, his back flat and calm.

"He isn't humping his back," she told Sean. "He has a really nice relaxed feel."

"Lucky him," Sean grumbled. "Tell me if you feel him start to hump up, though. If he bucks, you're going to go through the roof."

"I don't think he will—" But Finn cut off Nadine's optimistic words as he caught sight of a flicker of movement in the corner of the arena. He ducked his head, bringing his chin close to his chest, and rounded his back, trotting in place.

"It was just a mouse," Sean huffed, taking Finn by the bridle and tugging him forward. "We all saw it."

"He's okay." Nadine could already feel the horse's hunched spine relaxing beneath her. "Just got startled. And he's looking for trouble, anyway."

"I'll stay close anyway," Sean said, glancing up at her.

She was a little touched by how worried he seemed about her. And a little annoyed, too. Did he really think she was such a green rider, she couldn't handle a few antics from a young horse? A snappy retort was on the tip of her tongue, a reminder that *he* was the one who hadn't wanted to ride this horse, not her. But she bit it back. Sean was just being thoughtful.

Nice, even.

"Let's just do a couple circuits of the arena, and if he stays relaxed, I'll see how he trots," Nadine decided. "If he gets spooky, we'll chalk it up to cold weather and new places, and try him again tomorrow during the day, when it's warmer."

Sean agreed, but he didn't move away from the horse's head. He trudged alongside them, booted feet struggling through the cuppy clay footing alongside the rut where the horses had been working all evening, reminding Nadine of the sidewalkers from the therapeutic riding session. Which reminded her of Martha Lane.

She glanced down at the back of Sean's head. Was there something going on between those two?

It was none of her business. Probably. But then again, Martha was barn business. And barn business was her business.

Nadine felt utterly justified when she asked, "Sean, how was Martha?"

He kept his eyes forward. "Sorry?"

"Martha. Your student? You seem really protective of her. Just wondering how her ride went."

"It went... like a ride. What do you mean, protective?"

She could hear the note of defensiveness enter his voice. It was slightly high-pitched. Nadine thought she'd pricked a hole in his armor. It made her lean forward in the saddle, hungry to do more damage. Finn jigged a little, reacting to her shift in weight.

"Don't play dumb with me. You did a whole weird power play with Tiny today. And her attitude with you, in general, is awfully flirty. Is there... Sean Casey!" Nadine gasped, as if she'd just hit upon an incredible discovery. "Do you two have something going on?"

"Are you asking me if I'm having an affair with Martha Lane?" Sean managed to infuse his voice with an impressive amount of sarcasm.

Nadine was momentarily disappointed, but she bounced back quickly. "It wouldn't be an affair. Her divorce was literally covered in *The Washington Post*. Including the million-dollar settlement she got." Martha's very public split from a D.C. lobbyist had been the event which precipitated her initial arrival as a volunteer, and then taking up riding lessons, in the first place. She'd needed a distraction from the frenzy. Her therapist had suggested horses.

"Well, no. There's nothing going on." His words were stilted now. "I think that's ridiculous."

Nadine wasn't convinced, but she abandoned that line, anyway. He wasn't going to give her anything. "Well, why don't you want her to buy Chocolate Kiss?"

"I just think she could spend more if we held out for longer."

"Caitlin would say board money now is more important than an extra few grand in sales later."

"Well, maybe Caitlin is wrong this time, okay?"

"Oh, sorry!" Nadine stiffened at his retort, and beneath her, Finn did too. He flung up his head and tossed in a few dancing, sideways steps for good measure. "Settle down," she told the horse, patting his neck, while Sean grew flustered and grabbed at the reins. "It's nothing for you to worry about. People-stuff only."

"I think you should get off," Sean warned her. "He's getting antsy. A turn around the arena is good enough for tonight."

"It's nothing. Let us go. I'll trot him right now, take the edge off."

"No!" Sean clung to the reins tighter. Finn shied away from his sharp tone, turning his hindquarters sideways. His hind hooves hit the arena's wooden kick board, and he jumped forward, spooking himself.

Sean was quickly left behind, but Nadine wasn't worried about him. She pushed her hands forward, hoping her body weight would follow and she wouldn't tip out of the saddle backwards. Luckily, it worked. She ended up hunched over Finn's neck as he took off across the arena, his huge strides eating up the ground. The horse flattened his ears and tried to push his head down, so she yanked up, sticking her heels into his sides at the same time. The trick worked; he picked up his head quickly, hollowing his back, and Nadine relaxed a little. She didn't mind if he wanted to run, as long as he wasn't bucking.

A few turns around the arena came more quickly than she'd intended, and Sean stood in the center of the ring, hands on his hips, as she let him gallop down the long sides. At the corner of each short end she stood up in the stirrups, reining back hard, so that he had to slow down around the turns. After the third turn, he slowed to a trot, then shoved his head against the bit in a gesture which suggested he was tired of running away.

Nadine put her hands forward, giving him a little room to stretch, and rose with the trot. He had a huge step, she noticed. He'd be a beautiful mover, but it would be awfully hard for the average rider to sit this kind of trot. She was coming out of the saddle by miles every time she rose, borne upwards by the lift in his gait.

"What a star," she murmured, before slowly lifting her hands and sitting back in the saddle. Finn responded willingly, taking a few more steps of trot before he shambled down to a walk. Not a very tidy downward transition, but not completely raw and green, either. Nadine patted him on the neck, her hand slipping beneath the heavy fall of his black mane. "Well done, big boy."

She reined him into the center of the ring, where Sean was still standing in place, looking like a riding instructor who had given up trying to control his students. She thought his expression was strained. Had she frightened him? For a moment she felt bad, and then she was just amused that Caitlin thought Sean should be the one to start this horse. She didn't know what Sean Casey had lied about to get his job here, but if he'd said he was experienced with young horses, that was going on the list.

"Pretty easy ride once he got his jollies out," she said, walking the horse in a circle around Sean. "You want to try him?"

"No, thanks."

She didn't bother hiding her grin. "So he's mine for a little while longer?"

"You two seem to get along." Sean's taut expression told her he wasn't amused with her teasing.

What a shame. "You know, if you got a sense of humor you'd be a lot more fun to hang out with," she informed him.

"If you had any sense, you'd be a lot easier to hang out with," Sean retorted, and he marched out of the ring.

Nadine stared after him, surprised—and a little dismayed, too. What was that supposed to mean?

"Men are so weird," she muttered, and Finn snorted. Which might have been an agreement, but she didn't know if Finn was on her side, or Sean's.

Chapter Eight

Sean

Sean marched upstairs without bothering to help Nadine put Finn away. Since she was so smart and so good with green horses, she could handle it herself. He didn't have to sit around and babysit her. She'd wanted to be in charge of Finn? Fine. All hers. He was hungry and tired and cold. Good freaking night.

But once inside his bare little apartment, water heating on the burner to make a package of ramen, Sean didn't feel great about leaving Nadine to wrap up her ride on her own. He hadn't even waited for her to dismount! For all he knew, Finn had dumped her on the ground immediately, the very second he'd closed his door, and while he'd been tugging off his boots and yanking down his cold, sweaty socks, she was laying in the dirt, injured and alone.

Sean managed to build this up into quite a pathetic scene by the time he rushed to his door and tugged open his sticky door. But it turned out he was wrong. Nadine had Finn in the wash-rack and was rubbing his back with a towel dipped in a bucket of hot water. She looked up at him and paused in her work.

"Everything all right, Sean?"

He narrowed his eyes at her. Stupid competent blameless Nadine. "I guess you've used up all the hot water for the next hour," he snarled.

Nadine shook her head. "I only filled one bucket. You can still take a shower. I'll wait until later."

"No, I'm making supper." He went back inside, slamming the door behind him, and then stood still as the entire apartment seemed to wobble. It had a nasty habit of doing that when he was a little too violent with the door. Because Sean did not like earthquakes, he had been pretty careful about this effect for some months. But he guessed tonight he was just full of bad decisions.

The water was boiling, steam rising to the low ceiling. He turned the burner down and threw in the brick of noodles. Then he looked around and sighed.

A rectangle of dark tones and wood paneling. His apartment was a little like living inside a railroad car. Not a fancy, old-fashioned sleeper, either. Just the kind you'd slide open and fill with cans of beans or something. The kind a hobo would clamber into, finding a convenient pile of straw in one corner for sleeping as the train clicked over the rails all night long. At least the hobo would wake up somewhere new. Sean would creep beneath the covers of his bed tonight and wake up in the same place tomorrow.

And he was so tired of waking up here, when he was waiting for something so much more.

He thought about messaging Simone, but decided he was too blue; she didn't like it when he was anything but perfectly sunny and optimistic. Simone considered people with problems toxic; she said she couldn't afford for her positivity to be brought down by anyone else's bad attitudes. And she was alarmingly good at putting aside her own unhappiness. Look at what had happened with Winsome, the horse that Sean's father had bought for her. At first it had seemed like a friendly business venture between two families which had been friendly for years. But when the Casey horses were sold, Simone's horse went, too.

When his father informed them the farm was going to developers and the horses, Winsome included, were all shipping to new owners, Simone had cried briefly; he'd seen her red eyes when he'd gone to her apartment, desperate for someone to talk to. But even though she'd loved Winsome, and they'd qualified for several year-end championships which she would now miss, Simone pushed through the loss almost instantly. With dry eyes, she told Sean she was going to find some new horses, and he'd be smart to start looking for someone else to underwrite his showing career. And she made it clear he wasn't going to cry on her shoulder about any of it.

Sean had expected he might get a little sympathy—after all, Simone lost one horse, but he lost his home and an entire stable of horses. He also lost his parents, in a way, because they were in the Bahamas, living at the old beach house, unwilling and uninterested in giving him the support he needed to continue his American horse showing career. They seemed to think he could just walk away as simply as they had.

"There just isn't enough money for it, dear," his mother had told him. "Things didn't work out. I'm sorry."

He'd just stared at her, dazed.

Things didn't work out. Four simple words for the end of Sean's life as he'd known it. There'd been no plan. His father hadn't prepared him for the possibility of losing everything. And to be technical about it, his father *hadn't* lost everything. The things that were squirreled away, like the Bahamas house, were waiting for his parents when the farm was gone. They made their position quite clear. They were leaving. If Sean didn't go with them, if Sean didn't like the things they'd saved for themselves, well, then Sean was welcome to figure out his own way in the world.

He was trying. He really was.

Sean ladled soup into a mug and sat down on the sagging brown sofa. He tried to watch some TV, but the antenna was bad and there wasn't any cable, so he took out his laptop and streamed some shows instead. The Wi-Fi was slow and spotty up here, but he'd learned to live with the constantly stalling streams.

"See?" he told himself, chuckling ruefully as the video buffered yet again. "A person really can get used to anything."

In the quiet moments while the internet reset itself, Sean listened to the surrounding sounds. The wailing of pipes at the end of the apartment told him Nadine was using the hose in the washrack again, probably cleaning up for the night once she'd put Finn away. Then he heard her staircase creaking, like a distant ship groaning in heavy seas, before her door opened and closed. As he finished his soup, he listened to her steps moving around her apartment, just one wall away from her.

It was calming, having Nadine next door. Not because it was Nadine, of course. But just the presence of another person. He didn't know if he could manage to sleep in this apartment without someone on the other side of that wall. Not with that vast barn stretching out beneath him, filled with the odd raps and bangs of the night, impossible to tell if he was hearing horses kicking their walls, cats stalking rats, or—anything else. Nadine might not be the nicest person in the world, at least not to him, but she was another person, and sometimes that was all that mattered.

Today had been nice, though. At times. They'd had lunch together. They'd agreed on training Finn together. And even though she'd totally scared him while riding Finn, at least she'd done a nice job with the horse. He could probably learn a lot from her if she would be willing to teach him.

Sean put his dirty mug in the sink, ran water into it, and looked at the clock. Eight o'clock. Even with their late-evening ride on Finn extending the work day by an hour, he still felt at loose ends. What could he do between now and ten o'clock, when he'd try to fall asleep? Stare at the swirling little buffering symbol on his laptop screen? Drink a six-pack? Scream into the void?

He listened to Nadine's footsteps, so close, and then, without thinking, he knocked on the wall.

There was a moment's silence. Then her footsteps resumed, came closer. He felt like she was standing right next to him. Cautiously, with a long space between them, she made two quite knocks.

He knocked right back, laughing when he heard her step back. And then, like magic, he heard her laughter through the wall.

Suddenly, Sean felt better. About all of it: the night ahead of him, the prickly woman he worked with, even the drab little apartment. He knocked once more, and then he called, "Meet me downstairs in ten minutes."

He didn't know if she'd come, but after a few moments he heard her footsteps retreating into the bedroom. Sean followed suit, pulling a warm blue sweater over his t-shirt and tugging on a dry pair of socks. He didn't have a clear idea of what was coming next;

he just knew he didn't want to be alone—and with Nadine living right there, he didn't have to be.

He heard her before she appeared, her staircase creaking once more as she came lightly down the treads. He was leaning against the wall facing the wash-racks, horses moving in the stalls behind him, eating their hay and turning softly in their shavings. The barn was dark, with just a few lamps half-lit up in the rafters, casting a faint, ghostly glow across the aisles. When he called a quiet hello to her, his breath appeared in a blue fog.

The light was just enough to show her cautious smile.

"What are we doing?" she asked, keeping her voice low, as if she was afraid the horses would hear them and think it was time to eat. "It's too soon for night-check. Did you need something?"

"I needed company," Sean said, and then, seeing her expression slip into suspicion, he added, "I needed your company."

Her eyebrows came together. "Why mine?"

"I don't know," Sean laughed, feeling delighted to be around someone else. He couldn't believe how low his mood must have been, that he could suddenly be buoyed so high just by another person's presence. By her presence. "Dammit, Nadine, let's be friends. It's tiring, living here with a person who hates me."

She sighed. "I don't *hate* you."

"You hate me. Admit it."

Nadine dropped her eyes. "I may have thought I hated you."

"But you don't, not really?" Sean tipped his head at her, going for the puppy-dog look. "You're willing to give me a chance? I mean, if you overlook how I do everything wrong and make you mad all the time, I'm great."

She laughed despite herself, and he allowed himself a little grin. "Fine. We can be friends, but only because you let me ride Finn. And because you look really pathetic right now."

"I am pathetic," he assured her. "Very. What now? Should we go for a walk? I bet there's a moon. When's the last time you were outside at night?"

Nadine shook her head, thinking. "I honestly don't know. I'm always inside the barn after sunset. Until we start turning horses out at night, I have no reason to go out."

"Well, now you have one. Let's go look for the moon." Sean led the way, heading for the side door near the indoor arena's entrance. It would be easier, quieter, to slip out that way, rather than tugging open the big barn doors they closed each night after lessons ended.

"Okay, crazy person," she agreed, laughter in her voice, and he heard her steps chasing after him.

Sean pushed open the door, taking care to keep the lock unbuttoned. They stepped over the sill and looked across the outdoor arena, the jumps glistening white in the moonlight.

"You were right," Nadine sighed. "How did you know there'd be a moon? You checked your phone, didn't you?"

"No," Sean insisted, feeling elated by the blue glow of the moon. "I just felt it. I've got the moon in my blood."

She laughed again, pushing one hand against his arm, and he felt a warmth spread through his body at her touch. Startled, he glanced back, suddenly dying to see her pretty, pale features in the moon-glow. But Nadine was still standing in the shadow of the barn, and from there she looked like a spirit, her form just barely showing in the realm of men and horses. He reached back and clutched at her hand, pulling her forward into the moonlight. And then, without really knowing why, he started running.

Startled laughter bubbled from her throat as they went tripping through the night, passing the outdoor arena and running right up to the dark fence of the front pasture. The countryside spread out before them, slumbering silently under the silver-gold face of the moon. In the distance, a car drove along the main road, its headlights seeming to flicker as it passed each post of Elmwood's long, ramrod-straight fence. Off to their right, beyond the empty square of the parking lot, a sphere of golden light seemed to surround Caitlin's home, where strategic spotlights lit up the graceful frontage of the historic farmhouse that had been in her family for generations.

They leaned on the fence, his urge to run momentarily stilled by the wood against his chest. Much like a horse, he thought, chuckling to himself. The permanence of the surrounding countryside, the dips and hollows of the fields and foothills, all served as a balm to his spirit.

"What are we doing?" Nadine gasped. "I feel like we just went a little crazy."

"We should go all the way crazy," Sean said, with no idea what he meant, but sure she'd understand.

"Or maybe we shouldn't," she replied, and he looked at her with sudden disappointment. But she wasn't turning around. She wasn't abandoning him for the staid security of the barn. He looked over his shoulder, at the little rectangle of half-light where the open door stood against the dark hulk of the barn. When he turned back to Nadine, she was walking along the fence-line. Sean scrambled after her.

"Don't leave me out here in the dark," he called, just to hear her laugh again.

She didn't disappoint him. "I think if we go this way, behind the indoor, we can see more stars. We just need to blot out the lights around Caitlin's house. She lights it up that way so it looks too bright to rob at night, but it kills the view of the night sky on that side of the barn."

They emerged on the empty ground beyond the indoor. Ahead there was just another fence, separating them from the broad sweep of the north pasture. And sky: a dark velvet sky filled with a million points of light.

"Oh, wow," he murmured.

"I know." Nadine's voice was low in her throat, as if she was afraid to scare the stars away. "And if you look that way—" she pointed into the distance, "—you can see the Catoctin Mountains. Look, there are a couple of lights on them."

The low, dark mountains were at least ten miles away, but the moonlight still seemed to pick out the tree canopy of the thickly forested slopes. As Nadine had said, a few house lights gleamed into the distance.

"I love those mountains," she sighed. "I wish I lived right in their folds, like Rosemary does. Her back pasture slopes right up to Notch Gap. It's incredible. I've been looking at those mountains my whole life, but when I'm up in them, I feel like I'm just wrapped up, safe and protected."

Sean glanced at her, taking in the faraway look on her face. Her dark hair fell around her cheeks and curled over her shoulders, and he felt an inexplicable desire to wrap his hands in it. Then, without thinking, he did it, reaching out his left hand and sliding it right into those raven tresses.

Nadine shivered slightly, as if her hair had feelings of its own. And then, as he inadvertently tugged at a curl, she turned her head. Her eyes locked on his, wide and sparkling in the moonlight, so dark the green seemed changed to charcoal gray. Her lips parted. For a moment, Sean thought the unimaginable was going to happen.

And he wanted it to happen.

Then she stepped back, confusion taking over her features. "Sean," she said softly, his name a question. "What—"

He put his hands behind his back, as contrite as if she'd slapped him. "I'm sorry. I don't know what I was thinking."

Her gaze fell to the ground. Whatever spell the moonlight had woven, it was broken now. "I'm going to go back in," she said slowly.

"Me too," he agreed, but she shook her head softly.

"You don't have to follow me around," she told him. "I'm fine on my own."

Sean could take a hint. He tried his hardest not to watch her as she walked away from him, his eyes on the Catoctin Mountains, his ears attuned to every step she took.

Chapter Nine

Nadine

"I thought he was going to kiss me," Nadine whispered.

"Would you have let him?"

"Oh God, no. Come on, Avery. There's no chance in hell. This is *Sean Casey*."

"Whom I haven't met, because every time I suggest coming back to Catoctin Creek, you tell me to stay away."

"Well, I've told you plenty," Nadine grumbled. "You should know by now that he's not exactly boyfriend material. And you're better off out in the real world. You're a star now."

Avery's laugh was like sunlight sparkling over the satellite connection.

Nadine had been emailing, and then texting, her friend Avery nearly every day since the tenth grade—not coincidentally, the same year she had begun working at Mike and Joe's farm. That was also when Avery put all her efforts into the Catoctin Creek Players, an amateur drama group which was constantly putting on an ambitious schedule of shows very few Catoctin Creek residents bothered to see, but which made nice weekend amusements for out-of-towners up from D.C. or Baltimore for an antiquing weekend. With their after school and weekend pursuits suddenly miles apart (literally), their friendship outside of class went mostly virtual.

And it had stayed that way, even as Avery embarked on an exhaustingly ambitious theatrical career.

The phone call was out of the ordinary; Avery was often in a far-off time zone and Nadine went to bed pretty early, but the situation downstairs had been pretty out of the ordinary, too. Nadine had needed someone else's voice, and Avery's musical, professionally trained vocals were the only choice that would do.

"I'm halfway to accepting this Catoctin Creek Players alumni invitation," Avery warned her now, her voice tinkling with more suppressed laughter. "Maybe it's time to come home and see the old stomping grounds, sing a little duet with old Mr. Stanbaugh."

"You wouldn't." Nadine tipped her head back a little too quickly and thumped it against the hard back of the sofa. "Ouch!"

"Calm down, don't hurt yourself. I won't come back. They're just doing a revue, anyway, and I hate those. Give me a story, not a collection of songs. It's not a concert. Anyway, this Sean thing. Maybe you had him all wrong. I think you should see it through. Give him a chance."

"He's trying to seduce a middle-aged woman into buying him show horses," Nadine said flatly. "Or have you not been reading my emails?"

"I thought that was like, a euphemism."

"For *what?*"

"Let's not even pursue that. Forget I said anything. So okay. Sean wants some nice horses, and he's willing to put out to get them, *but* he also wants to kiss you. Well, he knows you can't buy him any horses. So maybe he's changing his priorities?"

Nadine huffed a sigh.

"What? People can change. You're in your late twenties now. This is prime change season."

"Have you changed?"

"I change every few weeks, Nadine. I'm an actress."

They both laughed.

"In all seriousness," Avery finally sighed. "Would it be so bad? I thought you said he was gorgeous."

"He is gorgeous. But all that hot just covers up his total lack of good. He's a big fake, Avery. It's hard to explain to someone who isn't in horses. But half the time, I feel like he's got no idea what he's doing. He can ride, from what I've seen, and he manages to teach people okay. But he fumbles around with stuff I can do in my sleep, like wrapping legs, or setting grain." Nadine tried to think of a suitable metaphor Avery would understand. "It's like, he can direct, but he can't act."

"That's normal, actually. But I can see where you're trying to go. I just don't think I understand what that has to do with being hot and being a good kissing candidate, I guess. Is he not nice? Big old meanie?"

Nadine listened to Sean's footsteps on the other side of the wall. He was walking from bedroom to kitchen. She wondered if he'd changed into some nice, cozy pajamas. Now, maybe, he was going into the little fridge with its tiny half-freezer compartment to get out a tub of ice cream. A little bedtime snack. She imagined him settling down on the sofa to work his way through a pint of— now, what would Sean's favorite ice cream be? Something chunky and crunchy, like that one she'd had last week that was stuffed full of peanut butter cups and pretzels? Or was he a smooth and staid vanilla kind of guy? No, not Sean. He was too adventurous—

"Nadine? You still there?"

"Sorry. Yeah. Thought I... uh... saw a mouse." Nadine's mind had gone inconveniently blank for a moment there.

"Gross! You have mice in your apartment?"

"Well, it's a *barn,*" Nadine reminded her, and the conversation derailed for several minutes.

"You've proven your point," Avery said eventually. "Barn cats are very important and they do deserve health insurance just like regular workers. I'm not sure how we reached that conclusion, but I'm with you now."

That was the fun of a chat with Avery. They always ended up heading off on weird avenues. Their conversations were impossible to keep on track. Nadine tugged a fleece throw up around her legs, hoping they'd talk longer, but Avery started bringing up her early alarm in the morning, so she guessed they were wrapping things up.

"You didn't tell me what to do about Sean," she complained as Avery finished describing her hellacious commute into the downtown theater where she would be working on sets the next day. "We're only talking about *your* problems and I think I made it pretty clear this call was about me."

"Oh, fine," Avery snorted. She thought for a moment. "I think you should kiss him and then decide."

"What? How is that a choice?"

"If you already made your mind up and you're going to turn him down, why are you asking me?"

"For back-up."

"No. You're not getting back-up on this. Nadine, you haven't been on a date in, what, five years?"

"Try *one,*" Nadine retorted, stung.

"Oh, *forgive* me. That is so much better."

"I keep to myself. You know I don't want to run into anyone from high school. I don't need to relive that period of my life."

"Which is why you should never have moved back. But *whatever.* I *digress.*" Avery's voice was reaching peak dramatic actress levels. The finale was coming now. "Kiss Sean Casey. Give yourself permission to have some fun. You *need* to have fun, and frankly he sounds like he could do that for you. So try it. Make things weird. Do everything you wouldn't normally do. And see what happens!"

"That's your advice?"

"Uh-huh."

"Are you done now?"

"Uh-huh."

Nadine sighed as loudly as she possibly could. It was possible Sean heard her through the wall. Or maybe he thought it was a gust of wind.

"Good luck, Nadine. Keep me posted!"

"Thanks, Avery. I think."

With a final peal of laughter, Avery hung up.

Nadine stared into the darkness of her bedroom for a few minutes, trying to absorb Avery's advice. Was there any good in it? Making things weird and doing everything she didn't normally do . . . these things all sounded like bad ideas. And yet . . . she *hadn't* kissed anyone in a year. Avery, she guessed, probably had.

It was funny, but, until tonight, Nadine hadn't felt lonely in a long, long time. She had been living alone for years now, bouncing from bad housing situations to slightly better ones as she upgraded jobs, worrying only about the lock on her door and the quality of her horse care. She hadn't had time to worry about things like friendships—anyway, her regular chats with Avery went a long way towards filling that void. Horses, requiring constant attention and limitless worry, erased the rest of it.

But now, she felt the quiet, especially when Sean's apartment didn't yield any creaks or groaning floorboards to let her know he was there. She felt the emptiness. She sensed the void.

She had a suspicion things had already gone too far, and despite her best intentions of doing otherwise, she was about to do some things she didn't normally do.

Not tonight, though.

Tonight, she was going to bed.

Nadine's phone buzzed with her boss's morning check-in earlier than usual. She ran a hand over her tired eyes as she pulled the phone from her jeans pocket. The sunrise was a particularly dazzling one, and she'd just turned out the ponies in the front field, where they'd galloped away, gilded with gold. She leaned against the fence and pressed the phone to her ear. "Hey, Caitlin."

"Hey, yourself. I have good news!"

Well, Caitlin was very awake this morning.

"What's up?"

"About half the course is ready! The contractor sent me an email last night, and I just spotted it. I need you and Sean to go ride over it today and let me know if any jumps need adjustments. He'll make changes we need while he's finishing up the second half."

It took Nadine a solid minute to realize Caitlin was talking about the hunter pace course. Someone had been out in the north pasture building? The crew must have been on the far side, beyond the creek. "I didn't even know there was construction going on out there."

"The hunter pace is in less than two months, Nadine! Of course they're doing construction! You guys just spend too much time inside. Seriously, move all the lessons outside. All of them. Unless it's raining, you're using the outdoor ring or the field. I want everyone comfortable outside. Tell Sean for me, okay?"

"Can't you tell him?" Nadine wasn't sure she was up to giving Sean that kind of news. The guy seemed married to the indoor arena.

"Can't. Meetings all day in Frederick today. Tell him. Bye!"

Nadine sighed into her empty speaker. Sometimes it felt better after she did that, as if she'd *actually* heaved a sigh at her boss. Not that she ever would.

Richie and Rose came out of the barn, leading a pair of lesson horses out to their paddock. "You look down," Richie observed. "Everything okay?"

"Fine, Richie, thanks." Nadine popped on an artificial grin and kept wearing it as she walked into the barn to fetch another horse.

She *was* a little down this morning, although she was trying not to show it. She couldn't exactly talk about it with Richie and Rose. What would she do, explain she had shared a weird moment with Sean last night and she was afraid they were both getting the wrong ideas about each other?

They'd have a field day with that kind of news.

"Come on, Finn," she said, opening the big horse's stall door. He came right over to her, lowering his head to nudge at the halter. "Thanks, that's very helpful, but if you could just—be—still—there. Okay. Come on, you can go into a paddock for a while and then when Seany-boy gets up, we'll go for a ride."

"You're going to ride him now?"

She turned. Sean was walking down the aisle. In a black hoodie and skinny jeans, he didn't look like he was planning on helping with stalls. Of course not.

"Not now, but Caitlin wants us to go ride over the hunter pace course, or half of it, anyway. She won't be here today, so I figure I'll take him. Unless you were planning on riding him today."

"No, that's fine." He stopped a few feet away, hands in pockets. "I was going to pick up some breakfast. What's your favorite kind of muffin?"

"Blueberry, but no one has muffins unless you're going all the way to Frederick." There were gas station muffins, wrapped in plastic, but Nadine would pass on that kind of offering.

"Nikki's making muffins this morning. Testing her new kitchen. She told me to come by early and she'd give me a half dozen."

This was a significant development. Nikki's muffins were rare treats. She made them for Sunday breakfast at the diner sometimes, but they quickly sold out, and Nadine rarely had Sunday mornings off. Thick tops, fat blueberries, crystallized sugar . . . Nadine's mouth was watering already. She tugged back on Finn's lead, stopping him from circling in front of Sean. "Well, don't let me keep you. That's important work."

He smiled. "Yeah. As soon as I saw the text, I hopped out of bed. I mean—I was going to come down and help you, anyway, but..."

"You don't have to help with stalls, Sean." For once, Nadine wasn't just being sarcastic about it. The potential for muffins changed their dynamic. Maybe last night did a little, too. But mainly, it was muffins. "Honestly. That's not your job. I just like to hassle you for sleeping in."

Sean's smile became a grin. "Figures. Don't you know I'm sensitive? I take everything to heart."

"A real softie."

They eyed each other for a moment, each daring the other to say the next thing, to decide whether to make it cute, make it flirty, or make it snarky. The decision was too big for either of them to handle on their own.

So Finn cut the moment short, tossing his head and pawing with one platter-sized hoof. Sean and Nadine both took quick steps back, just in case that massive foreleg ended up swinging in their direction, and then she gave the horse a quick tug on the lead, reminding him of his manners. "Stop that, Finn! I'll take you out, big impatient baby."

"I'd better go get those muffins," Sean said.

"See you in a few," Nadine called over her shoulder; Finn was already dragging her out of the barn, his ears pricked as some ponies did a few aerial movements in their paddock. "If she has good coffee, bring me back some of that, too!"

Chapter Ten

Sean

Nikki had only told a few friends about the bakery's soft run, and the lucky chosen ones were crowded on the front porch of the graceful old Schubert house. Sean exchanged soft good mornings with Gus, the farrier who took care of the Elmwood horses' hooves, and Kevin, Nikki's boyfriend (and Gus's apprentice), who was working on the renovation of the house. Stephen and Rosemary Beckett were sitting on the steps, looking out at the tulips coming up along the front walk, which sloped up from the sidewalk's end. The Schubert house was the last house on Main Street; after its graceful lawn ended, Catoctin Creek's little grid gave way to fields and forest.

Golden light found its way around the house's distinctive turret and the gingerbread detailing along the porch eaves, making the red and yellow tulips glow with a fresh spring energy that Sean only wished he could tap into. He settled down on the same step as Rosemary, who seemed to feel the same way.

"Can you believe that shade of red, Sean? I feel like it's going to burn itself into my retinas."

"Tulips are spring in a single bloom," Stephen said, leaning over to kiss his wife's ear.

"Oh, you're a poet now!" Rosemary laughed lightly. "You're full of surprises, husband."

Sean listened to the two of them banter. He liked Stephen and Rosemary together—Stephen seemed to bring out Rosemary from herself, give her more authority to say what she wanted even when there were other people around, a scenario she generally avoided.

It was interesting to watch them separately and together, and see the way being part of a couple could change a person. Simone had always said that relationships ruined friendships and made people jealous to the point of insanity. Of course, she usually said that during one of the many times Sean worked up the nerve to ask her on a date, or tried to turn a beautiful sunset into an intimate moment. If there was one thing Simone had taught him, it was that life was not a movie. You needed more than a beach weekend and a stunning view to get a woman to change her mind about you.

Which was why last night had been such a mistake on his part. He knew better.

Moonlight. Sean shook his head. What had he been thinking? Just because he'd felt like he was under some magical spell didn't automatically mean everyone else under the moon last night had felt it, too. Nadine certainly hadn't.

Although for a moment, the way she'd looked at him . . . well, she'd had him fooled. But he'd probably seen the things he wanted to see.

"Why so sorrowful, Seany-boy?" Rosemary turned her big blue eyes on him. "You look like someone kicked your dog."

"That's a terrible expression," Stephen complained. "If someone kicked my dog, I'd be *furious*. I'd be swinging fists."

"City boy," Rosemary chided. "So violent. It's more like, if the *cow* kicked your dog. You wouldn't beat up your cow. You'd just be sad the whole thing happened at all. Sad for your dog, sad for your cow. Just a sad situation, overall."

"Is that true?" Stephen demanded. "The expression means a cow kicked your dog?"

The door opened behind them, saving Sean from finding a way to back up Rosemary's claim. "Muffins are here," Nikki announced. "Get your muffins!"

Rosemary gave him an excited look as she scrambled to her feet. "If Nadine doesn't love you for bringing her these muffins, send her to me. I'll knock some sense into her."

Sean grinned. "Thanks. If this doesn't work, I'm in way over my head."

Rosemary laughed. "Boy, I'll say!"

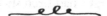

"Oh my God, Sean, these muffins are incredible." Nadine was practically moaning with happiness, which was quite a sound considering her mouth was full of muffin. "I owe you forever."

Close enough, Sean thought. He'd tell Rosemary the muffins worked their magic. Whatever weirdness had lingered between them earlier was gone now. Sometimes, all you needed was sugar. And butter. And blueberries. And whatever else went into muffins. He'd never actually made any. Luz had handled the cooking and baking at the Casey house.

Sean wondered who cooked for his mother and father now. Definitely not his mom. He cracked himself up just imagining it.

"Now I can't ride with you," Nadine sighed, wiping the smile from Sean's face.

"What? Why not?"

"Too... full... of... muffin..." She let herself go limp across the lounge sofa, eyes squeezing shut as if she was willing herself to fall asleep instantly.

"Come on. It's gorgeous out right now. Perfect sky. Perfect breeze. Perfect spring day. Don't deny me a ride on a beautiful April morning, Nadine. I'm begging you."

Nadine opened one of her eyes. "You know, you have very artistic ways of putting things. I've almost forgiven you for not bringing me coffee."

"There wasn't coffee," Sean reminded her. "As I told you three times already, Nikki didn't think to make enough for everyone. She feels very foolish. There will be coffee next time."

Nadine closed her eye again. "Then I'll forgive you after next time."

"Na*dine,* come on." Sean looked at the ceiling, sighing in mock frustration. "There will be coffee next time, but this beautiful day is fleeting."

"All right, all right." She sat up and smiled at him. "You big dork. Let's go riding. Who will you take?"

He'd been thinking about this. For his inaugural ride in the north pasture, which as far as he knew was just open land from here to Notch Gap, he would have preferred a quiet deadhead like Tiny.

But he also knew Nadine would laugh at him without mercy if he took such an easy horse out. "Calypso," he replied. "Just Thoroughbred enough to want to jump whatever he sees, but just lazy enough not to run off with me."

"A perfect choice. That's who I would have recommended, anyway. I need someone Finn can follow over fences."

"You've ridden this horse one time." Sean tilted his head. "You really think you should jump him on his second ride?"

"We'll find out what he knows." Nadine shrugged and stood up. "Remember, it's a hunter pace. There are no-jump options at every obstacle, for the flat riders. You *have* done a hunter pace before, right?"

Sean weighed his options and found the truth wanting. He hadn't been honest about his experience yet; no reason to start today. "Of course," he lied. "I didn't think about the flat options."

"Mm-hmm." Nadine gave him an appraising look. "Well, let's see what Finn knows. Hell, maybe he's an old hand at this. It's doubtful, but it's possible. I've been on worse horses who knew more than him."

Sean held up the paper bag with the remaining muffins. "Should I leave these for Richie and Rose? They'll be done with stalls in an hour or so."

Nadine eyed the bag for a moment. He saw the struggle in her eyes. She wanted those muffins.

"Yes," she said finally. "They can have them."

"I'm proud of you, Nadine."

"Shut up," she told him, heading out the lounge door. "I'm filled with muffin rage now."

Grinning, Sean followed her into the barn aisle.

When they weren't really fighting, Nadine *was* fun.

———❦———

The north pasture seemed to stretch for miles. In reality, it was about thirty acres—still, a massive chunk of open land.

"It's not open the whole way across, though," Nadine explained. Her voice had a catch in it; she was already out of breath from reining back Finn, who thought wide-open space meant wide-open galloping. "There's a wooded section in the middle, and a little brook that winds all through it."

Sean nodded, looking around at the green and blue day with pleasure. He really had been missing out by riding indoors—although it hadn't been this nice last month, he reminded himself. Their snowy winter had only just given way to the warming temperatures, and he was sure they'd see some leftover snow hiding beneath rocks and on sheltered hillsides. "Are you sure you're okay with Finn, though? He looks strong."

And the massive black horse made Nadine look tiny, Sean thought privately, though he wasn't foolish enough to say it out loud.

She just shook her head, smiling at him, and lifted her hands to make it a little tougher for Finn to tug on her. "We're fine, but if you want to canter, I'm game. It would be great to tire him out a little."

Sean laughed and moved in the saddle, letting Calypso grab at the bit. The Thoroughbred transitioned upwards into a long-striding canter, his hooves pounding with a satisfying rumble against the softening clay beneath them. But it was nothing compared to the thunder that Finn's big feet made as the draft cross leapt to catch up with them.

He looked over as Finn's black head reached a level with Calypso's dark brown one. Nadine was smiling from ear to ear, her eyes sparkling beneath the brim of her helmet. Her short black braid, bouncing on her back, was the same color as Finn's streaming mane and tail. The two of them suddenly looked perfect together—not too big, not too small, but a beautiful daredevil team, who couldn't be stopped by anything.

"The first jump is just up there," Nadine called, turning Finn slightly to the left. "You go ahead of us and hop the log. I'll send Finn through the little gate."

Sean saw the jump complex approaching rapidly. It was wide, almost out of place in the open field: an open gateway, flanked on either side by logs of differing heights. The small log would barely register as a jump to Calypso, but the oddity of its presence was making the Thoroughbred suck back, his ears pricked as he took in the scene. They were about ten strides out and Sean was just about to suggest they make a circle around the obstacle before jumping it, when Finn suddenly lengthened his stride and hauled Nadine towards it.

One—two—three strides ahead of Calypso, and Sean was fighting with the Thoroughbred to slacken his speed as Calypso sought to keep up with the out-of-control draft horse. And then Nadine and Finn were sailing together over the log—and not the little one, either. The large one, propped up in place by secure anchors, which had to be at least two and a half feet tall and just as wide.

"Wow!" He heard her shout as they landed with a rumble on the other side. "Woohoo!"

Calypso was really hauling on him now, so Sean let the Thoroughbred stretch out as he jumped the smaller log out of stride. Without Sean hauling back on his mouth, they caught up with Finn easily—Calypso wasn't a born and bred racehorse for nothing—and galloped alongside the big horse for another dozen or so strides. Nadine seemed keen to let them carry on, but now the ground sloped upward, and Finn was beginning to slow. By the time they reached the top of the hill, he was ready to break down to a trot, and then a walk.

Nadine patted him on the neck, laughing. "Well, that's it for Finn today. He's blowing hard now."

Sean let the reins slacken a little on Calypso, who was willing to stop as long as Finn wasn't outpacing him. "He jumped that fence like a pro."

"Right? It was *incredible*. One of the things I love about big horses is that when they jump, everything kind of stands still for a moment. I can't explain it. It's like they stay in the air longer or something."

"Not great for timed courses," Sean observed, thinking of his career in show jumping.

"No, definitely not—at least not for fast courses. But it's fine on something like this hunter pace, where the optimum time will be like, thirty minutes. And that works for his fitness level, too, which is . . . oh . . . nil?" She laughed again, clapping his neck. "Finn! You're already sweating, boy! And it's not even hot!"

"Poor Finn. He's out of shape. Don't make him feel bad about it."

"I won't," Nadine promised. She looked across the property. They were on the high point now, and Sean's gaze followed hers down to the woods below. New leaves wagged on the slim branches of trees, and he could see sunlight on water. "But we can do some walking and trotting to build him up a little. There will be some jumps down there around the brook and in the woods. He can hop through those. Who knows?" she added, looking fondly at the horse. "Maybe I could ride him in the pace."

Sean glanced at her nervously. That would require a number of things to happen: one, Finn wouldn't sell immediately, as Caitlin and Rosemary were hoping. And two, they'd have to be open about Nadine riding Finn, when the horse was his responsibility.

Sean didn't like to think about the can of worms this might open. If Caitlin found out he'd handed the ride over to Nadine, he wouldn't be in *trouble,* exactly, because Nadine was permitted to take out any of the horses she pleased. But there would be questions asked about why he'd done it, and Sean didn't want to answer something the wrong way. He'd made it this long at Elmwood; it would be a shame to get found out for a fraud now, when he was so close to the finish line.

He realized Nadine was looking at him, waiting for him to say something. "Yes," he said hastily. "Let's go down and jump the other fences. That's what we're supposed to be doing, right?"

"That's right," Nadine said with a happy smile, turning Finn to an old cow-path that zig-zagged down the steep slope towards the woods. "That's our job. Best job in the world, if you ask me."

Best job in the world, Sean thought glumly. *Unless you're me, trying to get out of it before someone finds out you were never qualified for it, in the first place.*

Chapter Eleven

Nadine

Riding Finn gave Nadine the most ridiculously happy sensations. She truly felt like she was floating above the world on his broad back. And when he jumped? Forget it. She entered another realm.

So as they rode back to the barn, ducking beneath branches dotted with green buds and running fingers along the velvety-soft blooms of flowering dogwood trees, Nadine was forced to consider what a terribly fragile joy this was. Not just the happiness that Finn had given her—although that was a sizable worry, since he was a sales horse and she was in no position to buy a horse—but the companionship between herself and Sean. For this moment, she felt like they were friends . . . the way she'd hoped for back when he first started working at Elmwood. She wasn't quite sure how they'd made this shift. And she wasn't sure how long it could last.

Maybe Avery was right, and she needed to give him a chance. If he tried to kiss her again, that is.

And maybe he wouldn't. She'd turned him down flat last night. What guy would come back for a second rejection?

She kept passing him little, worried glances, until finally he looked back at her, and his eyebrows arched in surprise. "What's the matter?" he asked, his voice so concerned that she felt a wobbling in her stomach. "You're okay, right?"

"I'm fine," she said hastily. "I was just thinking..."

"Don't do too much of that, myself."

She laughed despite herself. "It's hard to stop once you start. Zero stars, do not recommend."

"What are you thinking about?" He reached up to push a branch out of their way. In a moment they'd be out of the woods, with just the last green hillside to ride across. They'd be back in the barn in ten minutes. It would be lunchtime. Richie and Rose would be in the lounge, chatting about nothing. The afternoon would turn into a rush as she finished admin tasks, and he rode his other horses, and then the students would arrive. She felt overwhelmed with the predictable insanity on the other side of this ride.

"I'm thinking about last night," she said in a rush, hardly believing the words as they came out of her mouth. *Now* what could she say?

Sean looked at her quickly, and she thought he might rein back Calypso, demand she tell him why she'd run away from him last night. But he didn't. Instead, he said, "I feel really bad about that."

Her eyes widened, and she didn't know what to say. The sinking sensation in her chest was too much for her to think her way through.

"The moonlight made me read too much into things. I'm sorry. If I scared you, that was definitely not my intent." Sean swallowed and looked forward again. "Please forgive me."

Nadine found her voice. "I'm not mad," she told him. "I promise I'm not mad."

He glanced back at her. "But I scared you. You ran away."

"Well . . . yes." She gave him an uncertain smile. "It was just really sudden."

Sean looked her way, and for a moment she thought she saw a spark in his eyes. "It was really sudden," he agreed eventually. "I feel the same way."

They rode in silence for a few more minutes. Nadine thought about Avery's advice. Then she told herself she was crazy. And then she thought about it again.

Rinse, repeat.

Finally, she just said it. "Sean, do you want to try again?"

He reined back Calypso, and Finn halted alongside him, in no rush to leave behind his companion. Now his eyes really were glittering. "You're messing with me, Nadine," he said huskily. "What's your end goal?"

"More muffins," she told him. "They were amazing. If I let you kiss me, will you promise to get me more?"

"As soon as possible. I might even call Nikki and tell her that she has to whip up a batch this afternoon."

"Please do." Nadine leaned sideways in the saddle. "Okay. Are we doing this?"

Kissing on horseback is almost impossible. The horses have to be willing to stand still, but not only that, they have to be willing to stand close together. Luckily, both Finn and Calypso were pretty worn out. So when Sean eased Calypso close to Finn, his knee gently shoving against Nadine's, he was able to rise in his stirrups, lean over, and press the softest of kisses on her lips—all without getting a wiggle or wobble from the horses.

She closed her eyes and tightened her fingers as his lips touched hers, feeling a tingle zip through her entire body. The surge of electricity must have caused her to press her legs against Finn's sides, because the horse moved abruptly. They were separated before the kiss could escalate into something more—and Nadine supposed it was for the best. She blinked into the blue sky arching overhead, avoiding the glint in Sean's eyes as he watched her hungrily, trying to read her expression.

Suddenly, she felt like she should put some serious space between herself and Sean. What had they just done?

Things were going to get *so* complicated. *Avery,* she thought, *you gave me bad advice, girl.*

She reined Finn back again, straightening her helmet, then turned in the saddle. Sean was shaking his head slowly. When she tilted her head at him, he burst into rueful laughter. "I just wanted a movie scene to work in real life," he admitted. "Is that so much to ask?"

"With horses?" Nadine was highly amused. "You have to know it was impossible. I'm honestly shocked neither of us fell off." Finn tugged at her hands again, and she let him turn around, heading back towards the barn. "This guy's done," she called over her shoulder. "Rule number one of very large green horses, when they say they're done, believe them."

"Good advice, thanks." Sean trotted Calypso after them. "What else can you teach me about Finn?"

"Why? You planning on taking the ride back already?" Her voice was still purposefully light, but something in her seemed to tighten as she said the words. She'd just had a *very* good ride on this horse, capped with a pretty nice kiss. If Sean wanted to ruin her day, all he had to do was say yes, he wanted to ride Finn himself.

"Of course not," Sean said. Her shoulders sagged in relief. "I just want to know what I've been missing all these years, while you were riding scary untrained horses."

"So you admit it. You *don't* have experience on green horses." Nadine didn't mean to make things uncomfortable for Sean, but there was still something odd about his attitude towards Finn. She looked over at him again. He sat Calypso so beautifully—but almost rigidly, as if he had been positioned perfectly by an unseen hand. His seat in the saddle wasn't rigid, not exactly, but . . . not loose and natural, either. She'd held off asking for months, but now, Nadine's curiosity got the better of her. "Sean, where did you learn to ride?"

"At home," he said carelessly, eyes following a dragonfly buzzing near Calypso's waggling ears. "My mother hired a coach for me when I was . . . oh, four or five. I always rode at home, with my own trainer, unless I was at a show."

Nadine shook her head, unable to imagine such a lifestyle for herself. "And did you ever start a horse yourself? Or take a green-broke horse and train him to be, say, show-ready?"

There was a moment of silence.

She waited, knowing it was the question he had lied about to Caitlin when he'd interviewed. Would he lie to her? Now?

Did one kiss entitle her to the truth?

She rather thought it did. If Sean shrugged his way out of this question, she'd know she couldn't trust him.

Answer the right way, she thought, clenching her fingers tight on the reins. Finn felt her tension and tossed his head, jigging a little despite his fatigue.

"No," Sean finally replied, his voice strained. "Never. And I don't know what to do about it, because Caitlin thinks I'm training Finn, but it's going to be *you. All the way.*"

Nadine's heart lifted in her chest. Honesty! She could solve silly problems; it was finding a person worth her time that always posed the real issue. If Sean trusted her enough to tell her his secret—if Sean *respected* her enough to tell her his secret—then she could make a little sacrifice for him. Although, she thought, Finn was hardly little.

She reined Finn close to Calypso, letting her knee bump against Sean's. Their stirrups clanked, and he looked at her in surprise. She took the reins in one hand and reached out her free one. Sean took it, his eyes searching her face.

"If you want help, I'm offering," she told him. "I can help you learn to ride Finn—and teach him what he needs to know, too."

Sean's face was full of hope. "You mean that?"

"Of course. There are a few simple principles to training green horses. One of them is just to be kind, and you're already a kind rider." She smiled at him, letting go of his hand as Finn sidled away again. She missed the touch as soon as it was gone. "And it will give us something to do after everyone's gone for the night," she added. "I don't know how you felt about it, but I thought last night's walk got awfully chilly."

"The moonlight, though." Sean's expression turned mischievous. "You didn't enjoy the moonlight?"

"Talk to me in a month about the moon," Nadine laughed. "When the temperature stays above sixty-five or so."

"A Floridian at heart," Sean said. "I thought as much."

"Well, you teach me to jump big fences like you do, and we can winter in Florida next year," she said carelessly.

A beat of silence passed between them. Nadine turned in the saddle. Sean was watching her, eyes suspiciously bright.

It had been a throwaway line, but Nadine had a worried suspicion Sean was actually ready to take her up on the idea.

They dismounted behind the barn, so that no one would see Nadine had been the one riding Finn, and switched horses. She patted Calypso on his warm neck as they walked along the side of the barn. Beside them, the unused outdoor arena baked in the midday sun, a faint smell of tires rising from the shredded rubber mixed into the clay footing.

"I forgot to tell you," Nadine called over her shoulder. "Caitlin wants the lessons moved outside. You ready for that?"

"Well, at least it's better footing for jumping than what we've got inside," Sean observed, kicking at some shreds that had escaped the arena. "I'll ask Richie to give it a good grooming with the tractor before we use it, though."

"Can't you drive a tractor, either, Sean?" Nadine grinned. She pulled up Calypso so he could catch up with her. "I'm beginning to think you're a fake farmer."

"I never said I was a farmer," Sean growled. He pulled off his helmet and pushed back his blonde hair from his eyes. Nadine saw the mischief in his face right before he reached for her, wrapping his free arm around her waist and pulling her close. Without meaning to, she squealed, and Finn tugged back so fast the reins simply vanished from Sean's hands. He whirled and snatched at the flying reins—but Finn was too quick for him. Tail up, white rump shining under the sun, the big horse took off.

"Oh, no, no, no," Nadine muttered, throwing Calypso's reins at Sean and running after Finn. She knew better than to chase a horse—the best way to catch a loose horse was to be so easygoing about it, the horse didn't even think they were wanted—but in the narrow alleyway between the barn and the arena fence, she had no choice but to go after him. With any luck, he'd turn and head into the barn . . . hopefully *not* running over Richie or Rose, or anyone else who might be in the aisle.

"Turn, turn, turn—"

He didn't turn. He kept going, right across the parking lot, with his head high and his ears pricked, the reins trailing around his pounding front hooves. Nadine heard a shout from inside the barn and knew Richie and Rose had seen him, but she couldn't stop to form a plan of attack. Finn was heading right up the drive towards Caitlin's house, and Caitlin had several cameras mounted around her porch. If Finn went galloping past her front door, Caitlin would find out about it.

And Nadine didn't want to explain what Rosemary's precious sales horse was doing loose on the property.

Suddenly, a golf cart whirred past her—Richie was sitting in the driver's seat, leaning forward over the wheel, looking determined. Nadine watched him buzz after the horse, then pull wide, bouncing the cart through the grassy meadow between the barn and Caitlin's yard. She stopped running, winded and aware she'd never catch up to the horse, and stood with her hands on the small of her back, watching as Richie held out a scoop of grain with one hand and started shaking it.

"Listen to the grain scoop, horse," she said desperately.

Footsteps crunched across the gravel behind her. No hoofbeats came with them, so it must be Rose. "Richie'll get him with the grain scoop," Rose said, her reedy voice certain of victory. "That's a draft horse. Stomach first, brain later. He'll come around."

"I sure hope so," Nadine sighed. "Because Caitlin's going to kill me."

"You?" Rose tilted her head. "I was pretty sure Sean was riding him."

Nadine gave Rose a grateful smile. "That's right. I forgot. Caitlin's going to kill *Sean.*"

"Thanks," Sean called from behind them. "I heard that."

"Look! He's going to Richie!" Rose gave a satisfied nod and turned back to the barn. "Problem solved. Not much around a barn that a grain scoop can't solve."

Sean took her place, Calypso still tugging back on the reins. *He just wanted to go back to the barn. Finn should take some lessons from this horse,* Nadine thought. "Just kidding. Caitlin won't find out now. He didn't get far enough up the drive."

They watched the horse jog alongside the golf cart, ears pricked at the grain scoop Richie was holding out as he drove. In a few moments, Nadine would have to catch him. But she paused, looking at Sean. "I know it went wrong, but I had fun with you today."

His eyes lit up. "I had fun, too. Is work about to get more interesting?"

"Sadly, no." Sean's face turned puzzled. "Sean, come on. You know Caitlin has a rule against in-house dating." Nadine shook her head at him, suddenly wishing her boss wasn't such a stickler for appearances. "This is going to be one more secret you get to keep."

Chapter Twelve

Sean

Another secret. Sean knew there was supposed to be some level of sexiness about a forbidden romance, but at the moment, he just felt annoyed. *One more secret you get to keep,* she'd said, as if he loved living all these lies, as if he woke up every morning excited for another day of Let's Pretend.

Let's pretend he was a competent riding instructor, let's pretend he had experience with young horses, let's pretend he was committed to this farm for the long haul, let's pretend his parents didn't sell off their assets before the government investigated and *took* them, let's pretend he was at all certain, for a single second of the day, that he had any idea what he was doing anymore.

Because if before today, he'd at least been operating under the courage of his conviction that Martha Lane was his ticket back to the horse show life he'd been missing, now he had to contend with something completely new: feelings for another woman.

Feelings for *Nadine,* which made things even more confusing.

What made things even worse was that now he felt like he'd always seen her this way, which made him suspect he was remembering his own life wrong. It was as if he'd woken up one morning and the sky was green, and he'd nodded to himself and said, "yes, just like I remember," even though he *knew* the sky had been blue before.

It was like Nadine's kiss had rewritten history. As if all their bickering, all of her barbed little insults and digs at him, all of his irritation at her relentless work ethic and dedication to Caitlin's business, had simply vanished. A clean new slate stretched out before them, the resentments of before washed away.

Sean was baffled by the entire situation.

And then there was Martha.

What on earth was he going to do with the Martha problem?

Because he wasn't ready to give up on his dream of his own horses and his old life back—and that meant someone else's wallet had to do the heavy lifting. Martha was still the best shot he had at escaping life as a half-incompetent riding instructor.

Who was he kidding—a mostly incompetent riding instructor.

His future right now hinged on getting Martha to open her pocketbook and invest in his dreams... whatever it took.

Unfortunately, there was no way Nadine was going to be on board with those plans. For one thing, she seemed utterly committed to Elmwood. And for another, it was possible he'd need to pay Martha certain... favors.

Sean shook his head. Things wouldn't go that far.

They couldn't.

"Hand me the sweat scraper?"

Nadine was peeking around the wall between the two wash-racks. Sean handed her the sweat scraper and started to unhook Calypso from the cross-ties.

"Don't forget his cooler," Nadine said, popping back around. "It's still below seventy degrees."

"Right, of course." Sean snapped the cross-ties back in place and went for one of the coolers thrown over a nearby chair.

"Slap some liniment on his legs while you've got him there." Nadine was looking around the wall *again*. "The yellow bottle in the rack there."

"I got it." He knelt, bottle in hand, by Calypso's forelegs. The horse shifted and lipped at his hair while he rubbed the strong-smelling liquid into his legs.

"Don't wrap them, though," Nadine called over the wall.

"I *won't*," he insisted. "Even I know that if you rub, you don't wrap."

Nadine's face appeared again. "What's that supposed to mean?"

He sighed. "What's *what* supposed to mean?"

" 'Even I,' " she enunciated. "Do you have a problem with me giving you instructions? Like, do you think I'm dissing your horse knowledge?"

Sean found himself laughing. He pulled himself upright and leaned over Calypso's back, the soft fabric of the cooler beneath his arms. "*Now* you ask that question? You've been bossing me around for six months. I'm used to it, Nadine."

He was, mostly. Now that his brain had abruptly decided he was no longer offended by her religious adherence to her own horsekeeping tenets.

She lifted her eyebrows. "Because I don't want you to get mad —"

"I'm not mad."

"—But sometimes you forget to do things the right way."

He gazed at her, face blank, until she went back to her own horse. Then he laughed and shook his head. A few days ago, they would have descended into a shouting match. Today? Well, one kiss could change some things.

Two, he figured, could change the world.

Time to make that happen.

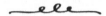

The next night saw Sean standing in the center of the indoor, watching Nadine trot Finn in big figure-eights. The evening had been wet; the sky weeping cool showers with an occasional rumble of thunder, which had undone all the good of Richie's careful harrowing in the outdoor arena. The footing was dotted with puddles, smaller bits of shredded rubber floating on top. Lessons had taken place inside as usual, and now Sean's ankles were tired with the effort of standing in the center of the ring all evening. But he was about to mount up on Finn himself, and he was reminding himself that standing on solid ground wasn't always the worst thing.

Nadine sat down and brought Finn to a gradual walk, although not without a lot of head-tossing and tooth-grinding (on Finn's part, not Nadine's). She patted him on the neck anyway and gave him a few effusive *good boys*. Sean found the show a little over the top for the kind of transition she'd gotten. But this was Nadine's lesson, not his. If she wanted him to treat the horse like he'd just solved world hunger instead of straggling down into an uneven walk, that was what Sean would do, as well.

She rode him over to Sean, dropping her stirrups. "You ready to get on him now? He's nice and warmed up. I think he'll be really good for you."

Sean looked at Finn, from giant feet to massive shoulder to huge head. "I'm really not," he admitted. It stung his pride to say so, but he was trying to be honest with Nadine—and not get killed.

Nadine tilted her head at him, smiling in that soft way she had, a sweet look she had previously saved for dogs and horses. Now it gave him a sweeping feeling of warmth, and maybe a little courage besides. Nadine believed he could do it. Didn't that mean he could?

Of course it didn't. Horses didn't care who believed in you. People attributed a lot of mystical powers to horses, but Sean had always found they were mostly interested in what a person could or couldn't do, and how they could get what they wanted with that knowledge.

Still, he found himself nodding, answering her unspoken question. "Okay, if you think I'm ready."

"I'm going to guide you through all of it," she told him, dismounting in supple motion. "Just forget everything you know about riding 'made' horses. No quick movements, no big, strong aids." She waved her hands and picked up one of her heels, demonstrating what she meant: quiet hands, quiet legs. "Sit in his center, and bring your lower legs just a little forward for safety, like you're going into the jumper ring on a super-hot horse who's just looking for trouble."

"Okay. That I know how to do."

"Safety seats are fundamental," Nadine said, winking. "You didn't get to this point in your life without it."

She held Finn while Sean brought over the mounting block, then stood at his head, hands on both reins to steady the horse, while he mounted. He tried to be slow and careful, but it still took a leap to get into the saddle. Finn shifted unhappily, swishing his tail. Strands of hair slapped against Sean's boot, startling him. He glanced back in astonishment.

"How long is this horse's tail?"

"The taller the horse, the longer the tail has to grow to reach the ground," Nadine said reasonably.

"That sounds like an ancient proverb."

"It's a Nadine proverb." She twinkled a smile up at him. "Gather your reins and walk him in a circle around me."

"We're doing this?" He took one last look at her. If Finn dumped him on the ground and trampled him into the dirt, at least he'd have this final vision of Nadine, with her black hair braided and falling over her shoulder, and her green eyes gleaming at him. Again, he wondered how he'd been immune to her charms for so many months. Nadine was beautiful! And he was an idiot.

An idiot on a giant horse with only basic training.

"We're doing this," Nadine told him. "Gentle hands, gentle leg."

She stepped back, setting them free.

⁓⁓⁓

They sat over pizza that night in Nadine's apartment (she had a slightly comfier couch, it was decided, after they tested both of them). Her laptop was open to a rom-com, but they were mostly ignoring it, swapping riding stories instead. Nadine's stories mostly involved wild horses she probably shouldn't have been anywhere near, in Sean's opinion, while his stories mostly involved silly decisions he shouldn't have made.

"Wait, wait," she choked, swallowing down a mouthful of pizza while she tried not to laugh, "are you actually saying you agreed to take the horse into the welcome stakes *after* the owner said he hadn't made it over a full course in a year?"

"Well, I figured the horse was bored and looking for a challenge," Sean defended himself. "He went over everything in the warm-up! But yeah, it should have been a warning when no one else in my group would ride him. Simone said the horse was a nightmare and I guess I just wanted to show her up."

"So the horse just . . . refused everything?"

"The second jump." Sean sighed at the memory. "Jumped the first fence beautifully, slid to a halt in front of the second one, wouldn't even *face* it the next time I presented, and then turned to leave. I mean literally tried to run out of the arena before we'd been eliminated. I think he was used to getting eliminated and just skipped the third refusal."

"Please tell me that's your most embarrassing story," Nadine begged him. "Because I don't know if I could handle anything worse."

"How is this worse than your bucking pony of death story? You were at a show with that thing, too?"

Nadine waved her hands no. "Rex was a talented pony! He was just talented at bucking, not jumping. That's not on him. That's on *society*."

They were laughing so loud, Sean figured the horses downstairs could hear them and wondered what was going on up there. Usually, the apartments were next to silent at night.

"This is more fun than my usual evening," he said suddenly, taking her hand. "We should have done this a long time ago."

Nadine turned a blushing cheek. "Who knew we were sitting here staring at the same wall every night when we could be eating pizza and telling our darkest secrets?"

"Seriously. I'm having a really nice time."

"I am, too." She lifted her eyes back to his. That emerald shimmer in their depths made him feel a little crazy. He was just thinking about leaning in for that second kiss he'd been dreaming of when his phone started to ring.

He nearly fell off the sofa as he tried to shut it up. "This thing's usually on silent," he fumed, slapping at the screen without seeing who was calling.

"Take it," Nadine said lightly. "I'll get us some more pizza." She hopped up, plates in hand, and went into the kitchen.

Sean looked at the screen. *Simone.* He considered it for a moment. The space wasn't exactly private—the kitchen was just a galley at the end of the room—but Sean decided whatever Simone had to say wouldn't be too bad. And it might be good—too good to wait until later. "Hey, Simone," he answered, just before the call went to voicemail. "What's up?"

"Sean!" Simone's voice was a little shouty. He winced and turned down the volume, hoping her voice wouldn't carry across the apartment. He glanced at Nadine; she was messing around with the pizza box, throwing away some things, basically trying to stay out of his way. Nice of her. "Sean, you have got to get to Saugerties this summer. I have the *best* house lined up. It's unbelievable. Just signed the lease and I'm getting *psyched.* What's the plan? Have you bagged the old lady with the big money yet? Because I know of three horses going up for sale in the next week and the guy will do an all-in-one deal. Two are totally ready for the one-twenty meter and one is a really flashy green hunter. You could be set for the summer! What do you think? Are you there? Hello?"

Sean fumbled for words. For once, he hadn't spent this evening thinking about his places for Martha—hadn't been thinking about getting back to Simone and his other riding buddies—hadn't been thinking about his future show career at all. And that was just one way this night differed from every other night he'd spent at Elmwood . . . as well as every night he'd spent since the day he'd learned his farm was gone.

"Sean?" Simone raised her voice. "Is this thing on?"

"Yeah, I'm here. Listen, I don't know—it's not a sure thing yet," he stammered. He glanced at Nadine. She turned her head away quickly, opening the fridge door and ducking down to look inside. *Ugh.* He couldn't let her hear any of this. And Simone was so loud! Was she always this loud? This was her champagne voice— the house rental must be *really* good, and she had been celebrating. "I'll definitely call you back in a few days, okay? I'll have to have a discussion." He tried to keep his words bland and hoped Simone didn't notice.

Luckily, champagne Simone was not too picky. "Perfect. I'll text you the info . . . I mean you're going to want these horses. If you haven't done the dirty with moneybags yet, you're going to when you see these guys."

"Oh . . . uh . . . sounds great," Sean hedged. He took another glance at Nadine. She was smiling at him uncertainly, and he knew she was out of reasons to stay in the kitchen. "I have to go, okay?"

"Bye, Sean! BYE!" Simone shrieked the last word, and even with the volume turned down, her voice crackled over the speaker.

Sean put the phone down and sighed heavily.

Nadine came back and set down the plates "I found some cheese to sprinkle on the pizza, if you want," she offered, clearly trying to change the subject.

He smiled gratefully at her. "I can explain."

"You don't have to tell me who you're talking to on the phone."

"My friend Simone is . . . over the top."

"It's *fine.*"

"No, listen." Sean tugged Nadine close, wrapping an arm around her shoulders. He felt her stiffen, then relax against him. "I come from a very noisy, ostentatious crowd. They have no manners. You would hate them."

She giggled, tipping her head against his. "Okay. So are you saying I shouldn't meet your friends—for my own sake, not for theirs?"

"Very much so," Sean assured her. "They're the worst. Please don't ever meet them."

"Sounds good," Nadine said. She wiggled free of his arm, turning her head to give him a reassuring smile.

The kind of smile which instantly made him feel terrible. Was he lying to Nadine by not telling her about Simone, or Martha, or any of it? That whole question of lying by omission or simply protecting someone seemed to have a lot of gray areas.

"What's going on?" she asked, her smile fading as she studied his face. "Did I say something wrong?"

"No," he told her. He had some thinking to do before he got her tangled up in any of this. "Simone just reminds me of a lot of problems I don't want to think about, that's all."

"Should I . . . do you want to talk about it?"

"No," he said again. "Thank you, though." He leaned back against the sofa's back and gave her the best smile he could muster. "It's fine, really."

"Eat your pizza," she told him. "It's getting cold."

He obeyed her at first, his mind ticking over while she paid deceptively close attention to the movie on her laptop. The deal they'd made in the field yesterday came back to him. She'd already begun to fulfill her end of it: she'd helped him ride Finn tonight, and things had gone really well. He was beginning to see that his fear of riding an inexperienced horse was more of a phobia than a well-founded concern—yes, he had things to learn, and she said he needed to be a lot more relaxed and natural in the saddle if he was going to help a baby horse learn to move its body properly, but he was still an accomplished rider, and he could figure these things out.

But her offer to help him ride Finn had overshadowed her request: to learn to jump big courses. Now he wondered if she'd really meant it.

"Hey Nadine?" he asked finally.

She turned immediately. "Yeah?"

"That thing you said yesterday . . . about jumping? About wintering in Florida?"

"I was only joking," she said quickly. "You don't have to teach me to jump big courses."

He sat back again. "Oh. I thought you might have been serious."

"I just meant, you're probably too busy."

"Lessons are fine," he said. "It's the winter I'm most interested in."

"I mean, showing in Florida all winter sounds great. But how could I ever afford it? How could *you* afford it, now? No offense," she added. "But showing with Caitlin is never going to reach that point. She's happy with keeping her clients at local shows for a reason. Once you're doing the A-circuit, you're not actually making money. You're just showing how much you have."

He thought about that. It was true, he realized. Really, awfully true. For the owners, anyway. For anyone footing the bills, the more expensive a horse was, the bigger the money-pit that horse represented.

Sean sighed, then smiled at her. "Well, I could still get you jumping bigger fences, if you want."

Nadine nodded. "Yeah. I'd like that."

Chapter Thirteen

Nadine

"I'm not so sure about this." Nadine shifted in the saddle, looking at the big course Sean had set up. The outdoor arena had dried up under a steady streak of sunny days, and a fresh, cool breeze was blowing across the countryside, rippling Calypso's mane. The dark bay Thoroughbred shifted beneath her. He was warmed up and ready to jump the fences, but Nadine had never faced a course so large, and she was having a hard time keeping her hands steady on the reins.

"Calypso can jump this course in his sleep," Sean assured her. He was standing at the horse's side, and now he put one hand on her knee, a familiar gesture which made Nadine's heart give an entirely different sort of flutter. "All you have to do is treat these fences the same way you would if they were a foot shorter. Start with that line right there to ease in." He pointed to two fences, spaced about six strides apart. They weren't high at all—the first one was set to about two-and-a-half feet, the second one a few inches higher. "Nice and easy two-six combo. Okay? And we'll work our way up to the three-six in no time."

Nadine knew she should be fine with jumping the higher fences. A person who had been riding for a decade now, and schooling every sort of horse, from just-saddled to made and staid, should have experience jumping above two-six. But she didn't. The trouble with riding sales and trade horses for her entire life was that Nadine had gotten really good with problem horses, but she'd never progressed to the complexities of riding *good* horses. Things like leveling up to higher fences or learning more difficult dressage moves were just not on the table.

But she'd told Sean she wanted to learn, and she hadn't been joking about that, even if the suggestion they winter in Florida together had been a throwaway line, an idea so silly it didn't even register as anything beyond a dream. Big time horse show life wasn't on her agenda. That was all Sean's.

And he was watching her expectantly.

So she gathered her reins, dropped her weight into her stirrups, and sent Calypso off into a canter with her chin held high. She wouldn't make a fool of herself, anyway. She'd get him over these fences.

They hopped over the lower jumps a few times without issue. She had to admit, he had Calypso going really well. A fine sheen of sweat soon covered the horse's neck, turning his coat an even darker shade of mahogany, but his attitude seemed to freshen with every fence, until he was tugging at the bit on each approach. She struggled a little to balance him before each jump, and the problem only grew as Sean directed her over progressively taller fences.

Finally, he all but hurled himself at a three-foot fence, and Nadine lost her balance. She didn't come out of the saddle, but she was rattled anyway, reining back and dropping her feet from the stirrups for a break. Calypso jigged impatiently beneath her. Nadine looked at Sean, hoping for some advice, but he just folded his arms across his chest and watched her, gaze still expectant, as if he was waiting for her to sort out her next move on her own.

Nadine was annoyed. For a riding instructor, Sean sure was being silent. "Any advice would be great," she called, an edge to her voice.

"You're doing fine," Sean replied. "Just stay out of your own head. Calypso's having fun."

"Fine? I nearly got dumped over that last fence." Sean had a weird definition of *fine*. "I feel like the distance is tougher to see with these bigger jumps."

"No, don't worry about that. Just go with your gut."

"My gut is getting us to the wrong spot and Calypso's getting antsy, so my gut's not the answer, Sean."

"Now, don't get mad. Just try it again."

Nadine glared at him. "Is this how you teach? For real?"

Sean held up his hands. "What do you want? You're doing fine. Just ride him to the base of the fence."

Nadine shook her head, astonished. "You really have no idea how to teach, do you? You're just winging it out there every day."

"Nadine—"

"And heaven help those kids when they actually get to the point where their horses need direction. As long as they're riding push-button horses who can jump two-six in their sleep, fine, but anything more than that? You're going to tell them to go with their gut? Come on, Sean."

Sean looked around as if he was afraid someone would hear her. But it was midday and their only company on the farm was the wind in the trees and the ponies in the paddocks. Richie and Rose weren't even there; they'd gone back to their RV for a midday break. Still, he stalked up to her, grabbing Calypso's reins as if he was going to pull them from her hands. "What's with you? I'm sorry if Calypso got a little hot, but I think you're just panicking. There's really nothing to this—"

"You can't teach by saying *there's nothing to it,* when clearly there is a skill, something you're supposed to be educating your students about." Nadine shook her head in disbelief. "Sean! Did you ever teach a single riding lesson before you came here? Be honest with me."

"Of course I did." But he dropped his eyes as he said it, and Nadine knew her suspicions about Sean had been well-founded from the start.

"Why would you lie about that?" She lowered her voice to a hushed whisper, but all she wanted to do was shout. "I was right all along. You don't have half the experience you claimed to! But Sean, people could get *hurt.* Horses could get hurt. Why would you lie?"

To me, she added, even though she knew the two words weren't worth saying out loud. When Sean had come here, he'd lied to everyone. He hadn't singled her out. Hadn't put her at risk.

Until today.

"Things were going fine," Sean muttered. "I didn't realize it was going to show."

"What? Your total lack of qualification?"

"Don't say it like that!" Sean looked up at her again, his gaze fierce. "I'm an experienced horseman. I have titles, I have championships, I have been showing double-A since I was a kid—"

"You're an experienced rider," Nadine corrected him. "But you're not an experienced *horseman*. And you're not an experienced instructor. Those are the parts you've been lying about." She sighed, turning Calypso's head so that the reins were tugged from Sean's limp fingers. "This horse is hot. He needs to walk."

And she needed to think.

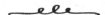

He left her to eat her lunch alone that afternoon. Nadine sat in her office and worked through the board bills for the month, slowly sipping at a mug of cold coffee. She'd propped her door open to let the mild air outside clear the room. The office was musty from a winter of heating elements and closed windows. Now, the barn scents of hay and shavings mingled with a floral fragrance on the breeze. With music humming gently from her phone, it should have been a pleasant afternoon. But every hour, on the hour, Sean walked by with a private lesson, and he made a point of keeping his gaze straight ahead when he passed her open door.

Nadine knew she'd hurt his feelings, and she could excuse his attitude. What she didn't know was how to move on from it. Their argument hadn't just been about a difference of opinion. She was genuinely concerned that Sean was doing a job he didn't really understand, and that if push came to shove, his lack of knowledge could get someone hurt.

And with lessons moving to the outdoor arena, the hunter pace coming up, and the prospect of teaching students to take on new challenges without the benefits of four walls or fences around them to contain their horses, she was afraid that a crisis might be just around the corner.

Finally, a lull came between lessons around five-thirty. With just one group session coming up, Sean opted to take a coffee break while Richie and Rose fed dinner to the horses who weren't about to be ridden. Nadine waited until she'd heard his footsteps on the lounge steps next to her office; then she closed her laptop and went after him.

He was pouring coffee into his mug. His glance, when it flicked to her, was cool. "Did you come in here to complain about something I said to my student? Because I think Amanda did a really nice job today."

"I was in my office while you were teaching, and you know it." Nadine couldn't help the sharpness in her tone, but she struggled to soften her voice before she went on. "Sean, listen, I didn't mean to accuse you of anything earlier to day. Or—hurt your feelings."

"Didn't you? When you told me I was a liar who didn't deserve my job?" Sean replaced the coffeepot with a bang.

"Be careful with that—it's the only one we have," she said quickly.

He shook his head and took his mug over to the couch facing the arena window. Flinging himself down against one armrest, he looked at her over the steaming coffee. "Look—you're right, okay? But I needed a job. Nothing was coming up, and I didn't expect to be here this long. Things escalated."

Nadine carefully sat at the other end of the couch. "We can work on it. There are guides, we can order the British Horse Society manual for instructors—"

"It's not important." Sean brushed aside her suggestions impatiently. "I won't be here much longer."

Nadine blinked at him. "Where are you going? Did you find another job?"

It had been a dream of hers for so long—for Sean Casey to get another job and get the heck out of her life. And now, when they were finally friends—and something more than friends—he was actually going to leave? Nadine felt a lump rise in her throat, and she swallowed angrily against it. *This is why you don't get close to people.*

Her brain was happy to offer up the reminder, as if it hadn't been at all involved with her sudden, satisfying deepening of feelings for Sean.

Sean was shaking his head. "Nothing's finalized yet, but my friend Simone has found some good horses and a place to stay this summer. If I want to get back to the circuit, I have to make a move right now. It's almost May, for heaven's sake."

"It's early April," Nadine offered, still working to push down the leaden feeling in her throat. "You have two months until summer. A lot could happen." She didn't know if she was talking to herself or to Sean.

Suddenly Sean sighed and put his coffee on the table next to the sofa. He leaned forward, taking Nadine's cold hands in his. She felt a flush of warmth travel through her skin, and her fingers curled over his involuntarily. "You're right. I don't know why I bother making plans." His chuckle was warm and rueful all at once. "I definitely didn't plan on trying to kiss you the other night, and look where we're at."

She flicked up her gaze to meet his, and just like that, the lump in her throat was gone. All that was left was a lift in her heart, a beating life in her chest. All that was left was the way his ice-blue eyes made her feel, and she knew that even if Sean left tomorrow, she'd still want this moment in her memories.

But she *really* didn't want him to leave.

"Let me help you with teaching," she whispered, her senses aware of the open door behind them, the possibility of eavesdroppers and curious eyes from the aisle. "Along with Finn. Just give us a chance, okay? Don't write off Elmwood because you had some other plan all along."

Sean nodded slowly, his lip caught between his teeth. "It's killing me not to kiss you right now," he murmured.

"You can't. Not when someone might see us. Caitlin would be furious."

"Good old Caitlin." Sean leaned forward, closing the inches between them with one swift movement, and brushed a soft kiss on her lips. "I'll risk it," he told her.

And as Nadine fought her warring emotions—one side of her wanted to yell at him, because *she* wasn't willing to risk her job for a stolen kiss, and one side of her wanted to jump him and plant a kiss of her own on those laughing lips—she barely noticed that Sean hadn't promised to stay.

Chapter Fourteen

Sean

Martha's regular riding lesson approached with a new significance this week. Sean got up on the appointed morning with a slightly sick feeling in his stomach. And it wasn't because he'd been up too late with Nadine the night before. He knew he had to talk to Martha today, and take his plan to the next level... or admit defeat.

He brushed his teeth carefully, as if Martha was going to arrive at eight o'clock instead of one, and checked the weather forecast before slipping on a silky tech-fabric riding polo and his favorite pair of Tailored Sportsmans. The breeches were almost old-fashioned in their severity, the buff fabric and darker leather knee patches a far cry from the fancy new high-tech tights and breeches that filled Sean's dresser drawers, but they gave him an air of tradition and permanence that would impress Martha while he was making his case.

Also, they were very sexy.

Sean turned back and forth in front of the mirrored closet door in his bedroom, hoping he looked good from every angle. He didn't *want* to make this transaction with Martha anything more than a business deal . . . but he had gone into this plan willing to do whatever it took. Until last week, he'd been perfectly fine with the idea.

Then things had started happening with Nadine, and with all these fireworks popping around his head, Sean barely knew which way to look anymore.

He went down the steps carefully, not wanting to bump his good boots against a single stair tread. Why was he even wearing his best field boots, the ones with his name stenciled inside by hand, the Italian leather so soft they cradled his calves like gloves? Why was he doing any of this?

Sean looked up and down the main aisle of Elmwood Equestrian Center, at the empty stalls and the grooms cheerfully walking their wheelbarrows out to the manure pile. This was a pleasant place. His colleagues were nice. His work wasn't overly taxing. He wondered why he couldn't just be content to stay here.

Eyes on the prize, he told himself. In a few hours, he'd have his answer. If Martha didn't want to finance a few jumpers for him, if her ambitions weren't what he'd thought, well, then at least he'd have a back-up plan.

It was more than he'd ever had before.

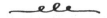

Sean had ridden Calypso, Chocolate Kiss, and another school horse named Pansy by the time Martha's allotted lesson hour rolled around. He'd begged off from lunch with Nadine, retreating upstairs to brush off his boots and breeches, give himself a pep talk, and drink a smoothie from his fridge—solid food wouldn't have stayed down, his stomach was quivering like he was at the in-gate before his first big adult jumper class. But Sean wasn't eighteen anymore—boy, was he aware of that—and all he wanted was to be back at that in-gate, the horse ahead rumbling around the course, maybe hearing that soft hiss of the crowd just before the *thudding sound* of a pole hitting the ground, putting Sean that much closer to the win. There were no nerves in Sean's memory of the show-circuit life. Just passion, excitement, and the ceaseless drive to take first place, again and again.

Soon, you'll have that back. He brushed off his breeches again, aware a few loose horsehairs and water spots made him look even more the accomplished professional, and headed down the stairs.

"Martha," he greeted her, because she was already heading up the aisle, wearing dark purple riding tights and a pair of field boots he'd recommended to her back when she'd started riding again. Her carefully highlighted hair was tugged back into a French braid, a few loose curls hanging suggestively around her thin face. Martha always made herself look good for lessons; Sean had figured it was for him and the idea had previously amused him—how easy this would be!—but now it just made him nervous.

Martha liked a nice embrace, and a peck on the cheek, as if she were European; he leaned in for the required greeting and over her left shoulder he spotted Nadine leaning against a stall front, a sardonic smile on her face. His heart surged in his chest, and he didn't know if it was from the pleasure of seeing her or the nerves of what he was about to do.

"Martha," he said, stepping back from his student, who surveyed him with a proprietary air, "I want to have a talk with you while we're tacking up."

She smiled as if she knew what was coming. "First things first, who am I riding today?"

He'd already ridden Chocolate Kiss, of course, and Nadine had put Martha and Tiny's name together in the lesson book without a peep of complaint when he'd asked her to. "Your usual horse," he said. "You're good with Tiny, aren't you?"

"I was wondering when you were going to offer me a challenge, Sean."

Was there an edge to her voice? Where had this rebellion come from? Sean felt like he was losing control of the conversation before it had even begun. "I just wanted you to be comfortable while we work on your equitation," he explained, his eyes flicking again to Nadine. Was she close enough to overhear? Judging by the smirk on her face, yes, absolutely. She was loving his discomfort right now. "Would you prefer to ride someone else next week?"

"I'd prefer to ride someone else when you think I'm ready," Martha said, with a little shrug of her shoulders. "But if you don't think I've improved enough . . ." She paused, leaving the door open for Sean.

He shoved through it. "I absolutely think you're improved enough. In fact, I want to talk to you about horses today—about what you want to do with them in the future. That kind of thing. Do you want to ride Tiny today, and we'll talk about what comes next? Then next week we can move forward . . . or even sooner, if you want." Sean wasn't talking about the school horse she'd ride in her next lesson, and he thought she knew it.

He'd laid the groundwork extremely well, he thought. If nothing else, Martha knew that he wanted her to invest in his future. The question was: could he make an appealing enough offer without putting himself on the table, too?

"Let's ride Tiny today," she agreed. "But any talk beyond what horse I'm riding next week isn't taking place in a barn aisle. Sean, let me take you to dinner tonight. My treat. We can have a frank talk when we aren't surrounded by curious coworkers." And Martha sent a pointed gaze over her shoulder, skewering Nadine.

Sean felt himself blushing for Nadine, but he shouldn't have bothered. She just tugged on a horse blanket she'd been toying with, said something about getting everyone into the tack room for a lesson on properly folding blankets over their bars, and proceeded to re-fold the offending article of horse clothing with beautiful straight lines. Sean was actually impressed by her aplomb.

Martha would have to work pretty hard to catch Nadine out. If the idea percolating in his mind had a shot at working, that would be important.

"Dinner," he agreed. "I finish at seven tonight."

Martha's smile was all teeth.

Martha was wearing a slinky black dress.

The moment Sean saw her standing by the bar, he realized his mistake. He shouldn't be out getting dinner with Martha—not at any point, but definitely not now, when things were changing so rapidly with Nadine. Hell, he was thinking about her now—

Sean shook his head. *Focus, man.* He had to get through this night without doing any damage to his business prospects with Martha, maybe even getting her to invest, but without pissing her off by passing on any physical stuff. And that dress told him he had a battle ahead.

Now he stood anxiously just inside the vestibule of the shadowy steakhouse Martha had selected. A bored-looking hostess in a white shirt and black skirt stood off to one side, waiting to take his jacket; finally she cleared her throat and Sean jumped. She held out her hands, head tipped inquiringly. "Are you coming in, sir?"

He shook his head, clutching at the lapels of his jacket. If he gave it up, he'd also give up the chance at a quick getaway. And this was looking like a situation which might require fast moves. "I'm just waiting for someone," he lied, watching Martha.

She was leaning back against the dramatically lit bar, one heeled foot tipped against the brass foot-rail, swinging a martini as she told the punchline of some joke to a silver-haired gent in a gray suit. Someone age-appropriate for her, Sean thought worriedly, someone she could easily pick up at a dark and elegant steakhouse, a place where he felt thirty years too young and thirty million too poor, give or take a zero. The whiskeys winking on the shelves behind the bar were labels he couldn't afford to look at; the entrees on the menu were priced in the vicinity of his weekly grocery budget. She had invited him here to show him her power.

So, yeah, Sean was leaving on the jacket. He might need to make a quick exit, and fumbling with coat-check wasn't time he could afford to waste.

He steeled himself, put back his shoulders like he was entering the show-ring for a medal class, and walked across the dark blue carpet. Martha's gaze swung toward him, and her smile widened.

"Sean Casey, look at you! In a suit, just the way I like them." Martha glanced back at the silver-haired man, whose own smile had grown strained. "Todd, this is Sean Casey, my horse trainer. The one I was telling you about."

Sean made an effort to provide a firm handshake, all the while wondering what was going on. There'd been no intimation that he'd be meeting anyone tonight. Maybe he'd read Martha's signals all wrong?

"Todd is a real estate man through and through, aren't you, Todd?" Martha laughed, a tinkly cocktail-party sound. "He's my silent partner, you know. And very picky. I look at properties. Todd finds faults *and* won't let me buy them. Very frustrating."

"She's completely unreasonable," Todd told him pleasantly. "Absolutely out of her mind. But you know that, don't you, Sean?"

"I . . . uh . . . ." Sean was at a total loss. Property? Silent partners? Sean had come here to talk about buying horses, not land, and Martha had never mentioned there was anyone else to reckon with on the way to getting a signed check.

"You're right not to answer," Martha told him, misjudging his silence. "Ignore Todd. He was just leaving. Ah-ah!" She preempted Todd, who was starting to protest. "You knew the rules when you waltzed over here, Toddy-boy. I told you no business tonight. Shoo. Off you go." She turned back to Sean as Todd waved a hand, evidently bearing no hard feelings, and went back to his table. Sean couldn't help but notice he was dining alone.

"That was surprising," he said. "This doesn't feel like the kind of place where you meet up with friends."

Martha looked around her. "Why not? It has booze, it has good lighting, it has music set at just the right level—enough to buzz in the ears and prevent too much eavesdropping, not so loud that you have to shout. I love this place. Always meeting friends here."

And so she'd brought him here, to show him off to everyone. Lovely. "It's very nice," he said, hoping she'd believe he'd amended his opinion so easily.

Luckily, Martha didn't really care about his feelings. "Let's get you a drink and then Rochelle will find us a table," she said breezily, snapping her fingers for a white-shirted bartender. While the man behind the bar was dutifully making Sean a drink, she fastened a glittering dinner-party smile on him. "So, the truth is, I didn't actually just meet Todd here tonight."

"Of course you didn't."

"Todd has some news today on a property, which makes me think we might invite him back over to talk more. If you want to."

Sean took the cocktail from the bartender, nodding briskly when it was suggested the drink go on Martha's tab. He didn't have enough money in his bank account to pay for it, so there was no point in trying to save face. "You're saying you found a place you want to buy? Like—a *farm?*"

"I think I have, yes! The place I want to buy, and the place I want you to run. So first, let's talk about you, and your role in all this. I know you don't want to teach little kids for pennies much longer. So let's set you up to make some real money. And me, of course." Martha's smile turned coy. "I have business ideas that Caitlin can't even conceive of."

Sean could have laughed if he wasn't so discomfited. He'd been played. While he'd been angling for the right moment to convince Martha to invest in his show career, she'd been making her own plots and plans for his future. And now he had no choice but to listen.

"Great," he said, tipping his glass. "Let's talk about me."

He ordered expensively, confident in Martha's platinum Amex and his ability to keep charming her through the duration of the meal. Sean was resolved to be receptive, interested, possibly even witty if he could manage it, right through coffee and dessert. He just needed Martha to believe he'd considered every angle of her proposal—so that she'd believe him when he turned her down.

Because of course he'd turn her down. He was trying to get to New York for the summer, and Florida for the winter—not settle forever in Maryland.

Todd was invited to join them and he came happily, the look of surprise on his face rehearsed and barely hiding his expectant attitude as he described the property to Sean. Paddocks. Stalls. Hot water wash-racks. Arenas, both outdoor and indoor. Everything a person would expect in an equestrian center. Sean nodded politely at every amenity, working his way through a steak that cost more than he'd made that day.

By the end of the presentation, Todd sounded a little hoarse and Martha stepped in. "Enough about the footing and the fencing," she told him. "What Sean really wants to know is how he's going to make money there." Martha twinkled at Sean. "Our Sean loves money."

He gave her a thin smile. "Just trying to make a living in a very expensive sport," he said.

"And you come from a pretty sweet set-up," Martha prompted him. "Right? Ashton Downs, that was your family's farm, wasn't it?"

Sean's smile slipped, his stomach lurched. What did she know about his family? "I grew up there," he allowed. "It's been sold."

"That's the short version." Martha waved her wineglass at him. "I won't waste Todd's time with the long one. But I think it proves my point . . . you're looking for better things than you've got at Elmwood. I'll bring you on as head trainer at this place. House, stalls, students, staff. Just keep everyone happy and keep the money flowing. The same as you're doing for Caitlin, but on a much larger scale, obviously."

Sean nodded slowly, fingering his own wine glass. There were so many wars raging in his mind now, he scarcely knew which was which. Voices shouting everything from, *You're not qualified for this job* to, *You'd be crazy to pass this up* to, *What about Nadine?*

He wanted to think the last voice was the one he should listen to. But it was hard to know for sure. Hard to know when he was sitting in a dark steakhouse, surrounded by opulence, with the lonesome, shabby barn apartment the only thing waiting at the end of this night.

Martha tipped her head to one side, smiling. "Sean? Did I lose you?"

"No, I'm so sorry." He tried to take a deep breath, fumbling for words and the air to speak them. "I just—wasn't expecting something like this."

"I suppose you weren't." Martha glanced at Todd, who looked a little puzzled by Sean's reaction. "Oh, I didn't warn him. This was a sneak attack."

Todd lifted his eyebrows.

"And I wasn't considering running a full-scale barn myself," Sean explained. "That's a lot of work."

"Oh, I see." Todd managed to look disapproving. "Not afraid of a little work, are ya, son?"

It was the kind of thing his father might have said, in the same kind of vaguely mocking tone. The implication was always that Sean had never worked hard, that everything had been handed to him. Sean had never been able to make his father understand that even with the best horses, even with the top trainers, he had always been working hard in the saddle. Riding wasn't a game of posing —or rather, the prettiest poses required the most strength.

But he was also well aware that was the only place he'd had to work, while people like Nadine did all the dirty work. He'd learned a lot over the past months at Elmwood, avoiding chores until he could teach himself to do them properly, not wanting to be caught as the so-called riding instructor who couldn't even muck out a stall, not wanting Nadine to find out he'd been riding all his life but couldn't properly wrap a horse's legs.

The truth was, *Nadine should be offered a job like this.*

Or at least, the horse management side of things. He imagined them as co-managers: Nadine could handle the horses and barn; he could handle teaching and training. *This could work.* It would be a stretch for him, but he could learn. He could put in the effort he hadn't bothered putting in for the past six months at Elmwood.

He could adjust his goalposts if it meant he could just get back to showing in some capacity.

"I'm not afraid of work," Sean told Todd. "But I'm not sure I'm the right person to handle *all* of it. But I know someone we could bring in. If we could get her interested—"

Martha leaned back in her chair, her eyes narrow. "No."

Todd glanced between the two of them. "I'm sorry?"

"He's trying to weasel out a job for his girlfriend. The answer is no. She's Caitlin's manager. She can stay there."

Sean nodded slowly, turning the facts over in his mind. He hated to admit it, but no Nadine, no deal. He couldn't run a place like that on his own. Finally, some clarity. He felt like his brain was just stretching, looking around, and wondering where the hell it had woken up. But at least now he knew his answer.

"It's not going to work, I'm afraid."

Martha pressed her lips together. She considered him for a long moment before saying, "She wouldn't choose you."

Heart thudding, Sean placed his napkin on the table and stood up. He went slowly, making sure his reaction didn't show in his movements, taking care not to bump the table. No one could know how well Martha's arrow had struck. No one had ever chosen him—but how did Martha know that?

"Leaving so soon?"

"I have to get up early," Sean said coolly. "Life on a farm. Thank you for dinner."

Martha looked up at him, smirking. She lifted a sheet of paper from the little stack by Todd's plate and passed it to him. "Call me when you're done feeling noble," she told him mockingly. "The offer stands. But not forever."

He took the paper and slipped it into his pocket, resolved not to look at it immediately. "I'm sorry we were on different pages, Martha."

She sighed, and for a moment the mocking look on her face smoothed away. "What did you really want from me, Sean?"

Hope, unreasonable as it was, sprung in his chest. "Three horses, show fees, and summer at the show circuit in Saugerties." The alliteration made it all sound so appealing. "You're the owner. I show them. Your stable name, your colors, yours to syndicate or sell."

Martha humped an eyebrow at that. "Hmm. Almost reasonable. You don't think we can reach a compromise?"

He hardly dared to breathe.

"I'll look at the horses," she decided. "Send me their info."

Chapter Fifteen

Nadine

"I heard Sean is going to dinner with Martha tonight."

Richie was leaning into the office, a big grin on his face.

Nadine put down her pen. She'd been trying to figure out how many more combinations she could fit into the hunter pace schedule. The event was only half-full but with a month left to get entries, she was still hoping she could fit in extra riders. Every penny that came in would help the therapeutic riding program, and by extension, help avoid any financial woes Caitlin might be anticipating.

"Any thoughts on that?" Richie asked.

"Are you trying to get me riled up about this, Richie?"

"A little bit," Richie said, unabashed. "Wanted to see what you'd say."

"You're a big gossip. Your wife should do something about you."

"I try!" Rose's voice floated from across the barn aisle. "Ain't nothing I can do with him!"

"He's just having dinner with her, Richie, it's perfectly innocent." Nadine spoke knowing her words were meaningless; it was highly unusual for a trainer and a student to have dinner together. The only reason there could possibly be was a potential business agreement, and if Sean was trading off the books with Martha, Caitlin was going to lose it on him.

She'd tried telling him as much before he went into the ring for his last lesson of the evening, but he'd brushed aside her concerns. "I've got this," he kept saying, as if Nadine had any reason to believe Sean could pull off a business dinner with one of the farm's clients and not get into trouble.

Maybe she should have—after all, he'd managed to get the job here with what she could only assume were fake references. But still, Nadine had little faith in Sean on this one. He was heading for a crash.

She didn't want to see it.

"I'm washing my hands of the whole affair," she told Richie, "and I think it would be great if you kept out of it, too."

"I thought you'd be worried about Seany-boy," Richie told her, acting wounded. "I thought you two were special friends."

"Richie, come on." Nadine gestured at her legal pad and the scribblings therein. "Can't you see I'm trying to do math here?"

"Oh!" Richie's Santa Claus-beard crumpled with silent laughter. "Wouldn't want to disturb you while you're doing *math*." He went back to the feed room, where Rose was setting up morning grain, his shoulders still shaking with hilarity.

"That man," Nadine muttered, picking up her pen again. There was nothing else to say about him, though. Richie was incorrigible. Rose had told them so many times.

Sean, on the other hand . . . she wanted to catch him before he left. See what he was really up to with Martha. So it was pretty disappointing when Caitlin waylaid her as she tried to finish up for the night, and kept her in the office until past seven-thirty, talking about horses she wanted to sell and students she wanted to advance. By the time she was free to go, the barn chores were done and the parking lot was empty.

Caitlin walked into the aisle and looked at the half-lit barn with surprise. "I didn't realize it was so late!"

Apparently not, Nadine thought grouchily. The depth of her annoyance startled her a little. She was used to thinking of Caitlin in a more respectful way. Almost as much her benefactor as her boss. After all, if it weren't for Caitlin, there was no telling where she'd be working. But it almost certainly wouldn't come with an office, a full apartment, or the peace of mind which came from knowing no one was going to bang on her door in the night.

She might even have ended up back at her mother's house. Which, she supposed, might have prevented Reg from coming back . . . but it wasn't likely.

"We should get dinner," Caitlin announced. "You want to go to the Blue Plate? My treat."

"We'd have to hustle," Nadine said doubtfully, but her stomach gave a resounding rumble at the thought of Nikki's meatloaf platter. The evening was cool, and the day had been long; diner food sounded like exactly the thing to fill her up. "Think we can make it?"

"I know we can." Caitlin's eyes twinkled. "Come on, let's run for it!"

They pelted down the barn aisle, past the pricked ears and wide eyes of the astonished horses, and slipped through the side door next to the big sliding doors, already closed and latched for the night. Caitlin's truck was parked out front, and in a matter of moments they were pealing out of the lot, sending gravel flying.

A spatter of rain hit the windshield; the cool evening was giving way to a chilly, wet night. "April showers," Caitlin muttered, flicking on the wipers. "We better get some *big* flowers, after the winter we just had."

"My mom said she'd never seen so much snow in her life," Nadine said absently, forgetting she never mentioned her mother.

She felt Caitlin's sharp glance. "How *is* your mother?" Caitlin had an idea of Kelly Blackwell, of what it meant to grow up in the battered townhouses of Wonder Avenue, a neither-suburb-nor-city subdivision stranded between the corn fields out on Old Frederick Road. But the two women were separated in age by ten years, so they'd never run into each other in school. By the time Kelly was in high school, Caitlin was finishing up college down in College Heights.

And even if they'd overlapped in age, they'd never have overlapped in social circles. Caitlin was Catoctin Creek gentry, or as close as the little town came to anything like a ruling class. There were layers to Catoctin Creek, just as there were any other old society which had been around since before the Revolutionary War, and the Blackwells, newcomers and poor, had never gotten closer than the peripheries.

So it was with all this history weighing heavy on Nadine's mind that she simply shrugged and said, "She's fine, I guess."

"Still with Reggie Vargas?"

Nadine stiffened. "Yes." How did Caitlin know about Reg?

"Relax. I've known Reg forever. He's done some odd jobs for me."

That didn't make Nadine feel better. Reg was a petty thief, at best. Every time he had the opportunity to work a normal job, live on the right side of the law, he chose not to do it. Instead, he waited for whatever job his "friends" had for him. That was how he'd just spent three years in prison. That was why he was on probation now. That was why Nadine was in Catoctin Creek, trying to keep her mother out of trouble simply by appealing to her maternal instincts: *If I go to jail, what does that do to Nadine's prospects?*

At least, that was what Nadine *hoped* her mother thought. But her doubts on this point were also why Nadine never spent the night in her old bedroom, and limited her visits to the townhouse where she'd grown up.

If she always had the alias of being hard at work at Elmwood, she couldn't be accused of anything.

But now, to find out Reg was involved with Elmwood sometimes, too? Nadine ground her teeth.

"If Reg ever did any jobs for you, that would be the one time he did something on the right side of the law," Nadine found herself saying.

Caitlin barked a laugh. "Oh, he's not so bad. You're probably not his biggest fan, I get it. But he does stuff no one else wants to do. For cheap. When you run a farm the size of Elmwood, a jack-of-all-trades comes in handy."

Nadine didn't ask what sort of jobs Reg was willing to do around the farm. The less she knew, the better.

Caitlin found her silence amusing. "You think Sean is so much better than Reggie? He's out right now getting wined and dined by the ex-wife of a lobbyist who doesn't know what to do with all her ill-gotten gains. Talk about dirty money. The least he could do is sell Martha one of *my* horses, like he's supposed to do."

Nadine looked at her then. "What do you know about Sean and Martha?"

"More than you, I'd bet."

Nadine didn't even know what to say.

The lights of Catoctin Creek drew them in, as dim as they were: streetlights orange against the blue dusk, moths batting themselves against the globes. The only businesses with their signs still lit were Trout's Market and the Blue Plate; as Caitlin parked, they saw Lauren look out the front door with a crease of annoyance in her forehead, wondering who was showing up so late. When the manager saw it was the Elmwood truck, her face relaxed, and she stood in the doorway as Caitlin and Nadine approached.

"You two are late tonight!" Lauren remarked. "I was fixing to close up shop."

"Take pity on us?" Caitlin asked humbly. "It's raining and we are hungry."

"As long as you don't mind me cleaning up around you," Lauren said, stepping back so they could come inside. "I sent the waitress home. No one here but me and Nikki, and a couple of folks in the kitchen."

"Sounds perfect. Let me save you time: I'll have a cheeseburger. Nadine, you know what you want?"

"Meatloaf, if there's any left," Nadine said meekly. She knew what it meant to stay open late for a customer. Sometimes boarders simply couldn't be induced to leave, especially on long summer evenings, and Nadine wasn't done until the barn was empty. "Or a burger's fine if there isn't."

"I think you might be in luck," Lauren told her. "I'll grab y'all some teas."

Caitlin slid into a booth near the kitchen doors to save Lauren a walk with their food. "Where d'you think the line is for *y'all* usage? Is it the Mason-Dixon? Did anyone use it when you lived up in PA?"

"Nope. We're what, ten miles from the Mason-Dixon? It's pretty hit or miss here."

"I could never imagine Catoctin Creek being part of the South," Caitlin laughed. "But I guess *y'all* is a good word. Covers a lot of ground."

"Tell me what you think Sean is doing tonight," Nadine blurted, unable to hold it back another moment.

Caitlin cocked her head, eyebrows lifted in gentle amusement. "Nadine! Please tell me no."

Nadine blinked at her. "No, what?"

"No, you're not crushing on Sean. Because he's about as reliable as Carrot," Caitlin went on, naming the farm's most notoriously naughty pony. "Sean is *why* I told you guys there's a no-dating rule. I didn't want him to . . . I don't know. Lead you on, or something. Whatever is the least old-fashioned way of saying that. And since you guys have basically been fighting since last fall, I wasn't too concerned. But now you have me worried."

"I'm not crushing on Sean," Nadine lied, because she didn't have a choice. "But it would make life complicated if he left. We have a lot of students."

"True." Caitlin accepted her iced tea from Lauren with a gracious smile. "Well, that's good. Because if he doesn't quit to go ride for Martha, I'm going to fire him."

"*What?*" Nadine couldn't help the panic in her voice. "You'd really fire him?"

"Unless he gets a lot better." Caitlin smirked. "He doesn't know it, but this hunter pace is his big trial. If my clients do great in their divisions, he can stay. I figure it's more fair than a horse show. Hunter paces are pretty even and objective: there aren't points for style, it's just about staying in the saddle under changing conditions while riding at a sensible pace. I'll accept that he needs to get better at teaching equitation, if I am convinced he can teach students to ride safely and effectively. But if he can't even manage that? He's out."

"I—I had no idea it was serious. I knew you wanted to see improvement, but . . ." Nadine thought of her previous offers to help Sean improve as an instructor. Now she had to force him to accept her help.

"I try to keep my cards close to my chest," Caitlin said. "And I expect you to do the same. No telling, Nadine. If he gets wind of this, I'll know why."

"Of course not," Nadine murmured, looking down.

"Thank you. And as for what I think he's doing tonight? He's trying to get Martha Lane to buy him some show horses and pack him off to the circuit to play with his old friends." Caitlin laughed and looked at her phone. "He thinks I don't see everything he does," she muttered, scrolling with one thumb. "People have always underestimated me. And they always regret it."

Nadine sat very still as Lauren appeared and placed their broad white diner plates in front of them. Her meatloaf steamed appetizingly from beneath a coat of brown gravy, and her mouth should have been watering, but suddenly, her desire to eat was gone. All she wanted to do was warn Sean—and figure out a way to save his job.

Assuming he wanted to stay.

Would he really leave and work for Martha instead? Even now, when they were just really getting to know each other?

Was she worth sticking around for?

Caitlin picked up her cheeseburger and surveyed it with deep pleasure. "I eat more salads than you'd care to know about," she told the burger. "Tonight, it's all about *you*." And she took a huge bite.

Nadine wished she could do the same, but she knew she could only pick at her food tonight. Until she got home and saw Sean, got some answers from him, she was going to be living with a whole swarm of butterflies in her stomach.

Halfway through her burger, Caitlin got a call she wanted to take. She left Nadine, telling her to clean her plate like a good girl, while she went out front to talk. Almost immediately, Nikki Mercer was sliding into the booth across from her, pushing Caitlin's plate to one side.

Nadine jumped. "Nikki! Where did you come from?"

"The kitchen." Nikki winked at her. "Listen, if Caitlin thinks she's the only one with bat-ears, she's the one underestimating people. What are you going to do about Sean?"

"I have no idea. I haven't even had time to think about it. I can't believe she wants to fire him!" Nadine looked both ways, as if

Caitlin would magically appear, but the dining room was empty, half the lights turned out as Lauren wiped tables with gusto.

"Believe it. Come on, you've known Caitlin a year now. She is capable of some amazing, generous things, but that's a recent development and I'm pretty sure there are ulterior motives at play. Caitlin is still Caitlin-first, at all times." Nikki stole a fry from Caitlin's plate. "You know anything about teaching kids to ride?"

"Not a lot," Nadine said honestly. "I can offer him suggestions, but I've never been an instructor, either."

Nikki shook her head, thinking. "Well, there must be books. Videos, too. Tell you what—you're more clued in to horse stuff than me. See what you can find. Send me the receipts and I'll pay you back."

"Why would you pay for Sean's books? I mean, that's really nice, but I'm just . . . a little surprised." And a little suspicious. Nadine remembered how much attention Sean had always paid Nikki.

"He's generous," Nikki replied, nabbing another fry. "He helped me a lot when I was trying to decide about starting the bakery. And I like him. I like both of you. *And* I don't want Caitlin getting too full of herself and messing up people's lives for sport. I'm afraid we're giving her too much power by letting her buy and sell half of Catoctin Creek, even if she's giving back to the town. Did you hear about the Foltzes?" Nadine shook her head. "Connie Foltz wanted to start an ice cream place. Rent was too expensive and the old ice cream parlor needed too much work. So her mom started asking around town, if anyone knew of a way to get the money. Meanwhile, Caitlin swooped in, bought the building, and she's putting in the work to renovate. She's going to rent it to Connie below-market."

Nadine glanced past Nikki. She could see Caitlin standing outside on the steps, talking away. In the distance, the dark frontage of the old ice cream parlor slept beneath the street-lights. "Why would she do that?"

Nikki shrugged. "Guilt over the way she treated most of us in high school? A really long-term business opportunity only she knows about? She just wants to control us? I really have no idea. But between the Schubert house where I'm building, and the ice cream parlor where Connie's going to open up—this summer by the way, it's going to be incredibly quick—and the therapeutic riding program at Elmwood, she's been spending a lot of time giving back. Honestly, that's why this Sean thing irritates me so much. She's inconsistent."

"She's always been inconsistent," Nadine allowed. "Working for her has been a challenge. But a good challenge."

"I know. You fit her really well. You're not demanding; you roll with the punches." Nikki gave her a sympathetic smile. "But Nadine—you might have to stand up for Sean."

"Maybe we can just make him a better trainer? Because I don't know what else I can do."

"We'll have to," Nikki agreed. "Because the only power you have is the power to walk. If he leaves, you leave, that kind of thing. Caitlin wouldn't give you up easily."

Maybe not, Nadine thought, as Nikki got up and Caitlin came back in, demanding that Nikki bring her replacement fries. But would she risk her job for Sean?

She liked him; she felt a horrible wrench at the idea of losing him. But she didn't know if she could give up everything she'd worked for to keep him around.

How could a person ever know the answer to that?

She'd just have to concentrate on making him a better trainer.

Chapter Sixteen

Sean

He saw her come into the barn through the side door, his heart lifting at the sight of her, then falling as he saw her expression. Something had happened tonight.

"Hey," he said, standing up to meet her. "Where were you tonight?"

She lifted her face, surprised he was in the shadowy barn aisle. "What are you doing down here?"

"I was waiting for you. I wanted to talk to you."

"I had dinner with Caitlin," she said. "At the Blue Plate. And she decided to sit around talking to Nikki after we were done. All about the Schubert house and Nikki's renovations. She wanted to know everything. I thought we'd never leave."

"Are you too tired to talk? I'll leave you alone if you just want to go to bed."

"No," she said, with a little sigh. "It's fine. I don't think I could just go right to bed after tonight."

"Something happened." He reached out without thinking, wrapped his arm around her thin shoulders. "You want to tell me about it? Over a beer, maybe?"

"That would be nice," Nadine agreed, giving him a tentative smile. "The beer, not the talking about it."

"Well then, I'll tell you my thing, and you can decide if you feel like telling me yours. No requirements." Sean took Nadine's hand and led her up the stairs to his apartment. When he had her settled on the couch, beer in hand, he opened his mouth to tell her about his night . . . and then realized he had no idea where to begin.

They looked at each other for a few moments. Nadine's face grew confused, and then she leaned forward, setting her beer bottle on the floor. "Sean, are you going to go work for Martha?"

He drew back as if she'd hit him. Who had told her? "I—I'm not sure," he said slowly. "We both went to the table with different proposals. I don't know if either will work out."

"What was yours?" Nadine asked pointedly, crossing one leg over the other. "Does it involve leaving Elmwood?"

"It did, yeah. Most likely," he hedged, as if he hadn't been dying to get out of this job. Before Nadine had taken a simple thing and made it complicated. "I gave her the information on three horses who would be perfect starters for an owner who wants to have fun on the circuit. I asked her to buy them for me."

Nadine's mouth dropped. He wondered what she'd expected.

"It's not that unusual a request," he went on. "Martha would be a great show-horse owner. She'd get to rub elbows with the kind of company she likes, and tell all her friends about how great her horses are, and we could do some buying and selling, as well."

"A way to show off how much money she has," Nadine said flatly.

He remembered her describing the show-circuit that way before, and he nodded. "It would be a win for both of us. I could show, she could have nice toys. But it doesn't necessarily mean I have to leave here forever."

"Saugerties," Nadine replied. "I'm really sorry, but I heard half of what your friend Simone said to you the other night." She rubbed her face. "She's loud on the phone."

"Yeah." There was no denying it, then. "It would be a summer circuit in upstate New York, for sure. So I'd be gone for that."

"And Florida in winter," Nadine continued. "Did you really want me to go with you? Is that why you brought it up again? Because you think you're going to leave?"

"Nadine, I would love for you to go to Florida with me." Sean didn't know if he was being too hasty. Didn't know the rules for this kind of thing. All he knew was that she seemed on the verge of agreeing with him, that she was on the edge of backing away from a certain argument, and that yes, he thought she'd be a really pleasant addition to any Florida trip.

"What was Martha's suggestion, then? She didn't show up ready to just buy you a couple of horses?"

"Shocking, I know." Sean made a face, but Nadine wasn't playing along. "Her idea wasn't nearly as much fun. She wants to buy a farm and have me run the training program."

He wasn't prepared for Nadine's bark of laughter.

"Hurtful," he said, when she was finished. "I know I'm not the world's best trainer, but—"

"Sean, my God." Nadine shook her head. "I was trying to find a way to tell you that we have to fix your teaching problem or find you a new job. Thanks for giving me the perfect segue into that conversation. Because you *cannot* go run training at another farm."

He stared at her. "Find me a new job?" he repeated, incredulous. "Did I miss something?"

"Afraid so. Obviously you're not supposed to know about this, but the hunter pace is a trial to see if you're a good enough trainer to keep around, or if Caitlin should just can you." Nadine picked up her beer bottle again and took a healthy swig. She seemed to have found her thirst, after all. "You have to get your students comfortable enough over the course to win their divisions. She wants to know you can teach safe, effective riding and—I'm dead serious, Sean! Why are you laughing?"

Sean didn't know why he was laughing. The urge just swept over him, impossible to deny. He shook his head, wiping his eyes as tears threatened to spill out. "I just—I should have known. She's so evil like that. She seems nice and then underneath there's just this current of darkness. And the whole thing with Martha is so ridiculous, and this just makes it even worse. To think I have been considering Martha's offer at all . . . crazy. Just think what Martha would say if Caitlin fired me and then I wanted to run training at her barn."

"You considered it?" Nadine's voice flattened again. "You would go work for her? Somewhere else?"

"I mean—*look* at this place." He pulled out the real estate listing Martha had handed him before he'd left the restaurant. "You'd consider it, too."

She took the paper from him and he watched her eyebrows go up as she took in the laundry list of amenities. "This is huge," she murmured.

"I asked if I could bring you along," he went on, thinking that would win him some points. "Because I'd need a really good barn manager, and you, obviously." Sean waved his hand. "You're good."

"Oh yeah? What did she say?"

He shrugged. "Too soon to make those kinds of decisions."

Nadine shook her head. "Please. She wouldn't have me. She's never been a fan of mine, and I saw the way she was looking at me in the aisle yesterday. But, Sean, even if you could do this successfully—you'd have yourself a big enemy in Caitlin. I wouldn't even consider starting a new barn in this part of Maryland."

He nodded. He should have figured Caitlin would be that kind of boss—the vindictive kind, who wouldn't take kindly to one of her employees starting up with a rival business. "That's a good argument against this whole thing to take back to Martha. I wasn't thinking clearly tonight. I didn't expect her to spring this kind of offer on me, honestly."

Nadine was looking at the real estate listing again. "I can see how this would be enticing. I just think you have to look farther away. Maybe closer to Baltimore."

He frowned at her. "Wait, are you suggesting I go farm-shopping with Martha?"

Nadine laughed at that. "No, of course not. But I feel like things are all confused right now. I came home tonight thinking we'd talk about ways to boost your teaching game so you wouldn't get fired, and you're already looking at your next job . . . for this *summer*, for heaven's sake. I guess I didn't realize you had one foot out the door."

Sean leaned forward, suddenly seized with worry. "But you'd miss me if I left," he said. "Wouldn't you?"

Her green eyes met his. "Of course I would."

He watched her tease her lower lip with her teeth. "I should say no."

"That's up to you."

"Stay here with you."

"If you can keep your job."

"You already said you'd help me. You can't take that back."

Nadine lowered her lashes, and Sean's heart skipped a beat.

Suddenly, he found himself slipping off the barstool and onto the couch next to Nadine, pressing himself close against her side. He wrapped one arm around her shoulders and she lifted her head slightly, giving him room to snuggle close. When her cheek tipped against his shoulder, he felt another squeeze in his heart, as if she'd physically reached inside his chest and clutched him there, as if she'd decided to keep him here beside her, and he didn't have a single say in the matter.

The feeling was as sweet as it was agonizing.

"I don't know what's going to happen," he murmured eventually. "But I wouldn't just leave you. I could try to find you a job on the circuit, or I could convince Martha to hire you, too—"

"No," she whispered.

"Or I could stay." He retreated effortlessly.

"Stop. Sean—we don't have to make any decisions tonight. Okay?"

"Okay," he replied, relieved to his core. "Let's leave it for tonight."

He woke in the night, the memory of her still so close she could have been in the room, and wondered how on earth they could have left it. They should have fought it out, they should have made their final decisions, they should have put all their demands on the table. That's what his parents would have done—and whoever had the most sound financial decision at the end of the argument would be proclaimed the winners.

That's why they were in their beach house in the Bahamas, and he was here in a barn apartment, trying to decide between which tyrant of a woman he'd work for next. Sean chuckled, a wry sound in the heavy silence. He didn't know what was coming next, and they couldn't possibly have made the right decisions tonight.

But as Sean rolled over, determined to get some more sleep before his alarm went off, he knew they'd have to start working towards their goals in the morning.

The first thing he'd do was solidify his job here. That way, no matter what, he'd have a place to live and money in his wallet.

After that?

Well, that depended on what Nadine wanted to do, he guessed.

He was beginning to think that wherever he went next, she had to be a part of it.

And on that frightening note, Sean realized he was not getting back to sleep.

Chapter Seventeen

Nadine

"Come on, loser, we're going shopping." Nadine held up her car keys, jingling them in front of Calypso's nose. The horse popped his lips together, trying to catch them, but she pocketed them and slipped him a baby carrot, instead.

"I take it you're talking to me and not my horse," Sean said with impressive dignity, considering where his hand was. He squeezed the sponge under Calypso's tail, and water streamed down, soaking his boots. "Why is it so cold that I'm reduced to giving this animal a sponge bath in April?"

"It's spring," Nadine said with a shrug. "This is what spring does. Anyway, finish him up, wash your hands, and come with me. I have to pick up some stuff at the tack shop in Frederick and this is the perfect chance to look at their horse books."

"Fine." Sean gave Calypso one more glance before unhooking him from the cross-ties. "I have to turn this guy out, though. Why are we looking at horse books, again?"

"Because we are giving you a crash course in effective riding instruction," Nadine replied. "Remember what I told you last night?"

Sean's expression reminded her a lot of things had been said last night.

"About the hunter pace, and teaching, and your job?" She looked around, lifting her eyebrows significantly. "The *secret?*"

"Oh right, the secret." Sean led Calypso out of the wash-rack. "Okay. Crash course it is. I'll be right there."

Nadine turned on her car and listened to the engine growl to itself as it warmed up. The day was bright, beautiful, and crazy cold. Last night's rain had given way to a shivering arctic wind which made the fuzz of new leaves on the trees look regretful they'd come out so soon. Nadine snuggled herself into a sweater and looked at the tulip blossoms blowing wildly in the flowerbed Rose had planted in front of the barn. She felt lucky she'd moved back to Maryland; there had been snow in parts of Pennsylvania. Snow after the tulips came out was inexcusable, Nadine thought.

When Sean finally arrived, she took off happily, ready for a change of scenery and a drive through the beautiful countryside. Lately, the only time she'd left the farm had been after dark, and then just for the quick drive into Catoctin Creek to eat at the Blue Plate. Now she looked out the side windows as much as she did the windshield, delighting in the fresh tint of green that had swept over the wooded hills and rolling fields.

Sean laughed at her every time she braked to point out a cluster of wild day lilies, or a flowering cherry tree, but she didn't even mind. "Spring is worth a little wear and tear on the brakes," she defended herself. "It's only this beautiful for a couple weeks every year."

"I like the way it shows off the lines of the trees and hills with just that little mist of green," Sean said dreamily, pointing at a cluster of trees crowning above a brown cornfield in the distance. "Even that weird subdivision in the middle of nowhere looks nice in spring."

Nadine felt her cheeks coloring, so she busied herself with the radio, letting her dark hair fall over her face. She didn't want to talk about Wonder Avenue. She didn't even like driving past it. If she did, she'd look down the road to the third house on the right, hoping she wouldn't see Reg's truck parked out front. And she figured it was almost certainly there. She had spoken to her mother twice in the past week, and both times she'd heard Reg in the background.

"What is this place, anyway?" Sean asked as the car approached the lonely lane of houses. "Who builds a single road of townhouses in the middle of cornfields?"

Nadine sighed. "It was built as government-assisted housing in the eighties," she explained. "But everyone in Catoctin Creek flipped out, and they managed to cancel the other streets. That whole field was supposed to be houses."

"Wow. I guess lucky for Catoctin Creek they canceled it."

"Why do you say that?" she asked sharply.

"Because look at that view." Sean pointed across the open fields. "You can see all the way down to Sugarloaf Mountain. If there were houses there, you'd lose this incredible angle."

And she realized he was right. Nadine felt her shoulders drop a little. "That's true. But the town wasn't trying to save the view, you know. They were trying to keep people out."

"It was the eighties," Sean said comfortably. "I'm sure it's different now."

Nadine shook her head, but she didn't pursue it. She didn't want her memories of growing up one of the unwanted outsiders from Wonder Avenue to ruin this beautiful day. But Sean wasn't through.

"I grew up on a huge farm," Sean began, looking carefully at the houses as they drew nearer. "It was outside of Middleburg, but so far outside, you could hardly say we were part of the community. Seems like if you had a little village of houses here and there, it might make things feel, I don't know, cozier? More tight-knit? Maybe things don't always have to be us versus them."

Nadine had to laugh at that. "Trust me, it's very *us versus them* in Catoctin Creek. I grew up here, remember? Did you ever notice how no one talks to me like they do to Rosemary or Nikki, or Caitlin for that matter? Those three can't get through the Blue Plate dining room without being stopped by half the people there."

"Well, I just figured it was because you're younger than they are. Everyone you just mentioned is in their thirties. There's not many people here who are our age."

"Connie Foltz is our age. The one I told you is opening the ice cream parlor, remember? And so is Roxie, who works at Trout's, and Melia, who teaches at the school. They're all from my senior class, did you know that? But none of them ever give me a second look. Not now, not then. The only friend I had in high school was Avery, and she left town."

Sean looked bewildered now. The houses of Wonder Avenue had flashed past; Nadine didn't even remember to look for Reg's truck. She realized she'd gotten herself worked up. "I'm sorry," she said. "It just didn't work out, that neighborhood. It wouldn't work now, either. I lived there, but it didn't make me a part of Catoctin Creek."

Sean stared at her. "Wait—you grew up—back there? On that street?"

She nodded.

"I had no idea. Every time I pass it, I think about what an odd, interesting place it must be . . ."

"It's just a street," Nadine said wearily. "It's not even an interesting street. My mom still lives there. She's why I wanted to move back here. Not because I'm *from* here, the way everyone always says. I don't think I'm really from anywhere."

The radio buzzed quietly to itself; a song gave way to a commercial for an auto body shop near the Francis Scott Key Mall. A DJ reminded them that the rest of the week would be cool, with periods of rain towards the weekend. "But don't forget, April showers bring May flowers!" she gushed in her lush radio voice.

Nadine switched the station. Classical. She left it there, a Bach concerto ringing through her car's tinny speakers.

Sean put his hand on her thigh. "It doesn't matter where you're from," he said softly. "I'm from a huge farm that's being plowed over to become a Wal-Mart Supercenter and three hundred tract homes. Home is where you make it."

She felt tears prick the back of her eyes, the old hurt welling up there. "I wanted to be from here," she whispered, hardly believing it could still sting so painfully.

"You can be from here, then," Sean told her. "Just like I can be. If this is where we want to stay."

She would have turned to him, then, but the country road was rapidly giving way to the traffic on the outskirts of Frederick, and so she just gave him a quick, watery smile, and let his soft touch on her leg sustain her all the way through the narrow city streets, until she pulled into the tack shop parking lot and could finally let down her guard.

—ele—

They had fun at the tack shop, trying out saddles and holding up show jackets, testing how they'd look in the latest styles. Sean put on a gaudy helmet blinged out with real crystals, and was bouncing around the store like it was Frederick's hottest nightclub before the sales clerk gently informed him the hat was six hundred and fifty dollars. Then he took it off, handed it over, and apologized with so much gravity that Nadine nearly fell off the bench where she'd been sitting, admiring a pair of boots she'd tried on, which cost nearly as much.

"Horse stuff is expensive when you don't have your dad's credit card," Sean confided, sitting next to her as she put the boots back into their box.

She snorted with laughter. "No kidding, little Lord Fauntleroy. I bet you don't even know how much money you asked Martha Lane to spend on show horses for you. It would be cheaper for her to just invest in a farm and let you run it into the ground like she wanted."

"Shhh! Someone's going to hear you." Sean looked around with wild eyes and Nadine felt herself dissolving into giggles again. Hard to believe she'd been such a freak show in the car, nearly crying over the way she'd been ostracized ten whole years ago.

With Sean, she realized, that stuff didn't matter. There was no baggage in the way. They were free to be whoever they wanted with each other. She wondered if he knew he couldn't have that with his old friends, the people who knew the Sean of free spending and zero cares.

She'd have to make sure he figured it out. Nostalgia could lead to all kinds of bad decisions.

"Okay, okay, let's be serious." She held out her hands as if trying to steady herself on a swaying ship. "We have to go look at the books and find a way to make you a good riding instructor overnight."

"Um, that's really harsh," Sean complained, but he followed her across the store. The bookshelves were laden with training books, but it took some work to find titles that addressed training people instead of horses.

"Here we go." She pulled out a spiral-bound book. *"101 Exercises for Riding Instructors.* This is a good place to start."

Sean opened the book and flipped through the pages. "Some of this stuff looks familiar. Wait. I've definitely done *that.*" He pointed to an exercise diagrammed on a page. "Why am I not teaching this already?"

"You probably just never thought of it as a specific exercise," Nadine said. "You're an instinctive rider, I think. You just *do* things. That's why you're good at riding horses like Calypso, who have a lot of training but need quirks ironed out. You can feel what they need. But most riders aren't like that. So you have to build all the tools for them and teach them how to use each one, and you have to be *really* specific."

"Sounds like a blast," Sean groaned, but he was already nodding at more exercises, flipping the pages and inspecting each image with interest, and she knew he was getting invested in the process already.

They found four more books, all of them filled with exercises and training philosophy and expansive metaphors designed to get through to the most uninspired of students, and Nadine paid for them herself, pocketing the receipt before Sean could stop her. He took the bag, along with the bridle strap-goods Caitlin had asked her to buy, and followed her out of the store. "That was too expensive," he told her as they settled into the car. "Let me pay you back."

"Don't worry about it. There's a fund already." She winked at him.

"What kind of fund? What does that mean?"

"I mean, a concerned citizen of Catoctin Creek has already stepped up to cover your expenses."

Sean groaned. "Don't tell me it's Nikki."

"Okay, I won't tell you. What do you want for lunch?"

"Really? It's Nikki?"

"I said I wouldn't tell you," Nadine repeated patiently. "But yes, it's Nikki. She says you were a big help with the bakery. And also, I think she wants to stick it to Caitlin for being so callous. And for having her fingers in so many pies in Catoctin Creek these days."

"But Caitlin's the reason Nikki is building the bakery." Sean seemed mystified. "She was at a standstill for a location before Caitlin offered the house."

"Exactly," Nadine agreed. "But Caitlin's getting a big head about all this charity. And she always has her own interests in mind, first. That's the way I understand it, anyway. She and Nikki go way back. There might be some old rivalry there, for all I know."

"Nadine, I don't see why you'd ever want to be part of Catoctin Creek society, or whatever it is," Sean complained. "Those women are all crazy, as far as I can tell. They're driven, and they're interesting, but they're crazy."

"It's not always easy living in a small town," Nadine admitted. "There's a lot more backbiting than most people would think. Now, can we get lunch already? I'm starving. Make a suggestion and I'll drive there; I know you eat out more than me."

"I don't have lessons for three more hours," Sean said contentedly. "Black Horse Pub. Pull out and take a left."

Chapter Eighteen

Sean

Maybe teaching wasn't so bad, after all.

Sean had put a week into his new leaf as a dedicated riding instructor, and so far, so good. With Nadine's help, he put together lesson plans before each session—"Just like a real teacher," he exclaimed once, earning himself a very astonished look from Nadine, who hadn't realized he'd never seen himself in that light.

But now he could recognize the sad truth: for as long as he'd been at Elmwood, he hadn't really seen himself as anything but a glorified babysitter, making sure kids and the occasional adult didn't fall off their horses. He'd thought his real work was schooling the sales horses into tractable prospects for the kids to buy. Maybe he should have realized he had the opportunity to make these students into riders, or that he was meant to be searching for nuggets of talent which could be polished into real winners in the show-ring, just as he had been. But somehow, for reasons Sean couldn't quite explain, he just hadn't seen the students of Elmwood that way.

"It's easy," Nadine told him when he tried to express this to her. "It's because you're a big old snob, and you thought a bunch of suburban kids at a riding school were beneath you."

"That's not it at all," Sean protested, but he knew she was probably right. He *was* a big old snob, just like she said. And he was having a hard time figuring out where that led him next.

Martha had been silent on the subject of the horses he'd asked her to consider. He didn't know if she'd looked at them. Didn't know if she'd contacted the seller. Didn't even know if the horses were still for sale. Simone pinged him a couple of times, wanting an update, claiming she needed to make arrangements for a roommate in the Saugerties house, and if he wasn't that person, she had to get someone else in the second bedroom, *pronto*. He begged off, asking her to wait, to consider his position, but she wasn't happy about it.

Simone had never been patient. She'd never had to be.

Nadine came into the office where Sean had been sitting over the lesson book, a few of the texts they'd bought at the tack store sitting open and sprawled across her desk. She was holding two coffees. "Thirsty?"

"Dying for caffeine," Sean admitted, accepting one of the mugs. "Although it's so warm out there today, I think we should consider moving into iced coffee season."

Nadine laughed, sitting at her desk chair. She scooted it close to Sean and looked over his mess, not seeming to mind that he'd spilled his work all over *her* desk. "And where are you planning on getting iced coffee in Catoctin Creek? That trend hasn't made it here. Wait a few years until the other millennials start moving back. Connie and I might just be the start of a migration home."

"Maybe Connie Foltz will sell it at the ice cream parlor."

"That's actually a really good suggestion." Nadine nodded at him. "Impressive, Sean! Tell her that. And I'm sure Nikki will, if she ever opens the bakery."

"I heard early June." Sean had been to the bakery for one other friends and family offering, bringing back a huge paper bag full of lemon and blueberry scones, which Nadine had been appropriately grateful for. He liked being the bringer of baked goods. It made him feel like he served a real purpose in her life. Nadine, unlike Simone, was not afraid of carbs, butter, or sugar.

"Just in time for the hunter pace madness to end." Nadine flicked her fingers across her desk calendar. "A month to go."

"Yup." Sean looked moodily at the lesson book again. "And that's what has me worried. I have four weeks to get these riders into winning shape, and I have no idea what I'm doing."

"Oh, it's not that bad." Nadine leaned over one of the guidebooks, flipping through pages. "Here. This is an exercise on pacing between fences. We can go out to the pasture and find some jump combinations you can use. Or we can throw some jump standards and poles in the back of the truck and take them out there, set up our own. What do you think? Which is easier?"

Sean looked at the diagrams, the jumps and the distances and the circles each rider should make all laid out in black-and-white. They were presented so matter-of-factly, but just looking at the drawings made him nervous. He wasn't afraid of the lesson plans themselves. He was afraid of what trouble the students might get into out in the pasture. Horses were different without fences to follow, boundaries to keep them in line.

"Sean?"

He sipped at his coffee, trying to buy time. Nadine put a hand on his knee, and he looked at her gratefully. "You know I'm just terrified I'm going to take someone out there and they're going to get run away with. Or bucked off. Or worse."

"Sean." Nadine's smile was tender. "I think you're developing a conscience."

He chuckled despite himself, and something more sarcastic curved her lips. She rubbed his leg comfortingly. "They're going to be fine. You've had them in the outdoor ring all week, just like Caitlin wanted, and everyone has adjusted. We've taken all the school horses out to the pasture to ride. Everyone has an idea of what's expected of them. Now it's just time to add the students. They can do this. It's their job, if they want to be riders. It's your job to show them the safe way to go about it, but it's their job to do the work."

That . . . made sense, actually. Sean let out a breath he hadn't realized he'd been holding. "Thanks, Nadine. That really helps put things in perspective."

"That's what I'm here for," she said, giving him one final slap on the leg. "And now, can you scooch all your things over? I have bills to write up."

They sat close together, side by side, until lessons began arriving and it was time to head out to work. Sean stretched, then turned and absently kissed Nadine on the cheek.

She turned her head, regarded him silently with those emerald eyes, and then leaned forward, giving him a kiss which took his breath away.

"Now go teach your lessons," she whispered as she pulled back. "I want those kids to win that hunter pace. You're not going anywhere, mister."

"You're not going anywhere." The words rang through Sean's mind as he took his students to the outdoor arena and began putting them through the exercises he'd written up for the lesson. *You're not going anywhere.* Wasn't that his worst fear, though? Wasn't that exactly the fate he had been trying to avoid?

Things were getting so complicated. He'd come to Elmwood with the intent of leaving before summer, before an entire year was out, and now he was hopelessly entangled with Nadine. They were spending all their time together; they were eating dinner together; they were falling asleep on the sofa together after watching a movie on her laptop, limbs entwined . . . in just a few short weeks, everything had changed.

"It must be spring fever," he muttered, shaking his head.

The rider trotting over cross-rails saw his head shake and pulled up her horse. "What?" she asked, teenage voice reedy with nerves. "Did I do something wrong?"

"No, I'm sorry." Sean waved his hand at her. "I was completely checked out. Start again, will you?"

The girl nodded and picked up her reins again, nudging her horse into a trot. They hopped over the cross-rails successfully, and Sean busied himself raising the fence heights by a hole.

Two-foot, three-inch jumps. He bit back a sigh as he pushed the pins through the holes in the jump standards, arranging the jump cups to hold the wooden poles. The holes at the very bottom of the standards were well-used here at Elmwood, but at his old farm, they'd rarely seen use.

Time to stop being such a snob, he reminded himself. If he did his job as a trainer, some of these students would rise to the top, achieving bigger and better things. He'd be able to raise their fences to three feet, three-three, three-six, and even higher. He could take them to the big shows he missed so much.

Well, he could if their parents had enough money, he supposed.

That was always the problem. He missed the days when he hadn't known how much things cost.

"Right lead canter in the top corner, then outside line, lead change if you have to, to inside diagonal, to next outside line. Got it?" The directions couldn't have been easier.

The teenager, a bright but nervous girl named Maya, paused and ran her finger through the air, pointing out the three lines he'd called. Then she nodded and pushed her horse into a trot. The other students clustered in a little group in the middle of the arena, out of the way. Sean stood a few dozen feet from them, arms crossed, boots planted in the rubbery arena footing, the way his own coaches had stood during his lessons.

Daily lessons. He'd gotten to the top hole on those jump standards through daily private training, unlimited show budgets, and priceless horses. How could he ever get a middle-class kid like Maya to that kind of level with such limited resources?

"This is pointless." His lips moved, but no sound came out. He watched Maya pick up the wrong lead at the canter, look down at her horse in confusion, sit down and bring him back down to the trot, pick up the correct lead on her second try. He sighed.

Even with lesson plans, even with the potential for growth, they were never going to take him back to the show circuits he'd left behind. Maya, like most of the riders here, was a local show kid.

Even if she had talent, she didn't have the garbage bags of cash she'd need to rise to the top.

These kids weren't his way out.

Without Nadine, his decision was obvious. Go with Martha, follow her money, wherever her money might lead. Even it felt wrong at first. He could iron things out somehow. But with Nadine, all he could hope was that he could convince her to follow him to greater things.

And she'd already said no once.

Nadine's eyes followed him when he came back into the barn. She moved to help the kids untack their horses, but as soon as she could escape, she ran up to Sean. "What's the problem?" She hissed. "Are you sick? You're completely pale. Maybe it's heat exhaustion?"

"It's not *that* hot," Sean said impatiently. He didn't want to talk about it—not right now, while he was trying to work things out in his head. Like how he'd convince Martha to send him to New York, and then he'd convince her to pay Nadine's way, too, and then he'd convince Nadine to come with him.

Wherever he went—to a new barn, to Saugerties, to join Simone, anywhere. He just needed Nadine to come along, and then everything would be fine.

She was the key.

She was also looking pretty annoyed. He realized his tone had been unacceptable and tried to mollify her. "Okay, maybe the heat got to me a little. I'll just sit down for a second and cool off."

"I'll get you a bottle of water." Nadine took off for the lounge, and Sean sat in a folding chair outside the tack room. He stretched out his legs, admiring his old field boots, which he thought somehow looked even classier when they were dusty with work. He'd had this pair for a solid six years and while they weren't as high end as his good show boots, they made him look extremely professional.

He squinted—was that a scuff on the left toe-cap? He'd have to buff that out—

"Sean."

His eyes shot up. "Martha . . . I didn't know you were coming tonight?" He was more familiar with the lesson book than ever before, and he knew Martha's name wasn't in it. "What's up? I don't think I can squeeze you into a lesson tonight."

"Did you even notice I'm not in riding clothes?" Martha did a little twirl, showing him her flowing blouse and capri pants. She looked ready to head to an art festival and buy some local watercolors. "Come on, I need you. Get Nadine to cover for you."

"What? Nadine's not an instructor. And I can't just leave. I have four students tacking up right now." *And fake heat exhaustion.* "What's going on, anyway?"

"I'm going to look at those horses, and I need you there, obviously. You can try them under saddle. They're down in Leesburg, so we have to hustle. Come on, tell Nadine."

"Tell me what?" Nadine approached cautiously, a water bottle in each hand.

"I need Sean," Martha informed her. "You can teach the rest of the lessons tonight."

Nadine actually laughed. She handed Sean a bottle of water, twisting the lid off as she gave it to him, as if he wasn't able to open it himself. He felt worse about his fake heat exhaustion. "Excuse me? Sean has a job. He can't just run around the countryside with you. Make an appointment with Caitlin if you want him to look at horses with you."

"This doesn't concern Caitlin," Martha replied, eyebrows arching dangerously.

Sean stood up before anyone said something that could get him into trouble. "Martha, I'm really sorry, but Nadine is right. I have commitments to all of these students tacking up right now. And the lesson after that. I can't just leave." He avoided saying he had a job, or bringing up Caitlin. He was too worried Martha might say something about him working for *her* and send Nadine over the edge.

The timing on this was all wrong. And if Nadine would just walk away, leave him to deal with Martha, he'd tell the older woman that she needed to let him work this out on his own time.

As if Martha would listen to you. His inner voice spoke up. *She wants to run your life, not take your advice.*

Martha was eyeing him with something like disappointment. "Well, I guess I'll cancel with him, then," she said finally. "I hope he doesn't sell before I can get a good look, but that's the way things shake out sometimes."

"We can set up a time that works for everyone," Sean attempted, but Martha had already turned on her heel and was marching out of the barn.

He looked back at Nadine. She was staring after Martha with narrowed eyes, her jaw set, her arms folded over her chest. She looked very formidable. But Sean didn't like her chances in a battle with Martha. That woman had been places, seen things, *done* things that Nadine probably couldn't even imagine. She was a scary enemy.

That was why Sean was trying so hard to keep her close. And he'd keep trying, if Martha wouldn't push things so hard that they all lost their chance.

Chapter Nineteen

Nadine

The day had been unseasonably warm, still air gathering in the aisles and growing stale as the hours wore on, and now Nadine pushed through the side door of the empty barn in search of a cool breeze. She gazed at the pink and yellow sunset gathering above the Catoctin Mountains. The horses had been switched to night turnout, and they flicked their tails against the last flies of the dying day as they grazed in the paddocks. Beyond the indoor arena, the open spaces of the north pasture seemed to beckon, a few early lightning bugs pulsing against the dusky trees in the distance.

Nadine ducked through the fence rails and walked through the new grass, which was growing thick and rich thanks to the warm days and the cool rains they'd had so far this April. The month had its share of stormy moments, but for the most part it had been a pleasant enough start to spring. In a short week, April would be gone, and May would dawn over Catoctin Creek. May, the month of the hunter pace. May, the last month before summer.

The hot months loomed large in her mind already. Elmwood would be busy all summer; Caitlin had her booking summer camps, which would bring in new students and keep the current ones hooked. She wasn't sure how she felt about the prospect of a barn-full of children. Last summer had been lazy, quiet even; Sean hadn't been here yet, and the focus had been on the therapeutic riding program. Nadine had spent a lot of time in her office, the air conditioner installed in her window humming pleasantly, while she worked on funding and scheduling for the program.

It was odd to think that work might all have been for nothing.

Well, not *nothing*, she supposed, walking down the hillside towards the hidden creek that tumbled through the north pasture. They had helped a lot of kids—and adults, too—who needed the physical and mental benefits of riding. They had introduced a lot of adults to the pleasures of horses, and some had even gone off to adopt their own horses, learning the art of horse-keeping from Rosemary. So the program had helped Rosemary's equine sanctuary as well, the volunteers paying her for the horsemanship seminars Caitlin had come up with in the first place.

And of course, with her newfound authority in the local community, Caitlin had channeled her interests into real estate and investing, and now Nikki was building her bakery, and Connie was building her ice cream parlor, and who knew what Catoctin Creek dreamer was next in line for their very own angel investor?

And she'd brought Sean here, and now Nadine felt like life was changed in a way she'd never really expected. The very sunset was more beautiful, the golden light more spectacular shining on the trees, their crowns of leaves more full and rich than in any spring ever before, because Sean was here.

"Hey, Nadine."

His voice arrested her in her tracks; she spun around and saw him half-running, half-falling down the steep embankment. He panted as he caught up to her. "You know, there are easier trails down to the creek," he told her, steadying himself with one hand on her shoulder.

"This is the fastest one," she told him, leaning forward to press a quick kiss of hello on his lips. "And I really wanted to get down there before the light was gone."

Sean looked at the cotton-candy clouds unspooling themselves above the golden light above Notch Gap, then back at her. "This is a nice little spot to watch sunset," he said.

"And an even better place to watch dusk," she told him. "Come on."

She took his hand and tugged him down the rest of the hillside, their boots slipping a little on the steep, slick clay path. They heard the creek babbling away, then pushed through some shrubs and low-hanging tree branches to find the water, seeming to glow with the last light of evening as it threw itself over smooth rocks.

She heard Sean suck in his breath. "What a beautiful little spot."

"And here is the perfect rock to sit on," she said, showing off a flat rock, smooth with age and warm with the day's sunshine. "Hop up and sit awhile. The lightning bugs are coming out."

Sean followed her, settling down close beside her on the big stone. She took a few deep breaths, waiting for the blue dusk to replace the shimmering afterglow of sunset, waiting for him to say something which would break the spell.

Because as much as she cared for Sean, she knew he was going to spoil things.

She could feel it, waiting there in the tension of his shoulders as she leaned against him.

"Sean," she said finally, "what's wrong?"

"There's nothing wrong," he replied, his voice low. "This is wonderful."

"Tell me the truth." She turned from the creek to him, her eyes searching his face. "What did Martha really want from you this afternoon?"

He looked away from her instantly, and she felt the gravity of the moment weighing on her shoulders. He could be honest with her now, and they'd have something real. Or he could lie to her, and she'd know that this was just a fling. Maybe she'd gotten too attached, but it would still be nothing if he couldn't tell her the truth.

She waited, breathless, feeling as if she was teetering on the edge of a cliff, not sitting on a warm, solid slab of granite.

She *so wanted* this to be real.

Sean finally parted his lips, though his eyes remained fixed on the stream—or maybe something beyond the water, something she couldn't even see. "She wanted to take me to see those horses," he admitted, voice gravelly, almost as if there were unshed tears. "The ones I wanted her to buy, that I could take on the circuit this summer."

Nadine's fingers dug into the rock's crumbling seams. She felt grit finding its way beneath her fingernails. "But you didn't go. Why didn't you go, if you were so set on leaving this summer?"

Sean turned to her then, his face sagging with emotion. "You *know* why I didn't go," he told her. "Because of *you.*"

And he swept her into his arms, pressing her close to him.

The dusk fell all around; the lightning bugs came out and lit the woods with their little golden tails, and Nadine wrapped her arms around Sean, and knew it was real.

"I need a favor. Two favors."

Nadine looked up from her paperwork. She'd been bent over the hunter pace schedule for the past hour, working out teams and ride times. The event was nearly full, but Caitlin was determined they wouldn't turn away a single rider who wanted to enter. It was making scheduling ahead impossible, but Nadine knew she had to stay on top of it or she'd be confronted with an unholy mess when she sent out ride times a few days ahead of the event.

So she'd spent the middle part of her day hunched over the spreadsheets and entry forms, while Sean waved his whip at her once an hour or so, heading out to ride another horse. She was actually jealous of him, spending a beautiful April day in the saddle while she was stuck at her desk, bleary-eyed from squinting at numbers and names.

"What's up, Caitlin," she said, leaning back in her chair and stretching. Her spine popped obligingly.

"Woof, listen to you," Caitlin snorted, wrinkling her nose. "Someone needs to get out and ride a horse."

"I might, when I'm done with this."

"Good. Take Sean along and go for a spin in the field. It's beautiful out. But anyway, listen." Caitlin sat down in a creaking leather chair. "Favor one: I need you to house-sit for me. I'm taking the dogs and going to a friend's house over on the Eastern Shore. Little mini-break before summer madness gets here. I'll only be gone three days, but the cats and fish need fed, and I just like to know there's someone in there in case . . . you know, anything happens. Can you manage that for me?"

Nadine imagined three days in Caitlin's beautiful farmhouse. "I can manage," she replied gravely, as if it this was a big task she was only just capable of.

"Good, thanks. I'm leaving Thursday. The other thing is, on the *Saturday* night, I need you and Sean to go to the Catoctin Hunt Spring Ball."

This made Nadine's eyebrows go up. "The what now?"

"Don't let the word *ball* scare you. This isn't like *Cinderella*. Unless you meet a rich guy there, in which case, be my guest, make it your own personal fairy tale." Caitlin's smile glimmered at her. "I fully support your rags to riches story as long as you don't quit on me or anything."

"Let me make a note of that," Nadine said drily. *"Fall in love with prince. Keep job.* Got it. And *why* am I taking Sean to a hunt—I'm sorry, a hunt *ball?* Why are we using that word?"

"It's some leftover thing from debutante days, I don't know. It's just a party at one of their big mansions. Music, dancing, drinks. And it's the perfect place to advertise the hunter pace. Everyone who hunts loves a good hunter pace. They can bring out their young horses, show off a little, maybe recruit some new members for when hunting season starts up in fall. I don't care," Caitlin went on. "Whatever they want to do. You and Sean can dress up, go to the party, and talk up the hunter pace to everyone you can. That should do the job of filling up the last spaces."

"And then some. We only have fifteen spaces left."

"Work your magic if we get more than that."

Nadine was not aware of any magic, but she nodded, because there was no point in telling Caitlin no. She focused on more immediate problems. "I don't have anything to wear to a hunt ball, and I bet Sean doesn't, either."

Caitlin's laugh was knowing. "I'll bet Seany-boy has a tux hidden away in his closet. This won't be his first ball. As for you, I called Macy down at the dress shop on Market Street in Frederick. Go there. She'll dress you up, and I've got the tab. It's a marketing expense."

"That's . . . incredible. Thank you." Nadine knew the dress shop she meant. Macy was a friend of Caitlin's from their high school days, and her boutique on Market Street was filled with beautiful, dainty, feminine things that Nadine could only dream of wearing.

"It's my pleasure. Sean can rent a tux and send me the receipt, if he has to. Well, I have places to be, people to see." Caitlin stood. "I'll bring you the invitation later. You're already RSVP'd, so don't worry about that. It has directions on the back."

Nadine leaned back in her chair and sat quietly for a while, her mind ticking over the unbelievable weekend unfolding ahead of her. The farmhouse was hers for three days. She was going to get a new dress and go to a *ball*. With Sean. In a tux!

This might feel like a Cinderella story, even if she already had her prince.

When he walked by with his next horse, tipping his whip to her, she ran out of the office and startled him with a huge hug and kiss.

"What's that for?" he asked, astonished.

"We're about to have the most amazing weekend," she told him. "You won't even believe it."

They moved themselves into Caitlin's house the moment her truck disappeared through the farm gates, laughing like naughty kids as they lugged their bags up the driveway and onto the front porch. Nadine opened the door with the key Caitlin had left her, and they tumbled inside. Sean stood in the big central hall as Nadine headed for the stairs, looking around with his mouth open.

"You've never been in here before?" Nadine asked, pausing at the foot of the staircase. She ran her hand over the polished dark wood of the bannister, savoring the feel. Someday, she thought, she'd have a farmhouse of her own. The idea was almost startling, and she realized with shock that she'd never allowed herself to imagine such a thing.

But maybe Nadine of Wonder Avenue *could* have a farmhouse. She'd made it this far, hadn't she? After everyone had told her that horses weren't for girls like her?

Who knew what else was waiting for her? Suddenly, Nadine felt capable of dreaming of a bigger, brighter future than she had ever contemplated before.

Sean turned in a slow circle, gaze taking in the big front living room to his left, the gracefully decorated office to his right, the light-filled kitchen just visible at the end of the hall. "This place is incredible," he said finally. "From the outside, it looks like just another brick farmhouse."

"This was always one of the most prosperous farms in Catoctin Creek," Nadine explained. "Most of the furnishings are from Caitlin's grandparents and great-grandparents. It didn't become a horse farm until Caitlin's mother took it over and leased out a lot of the cropland and grazing to other farmers. She was the one who wanted to concentrate on pony breeding."

"It's amazing," Sean said again. He put down his bag and walked into the living room, taking care not to tread on the antique carpet in the center of the room. He touched an elegant side-table, his fingers just grazing the inlaid wood. "Back at my old house—the living room had a table just like this. It could be from the same carpenter."

Nadine stood in the doorway, waiting for him to come back from memory lane. She had pushed past her own admiration—and envy—of Caitlin's house a long time ago. Caitlin hadn't earned any of it; this was her family's work. Nadine was not prepared to be impressed by anything which was handed down through generations. What good would it do her? She'd never inherit anything from her family.

If Nadine ever had a living room like this, filled with antiques and light, she would have *earned* it.

"Come on," she said eventually. "If you like this living room, wait until you see the sleigh bed in the guest room."

That got Sean's attention. "I like a nice sleigh bed," he told her, eyes twinkling with sudden mischief.

"You're going to *love* this one," Nadine laughed, and she bolted up the stairs, delighted to hear his boots coming fast on the steps behind her.

Chapter Twenty

Sean

Sean sat at a curving breakfast table set in a nook of windows overlooking the shady backyard, watching Nadine make grilled cheese sandwiches on the gleaming stovetop. The formal dining room glimmered darkly through the doorway, but Nadine insisted no one ever went in there, and the breakfast nook was one of the nicest spots in the house—a fact Sean was prepared to acknowledge. They had explored the guest bedroom thoroughly —the sleigh bed *was* very nice, and soft and welcoming, besides— and afterwards they'd prowled around the upstairs, admiring the newer, but traditional furniture Caitlin had chosen for the master bedroom, and exclaiming over the views of the farm and the surrounding countryside from the windows. Then, they'd come downstairs to raid the refrigerator, finding some very nice varieties of cheese in the cold cuts drawer.

"Here is your sandwich, sir," Nadine announced, sliding a beautifully browned grilled cheese in front of him. "This stovetop is a dream. I can't get bread to brown this evenly up in my apartment."

"You should demand a better stove, if this is the kind of results you can get with nice equipment," Sean told her, genuinely impressed with the sandwich.

Nadine sat down across from him and looked at her own golden-brown sandwich. "I really should. But unfortunately, this is the only thing I'm really good at cooking. Everything else is coming out of a can or getting popped in the oven. I've never had time to learn, or the space to do it. All the travel trailers I've lived in!" Nadine shook her head. "Half of them didn't even have working gas, so I ended up buying a tiny microwave and I took it everywhere I moved."

Sean gazed at her in admiration. "You're so tough. I can't believe you lived in travel trailers."

"Believe it. I've also lived in partially finished garages, feed rooms with a cot in the corner, and dorms." She gave a theatrical shiver. "The dorm was the worst. I only lasted a couple of weeks before I found something else. You do not want to live at a down-at-the-heels racetrack dorm."

"I literally couldn't even imagine it," he said. "You're amazing."

She picked up her sandwich and regarded him over it. "You're ridiculous," she said finally.

"No, I mean it. I can't believe the places you've lived, the things you've put up with. That apartment over there—" he pointed towards the barn, somewhere beyond the kitchen walls, "—is the closest thing to roughing it I've ever experienced. I've never even stayed in an RV at a *horse show*. I've always had a condo nearby, or a house rental, or just a hotel."

"Well, you've been lucky." Nadine shrugged and bit into her sandwich.

But Sean couldn't let it go. He needed her to know that she inspired him, that she was resilient and strong and as different from him as a person could be. That he could never, ever live up to her example—all he could do was try and hope he was enough. Being in this beautiful house, seeing a trace of the way he used to live, of the comfort he was used to, really put a spotlight on this fact. Nadine was tough and gritty; he was soft and coddled. And somehow, Sean was envious of her without ever wanting to experience what she had.

"You're just so strong," he told her now. "You saw the life you wanted, and you went out and took it. You did whatever it took. And me, I've spent all my time here feeling sorry for myself, trying to get someone else to buy me horses, not even bothering to do my job right, because I was so sure it was just a temporary setback."

"You couldn't know it *wasn't* a temporary setback," Nadine said reasonably. "I think you had every right, at first, to think you were leaving soon."

"No, don't excuse it. I was the worst. I'm embarrassed, honestly."

"You were the worst," Nadine agreed. "But you're getting much better. I like you a lot now, and that's saying something, because I couldn't stand you for a long time." Her smile twinkled at him, her eyes filled with fun.

Sean looked at her sparkling expression, her dark hair falling over her pale cheeks, freckles just popping on her nose thanks to all that spring sunshine. And he had a new, terrifying, wonderful thought: *he loved her.*

The idea was so astonishing he had to put his sandwich down. He leaned back in his chair and stared at her, immobilized by the sudden rush of emotion.

He loved her—every bit of her—her laugh, her sarcastic smirks, her grim determination, her brimming generosity. The way she decided he would succeed and set about making him a success. The way she looked down at her horse when she rode, despite everything he said, because she was used to keeping her eye on young horses who might suddenly duck and buck. The way she ran her fingers so lovingly over Finn's muzzle, and the big horse leaned down to ask for more attention, and she gave it willingly, until someone, Richie or Rose or Caitlin or a client, called her away. The way she saw the world as a place which owed her nothing, but from which she would extract every last drop of excitement and success and joy.

Her lashes brushed her cheeks as she cast down her eyes. "Sean, you're making me blush with this stare of yours. Stop it."

"I'm sorry," he managed to say, which wasn't the right thing, which wasn't at all what he wanted to tell her, because he didn't know what to do with this newfound knowledge—how she'd take it, what she'd say in return. The possibilities loomed in his mind, specters he'd never beheld before. Simone had laughingly turned down his repeated requests for dates, and he'd just come back for more, but if he told Nadine he loved her, and she turned her cheek to him, he wasn't sure what he'd do.

So with an effort, Sean forced his attention back down to the sandwich—the lunch she'd made him, and he loved her for making him a perfect, gorgeous grilled cheese sandwich—and he took a big bite, and let Nadine's soft breathing and the tapping of branches on the windows and the steady bubble of the fish tank in the living room fill the silence between them.

A knocking at the front door woke them both at the same time. Sean jolted upright, rubbing his face. Half beneath him, a throw blanket tugged over her, Nadine gasped and pushed him aside. Sean found himself falling and resigned himself to his fate.

From the beautiful Persian carpet where he'd landed, he looked up at Nadine, who was peering over the side of the sofa at him with horrified eyes. "Did I just knock you off the couch?" she asked.

"It seems that way." Sean grinned to let her know it was okay. "I heard something, like a knocking?"

"Let's just stay put," Nadine suggested. "Until whoever it is goes away." A frown came to her brow. "Unless it's Richie or Rose with a problem in the barn. What time is it? Jeez, we fell asleep after lunch." She tugged out her phone. "Two o'clock. That's not so bad. But no one has tried calling me."

"Shh—I hear something on the porch."

They sat very still, and then Sean's stomach flipped over as the front door was slowly unlocked and opened. Nadine looked at him frantically. He shook his head to indicate that no, he had *no* idea what to do. Then Nadine looked past him, and her face changed to an expression he couldn't read.

"Reg?" she asked, voice incredulous. "What are *you* doing here?"

Chapter Twenty-One

Nadine

Of all the people she might have expected to come through that door, Reg was definitely the last one. Nadine stared at him in utter shock, wishing he'd just vanish, like a figment of her imagination. What on earth could he be doing here? Was he breaking into the house? No—it was the middle of the day. Reg was an idiot, but even he wasn't *that* dumb. And Caitlin had said he did odd jobs for her sometimes. Was he working right now? Wouldn't she have told Nadine?

Reg grinned at this silent reception, his eyes shifting from Sean back before resting, pointedly, on her outraged face. "Caitlin told me you'd be here tonight," he said. "I didn't expect you to be here quite so early ... or with company."

So that was it. Caitlin hadn't expected her to come racing over the moment she set off for the Eastern Shore. Nadine sighed, dropping her gaze to Sean, who was looking up at her with confusion on his face. "Well, you caught us," she said reluctantly. "We—I was taking a little nap, and Sean came to get me. So we can go back to work. Which, I assume, is what you're doing? Working?"

"Picking up some boxes in the basement," Reg said mysteriously. "I don't suppose you'd help an old man carry them out?"

"Absolutely not," Nadine snapped. "Deal with it yourself."

She was aware Sean was looking back and forth between them with utter befuddlement. Well, she'd tell him when they'd gotten some distance. Because she wasn't staying in this house for one more second with Reg. "Come on, Sean," she said as regally as possible, dropping the throw blanket from her arm as if it was a cast-off robe. "Let's go riding. If Reg has a key, I guess he's not doing anything *too* illegal."

She studied Reg's long-jawed face as she said the last word, hoping to see his cheerful expression shift. But if Reg was stealing from her boss, he certainly didn't feel guilty about it. That, or he'd mastered the empty-headed *who me?* look. Probably not a big leap for him, she thought bitterly.

They trooped out of the house, snatching their boots from where they'd been left by the front door. Nadine sat on the steps to pull her short paddock boots on and waited while Sean zipped up the backs of his tall boots. Then they walked from the shade of the trees surrounding Caitlin's house into the bright sunlight gleaming on the farm drive.

"That was weird," Sean ventured eventually. "Who is that guy?"

He'd been honest with her, so now she would be honest with him. "That's my mom's criminal boyfriend," Nadine told him, clenching her fists at her sides. The pain of her nails pressing into her palms did a little to relieve her pent-up feelings. "I've known him since I was a teenager. And he does some work for Caitlin, apparently. I just found out a couple weeks ago."

She felt Sean's gaze burning into the side of her face, but she didn't look at him. It was too embarrassing—first telling him about her life before, living in travel trailers and dorms, then confessing that rough guy back in Caitlin's house was not only her mom's boyfriend, practically her stepfather, but also a person who lived outside the law. He had to be thinking she wasn't the girl he'd thought; he had to be questioning if he should be hanging out with her at all.

Then she felt his fingers on hers, prying them apart, until they were walking hand in hand. She felt an unexpected prickling at the back of her eyes, a heat that threatened to spill over into real, actual tears. When was the last time she'd cried? And now Sean had her weepy with his sympathy over Wonder Avenue and Reg. Nadine didn't she how she could possibly have time for that kind of emotion, and she fought to control herself.

Sean squeezed her hand. "Hey," he whispered. "I'm really sorry that guy showed up and ruined our nice time. I'd offer to go beat him up, but I think we both know I can't do that."

She gasped with laughter. "Oh my God, Sean, you probably could. He's *such* a wuss, seriously. Reg is the kind of guy that real criminals leave behind to get caught by the police and give them time to get away."

"Well, that's kind of sad, don't you think? Being the nerd of a crime syndicate? It must be terrible for his self-esteem." Sean's voice was light now, tripping her up with his jokes, and she turned to him, thankful for such a kind, understanding man in her life.

The first one, if she was being honest.

"I never thought of it that way," she said, smiling through her tears. "You're right. It would be sad to be such a loser."

"I didn't say he was a *loser.*" Sean's eyes sparkled with laughter. "Did you know I was the guy who got left behind to get caught? Every single time my friends smoked behind the barn, they scrambled before I knew what was happening. I always got in trouble."

"Well, if you smoked behind the barn, you got what was coming to you."

"I knew you'd be on my mom's side."

"Nasty habit." Nadine winked. "But I'm sorry you had such mean friends."

"Me, too. Jeez. I hope you'd never do that?"

"Leave you behind to get caught?" Nadine studied his face and thought she saw a real question in those ice-blue eyes. "Never, Sean."

She tacked up Finn; he decided to ride Calypso. Nadine watched him as he groomed the dark bay horse and wondered if he was developing a special relationship with him. It might be nice if Sean had a horse to show for Elmwood, she thought. Calypso was very athletic, and Sean's training and conditioning was actually making the horse a little too hot for the majority of their students to ride. He was looking for a rider who could push him and challenge him; like a lot of Thoroughbreds, he had the work ethic of an athlete who was eager to push himself to the edge.

Finn wasn't quite so high-strung; being part Percheron meant the horse had a slow, stubborn side which preferred stopping for a bite to eat over galloping up to a jump. Nadine had been finessing the horse's flatwork for the past few weeks, and had taken him over a few small jumps the day before. Now, she thought he'd like to try some of the smaller logs and coops out on the hunter pace course. After all, he'd already jumped a few of them the first day they'd gone out to the pasture. By accident, of course. But still, he'd been pretty capable.

"I wonder if I could ride him in the hunter pace," she said as they mounted up outside the barn.

Sean looked at her, surprised. "But you're only just taking him over baby jumps now."

"Well, we could do the flat division if we had to," she said, shrugging as if it didn't matter. But secretly, she really wanted to jump him. "But we know he can jump. Anyway, let's see how he does out there today. He can follow Calypso over some fences."

"If you're sure." Sean still looked doubtful, but Nadine had experience on her side. Sean might be more capable of getting a hot-blooded horse over a course of four-foot jumps than her, but he couldn't match her track record for schooling green horses.

They complemented each other pretty well, now that she thought about it. Maybe the bargain they'd made a few weeks ago had been kind of silly. She didn't need to learn how to show over big fences, the way Sean could, and he didn't need to learn how to train young horses. Together, they could handle everything a barn full of horses could throw at them.

It was an intriguing thought. Once more, Nadine found herself thinking of an entirely new future . . . one she'd never considered before.

Finn was surprised by the first log.

Calypso trotted over it with barely a thought, not even bothering to jump—he just lifted his legs and hooves extra-high to clear the low log. Finn stared at it, astonished, then flicked his ears back to Nadine as if he wanted to be *absolutely certain* she knew there was a log in his way, with perfectly good grass to trot through on either side of it. Nadine put her heels to his sides and pressed her hands against his neck. "That's where we're going, buddy. Right after Calypso. Come on, you've done this before."

"He was in a hurry to get somewhere before," Sean called, looking over his shoulder.

"I promise this is the fun stuff," Nadine told Finn encouragingly. "Up and over—"

With a snort, Finn lifted himself in the air and launched over the log. Nadine laughed, pressing her legs against his side from knee to heel. It was the only shot she had at staying mounted with the deer-jump he threw at her. She landed in the saddle again with an inelegant grunt as Finn cantered away on the other side.

"Very . . . something!" Sean called, having turned in the saddle to watch her. "Absolutely no points for equitation, but I'll give you a ten for originality."

"That was too funny," she chortled, letting Finn stretch his legs for a moment before she brought him down to a walk alongside Calypso. "I wish I could have seen his face."

"You should have seen *yours.*"

"Shut up!" Nadine leaned over and slapped his leg, which earned her some anxious jigging from Finn. "Oh, I'm sorry, baby. Sean, look what you made me do. I scared my sweet little Finn."

"Sweet little... have you *seen* this horse? He's like a dinosaur."

"You're still afraid of him? Look at him." Nadine draped herself over his neck. "Just a little noodle."

"I'm not afraid," Sean retorted. "I'm just... cautious. One of us has to be. You can't have two horse-people in a relationship who are both insane."

She smiled at him, pushing off Finn's neck. *In a relationship.* She liked the sound of that. "Come and jump it with me again," she urged him. "This time won't be so dramatic."

"Everything with that horse is dramatic," Sean grumbled, but he picked up Calypso's reins and turned the horse around to trot over the log again. Nadine smiled to herself as she let Finn bounce into a trot after him. They were a good team, she thought. In more ways than one.

By the time the hour was up, Finn was happily jumping over all the low obstacles, and had even splashed through the brook a few times. Nadine was hot and happy, and even though she knew she was a mess, with her bun straggling from beneath her helmet and her face red with the afternoon heat, she liked the way Sean seemed to be watching her every time her gaze flicked his way. His attention was a steady thing, and she felt as if something very real had happened to them today, something which had made all of their emotions bubble to just below the surface.

"I'm sorry to go back in," she sighed as they rode towards the barn. "But Finn is wiped out, aren't you, buddy?" She patted his sweaty neck.

"When he stopped pulling you to every jump, I figured you'd finally worn him out," Sean said, his voice amused. "He liked it out there, though. I think you *can* take him in the hunter pace."

"I'll have to get permission from Rosemary," Nadine mused. "And admit to Caitlin that I've been riding him all along, not you. Unless you want to take credit for this," she added quickly. "I don't want you to get in trouble."

"Nadine, I can't take credit for what you've done with Finn. That's crazy. You've done an amazing job. Don't just hand all the work you've done to me like it doesn't matter."

She smiled at him. "But it doesn't matter. You, me, who cares? The horse is going well. Rosemary will be happy. I didn't train him for my pride, Sean. I trained him because I love him." She paused, trying to decide if she wanted to finish her thought. She decided to go for it. "And because I didn't want to see you forced into something you weren't comfortable with," she added, keeping her tone light. "I could see you didn't want to ride him from the moment you saw him, and I felt bad. No one should have to ride a horse that makes them anxious. It's bad for everyone," she went on, feeling Sean's gaze on her, hot and intense. "The horse, the rider—"

"You took on this great big green horse because you didn't want me to feel uncomfortable on him? Without knowing if he was dangerous or anything?"

"I mean, like I said, I liked him from the start," Nadine said dismissively.

"But you got right on him. The first day. Because you knew Caitlin expected me to start him immediately. You wanted to wait, remember? Let him settle in?"

Nadine chewed at her lip. She shouldn't have said anything. Now Sean was going to be mad that she'd thought he was scared of the horse, and—

"Nadine, to take on a horse like that and then to offer to give me all the credit is just . . . it's really selfless. I don't even know how to react."

They were at the pasture gate; Finn stopped and touched his nose to the bars. Beside him, Calypso ducked his head to snag some grass, and Sean didn't stop him. He was staring at Nadine, emotion written across his face. She didn't know what to say.

"No one has ever done anything like that for me."

"It's—it's nothing," Nadine faltered.

"It's *not* nothing. It matters." Sean kicked his feet free of the stirrups and dismounted; after a pause, so did Nadine.

They met between the two horses. Sean unclipped his helmet and took it off; she didn't notice the sweat darkening his hair. She was too busy taking off her own helmet. When his lips claimed hers, she let the hard hat fall to the ground, forgotten, her freed hand twining around his neck, the back of his head, pulling him closer to her.

They were still locked in an embrace when Calypso apparently figured out how to unlatch the gate with his nimble Thoroughbred lips and ran back to the barn, taking Finn with him.

Nadine and Sean watched the horses gallop headlong away from them, apparently possessed of boundless energy once again.

"Well, that's what we get," she said eventually. "Kissing on the job."

"I guess this is why we aren't allowed to date," Sean agreed.

"A good rule."

They looked at each other and laughed.

It wasn't until they rounded the corner and Nadine noticed the truck parked in front of Caitlin's house that she remembered her worries about Reg.

Chapter Twenty-Two

Sean

"I just think it was weird, that he was in her house. I wish I'd called her or something."

Sean fumbled the knot in his bowtie yet again. He cursed and shook out the silk fabric. "Nadine, it was yesterday. You have to stop fixating on this," he called through her open door. She was in her bedroom, changing into the dress she'd picked up in Frederick. Sean hadn't seen it yet, but he was almost nervous with anticipation. What would rough-and-tumble Nadine look like in a formal gown?

And what would she think of him in a tux?

It wasn't that big of a stretch, really; formal riding wear was already a dark jacket and white shirt and tie, and there were several photos of him in his show clothes scattered around his living room. After ten years in the business, Nadine would be used to men in riding habits.

But he'd never so much as seen Nadine in a skirt—just jeans, breeches, and once, on a very warm October day, a pair of cut-offs. She hadn't broken those out yet this spring, either. Nadine lived in work clothes, but as beautiful as she was to him in her battered barn attire, he knew she'd be absolutely breathtaking when she cleaned herself up in civilian clothes.

The idea of it made his fingers slip yet again. He put the bowtie down on the arm of her sofa and glared at it, as if a time-out was what was needed.

"What are you doing?"

She was in the room. She was loose. She was—

Stunning.

Sean fought to keep his jaw from hitting the floor. He'd seen a lot of women in formalwear over the years, and privately he'd thought quite a few looked like a Barbie doll heading off to prom. Not now. Nadine had been expertly dressed by a woman with an eye for style and shape. The tea-length dress was perfect for her slight frame and short stature; she would have been swamped in anything longer. The slight flare of the skirt made her waist seem narrow, and the square-cut bodice and cap sleeves made her chest seem full. The lavender color, banded with darker purple in something shiny like satin, was perfect with her dark hair and green eyes.

"Well, if you're not going to say anything . . ." Nadine turned to march back into the bedroom.

"Nadine . . ."

She turned and looked at him, one hand on the doorframe. "Yes?"

Sean didn't know how to say it. How do you tell a woman she's the most beautiful thing you've ever seen? Surely you didn't just blurt it all out?

His silence was making her uneasy. She smoothed the skirt with her free hand. "Does it *really* look okay? I was afraid it was a bit much, but Macy insisted on this one. She said the color was right, whatever that means."

Sean looked at the way the lavender brought out the darkness of Nadine's eyes, the smokiness of her hair, and he knew Macy deserved his thanks. Macy deserved the thanks of *everyone* who was going to see Nadine tonight. "It looks amazing, and you look beautiful," he told her. "I am absolutely blown away."

Nadine smiled gratefully. "That's really nice of you, Sean."

"Absolutely incredible," he said, as if to cement his earlier words. As if he could think of anything else to say.

She gave him a bright smile. "I FaceTimed my friend Avery, and she said I look like she dressed me from her theater wardrobe. She's in a play set in the fifties right now," she added. "So it's a compliment."

"It's the perfect dress for you. Give me a twirl."

Nadine obliged, the skirt belling out as she spun in a quick circle. Sean's heart flipped over.

"Oh lord, can you dance?"

She shook her head. "Afraid not."

"A shame. Well, we can probably shake a few steps out of you tonight. Hopefully the champagne will be free-flowing; it usually is at these things."

"You're going to get me drunk and make me dance?"

Sean grinned. "That's the plan."

Nadine giggled.

He couldn't take it anymore. Crossing the little room in a few short strides, Sean tugged her close and indulged himself in a long, luxurious kiss. When they finally separated, she was looking at him with so much passion in those emerald eyes, Sean began to fear for the future of that pretty new dress. "We'd better go," he said huskily. "Or else I'm not sure we'll make it at all."

Nadine granted him a smile of such extraordinary sultriness, he nearly lost the ability to walk. But then she tugged at his hand. "If it's that good, let me finish with my hair and we'll go. Don't worry! I'll hurry. I've never made a stylish entry into a ball before."

Sean watched her go. Then he turned and picked up the discarded bowtie. "I hope you've learned your lesson," he told the scrap of satin.

The Catoctin Hunt was a local institution, the kind of hunt club which had been around since before the Civil War and wasn't afraid to brandish their blueblood credentials with exclusive events like the Spring Ball. The house chosen for the event was a graceful brick mansion, which for the past two hundred years had sat serenely atop its hill, overlooking several hundred acres of green spring grass, nodding tulips, and blooming trees. Sean drove up the driveway in the Elmwood farm truck, borrowed for the occasion as it was the sort of large, shiny equipage a hunt club would approve of. The two of them gazed out across the rolling pastures on either side of the drive, where Charolais cattle grazed the groomed grounds.

"Charolais always seemed like *fancy* cattle to me," Nadine ventured. "Since they're white, which means extra work to keep them clean."

"Do you think someone comes out here and scrubs the cattle before anyone arrives for a party?"

"Honestly, it wouldn't surprise me."

A valet well-used to big trucks took the keys from Sean and drove away with competence while they paused before the wide, shallow steps. Sean sensed Nadine needed a moment to catch her breath before they went inside. The house was intimidating enough, but more so was everything it represented: inside there was a group of people neither of them had ever met, and their job was to charm them into entering a hunter pace, while never giving away that they were emissaries sent by a barn which wasn't even part of their august assemblage.

Sean himself felt like a bit of an interloper, and he was used to these sorts of events and the people they'd find inside. He couldn't even imagine how Nadine must feel. He squeezed her hand, and she gave it a squeeze back. He felt her roll back her shoulders and take a deep breath, then another, as if she was about to enter the show-ring. He imagined a voice from within the house's wide front hall: "Riders, you are being judged."

The familiar words would have rung true in this setting.

The front doors were flung open to the cool evening, and golden light spilled out to meet them, mingling momentarily with the mellow light just before sunset. Inside there was laughter, the insistent bass thrumming of a jazz band, the promise of people richer and more self-assured than either of them had ever been. Sean almost wished they hadn't had to come; he wished he could just take Nadine, in all of her finery, to an outdoor table at the nearest Dairy Queen, where they could watch the sunset over the mountains while they ate marshmallow sundaes with plenty of hot fudge. For the first time, the return to his old world really, truly stood before him... and he didn't feel ready to go back.

Then she tugged gently at his hand, turning to look at him with her fresh face sparkling with excitement, and he realized she didn't feel the same as him at *all*. She was ready, willing, thrilled even, to enter this grand old house and speak to people who were in their own ways just as grand, just as old as the antique furnishings, the mellow bricks, the wavy glass. And he would go with her. Even if it scared him.

Well, he wasn't going to let her down.

"Here we go, princess," he told her warmly, and with their invitation brandished in one hand, and the other tucked around Nadine's arm, he led the way through the doors.

The first impression he had was one of dazzle: good looks, good breeding, good gowns, good suits. Drinks on trays, shining beneath expertly placed lighting. Potted palms, a grand piano, a terrace overlooking the darkening eastern sky, the azure blue accented with candy-pink clouds as if their hosts had ordered a perfect spring sunset to entertain their party. Hunting prints on the wall (of course) and bronze sculptures on the mahogany mantelpieces, a miniature herd spread about with abandon: mares and foals, jumping hunters, galloping racehorses. Sean was reminded immediately of home; the owner of this farm and his mother could have shared the same designer.

He had just released Nadine's hand to find her a glass of champagne when the first terrible thing happened.

He saw Simone.

Sean drew back in shock, nearly heading right back into the entrance hall, but Nadine was suddenly gripping his arm with her terrifically strong hands. "Where are you going?" she hissed. "We can't go wandering around this house!"

He shook his head frantically. "That wasn't—I can't be here, okay? Not like this."

Her face changed. "Not like . . . *this? You mean . . . with me?*"

And Nadine looked down at her pretty gown, her face changing slowly from delight to slow devastation.

"No," Sean hissed. "It's not you—believe me, I'd love to show you off. But it's just—as a shill for the farm where I'm the riding instructor? In front of *her?* I can't do it."

Nadine's eyes narrowed as she looked back at him. "In front of *who?*"

Chapter Twenty-Three

Nadine

She was going to kill him. That was all, just murder him. There were probably plenty of places she could leave his scrawny little body. This was a big farm. She'd tell Caitlin he'd wandered off, and she didn't know what had become of him. They'd hire a new riding instructor. It wouldn't be hard to replace him.

As a riding instructor. It would be very hard to replace him as a human, as the man she suspected she was falling in love with. No—she had already fallen for him. She knew it, and she hated it. Nothing good could come of falling in love—hadn't her mother taught her that every day she'd been with Reg?

But Sean was nothing like Reg. He had a heart and feelings which could be hurt. A past which had scarred him, although he didn't want to admit it. And that knowledge made her realize she had to deal with this moment with something like humanity. If he'd hurt her feelings, chances were he hadn't meant it. He'd simply had a shock and forgotten how to behave. She worked to control her temper, but she knew her voice was still stiff when she asked, "Just who is causing you so much stress?"

Sean's face was positively haunted, and as the silent seconds ticked between them, Nadine began to wonder if maybe he'd *actually* seen a ghost. A nice historic place like this was sure to have a few haunts. Mad spinster aunts shut away in the attic a hundred years ago, maybe a lost Union soldier—that sort of thing was actually common around here, to believe some of the stories she'd heard.

But Sean's specter was all too alive. "Simone," Sean sighed. "I saw Simone."

She'd been prepared to excuse a ghost. But no, he'd seen a real person. And not just any person, but the lovely young woman who wanted him to move to New York with her for the summer. Ah, yes, Nadine thought. Killing him was definitely back on the table.

"And if Simone meets me, you will . . . die? Sean. Be honest. Is there something else I should know about you and Simone?"

Sean shook his head. "It's not like that. Trust me when I say you're not the problem here. It's me, it's . . ." he pulled the handful of Elmwood business cards from his pocket, the ones that Caitlin had insisted they both come armed with, and hand out to everyone and sundry. "Look at this, Nadine. We came here to solicit these people into coming to a *horse show*. We're on the clock. Simone is here as a real guest. We're not on the same terms now and . . . it's embarrassing. Do you understand what I mean?"

Nadine was pretty sure she understood enough. He was still more concerned about Simone's opinion than anyone else's. The idea of it made her cheeks feel flaming hot, which was unfortunate

—red would clash with the lavender. She decided she'd given him enough benefit of the doubt. "So you're embarrassed about Elmwood. Well, I'm sorry we aren't good enough for you in Catoctin Creek, Sean Casey. But I came here to do a job, and I'm going to do it. You want to avoid Simone? Stay here, go hide in the barn, I don't care. I'm getting a drink, I'm getting a good buzz on, and then I'm going to convince half of this room to fill up our entries for the hunter pace. See ya."

It hurt more than it should have to walk away from him, and not just because her heels were pinching.

Nadine didn't know which one of the gorgeous creatures in the room tonight was Sean's old friend Simone, and she decided she wouldn't worry her head about it. She just set about doing exactly what she'd told Sean she'd do, in exactly the right order. She drained a glass of champagne, smiled at the caterer holding the tray as he took her empty, then snatched another filled glass and made her way over to the buffet, sipping appreciatively as she moved through the well-dressed crowd. She topped off a little plate. A few shrimps, a few of those stuffed dates, a nice piece of crusty bread, and she had just enough in her stomach to absorb some bubbly without making her dress feel tight. Now that was careful planning for a night of networking. She fingered the clutch where her own stack of business cards had been stashed.

Let's make some hunter pace entries happen, she thought determinedly, and looked expectantly around the room.

Holding her own was not hard in a room full of horsemen, she thought later, happy with the work she'd done so far. Everyone in the room looked fancy on the outside, but they were just oats, hay, and water on the inside. Just like she was, she thought, giving herself a pleased perusal in a bathroom mirror. She picked up her clutch and went back into the fray, thinking that champagne had a unique ability to make a girl have to pee *and* to give her a powerful thirst at the same time. She went back to the buffet and poured herself a mineral water, then found a nice corner near a palm where she could survey the room, look for a few victims she hadn't hit yet.

Then she saw Sean.

He was talking to a gorgeous young woman in the corner near the piano, one hand on the wall near her shoulder, leaning intimately toward her. If he'd been uncomfortable before, he seemed to be over it now. His face was animated, even alight, as he spoke; his eyes were fastened on her face as if she was the most interesting person he'd ever spoken to.

Nadine knew that it was Simone. *Had* to be Simone. And her insides coiled up so tightly she couldn't even finish the glass of mineral water. She put it down and stalked out the nearest door, which happened to open onto the stone terrace behind the house.

A blue dusk had fallen, and the brightest stars were picking their way through the lantern-light on the terrace. She felt like she needed proper night, though, so she found the stairs leading down to the lawn and headed down. When she was alone, without distractions, she could deal with these emotions properly. She was sure of it.

In the dewy garden, where the bright heads of the tulips and daffodils were visible through the half-light, the brightest glow from the house was nicely blocked by the trees growing around the base of the terrace. She found a bench, swept it clean with one hand, and sat down on the chilly wooden slats, hoping she wouldn't mark up the dress with anything. Macy would be so upset if she returned it damaged.

Although maybe Caitlin would just pay for the damages and own a new lavender-colored ballgown. She could afford it, surely. It might even fit her.

Nadine sighed and gazed into the darkness. Why did Sean's talking to Simone put her into such an instantly bad mood? Was she really that insecure?

Well, yes, she was a bit—but he'd cemented the feeling by clearly being embarrassed by his situation at Elmwood.

A situation which had been a godsend for Nadine.

And therein lay the problem between herself and Sean. She'd known it all along, although she'd never cared to pull at that particular thread. They'd been having too much fun together for her to face facts. But now she had to admit it was just fun. She could look at their relationship and see for herself that this was not a made-in-heaven match.

Sean wanted more than she wanted. She looked at Caitlin's house and imagined herself in a lovely farmhouse someday. Sean looked at Caitlin's house and imagined himself getting back all the glittering things she'd furnished it with.

Nadine wanted the substance; Sean wanted the style.

Voices floated down from the terrace and Nadine writhed. Sean and Simone had come outside, because of course they had. But she wasn't going to sit down here and eavesdrop. She rose to leave, to go deeper into the garden.

"But Sean, be serious—you're not going to stay there forever. The woman with the money—what happened with her?"

Too late. Nadine froze, waiting for his answer.

"She's tricky," Sean answered. "She wanted to be in control of everything. I had to tell her to back off."

"That was a mistake. Those horses sold. Where are you going to be all summer? Teaching summer camp? *Really,* Sean? What a waste of your talents. And time. We could be having a blast on the circuit. Tell me you'll call this woman back and get something moving again. *Please.*"

"It's not that simple," Sean said.

"You don't *want* to teach summer camp instead of showing with me..."

"No, of course not."

That was enough. With a determined sniff, Nadine shook out her skirt, darted back up the stairs, and was inside the house again before anyone could see her—hopefully. Whether Sean had recognized her as she'd flown past was anyone's guess. Nadine was already racing to the front door, where the valet was sitting on a cane-backed chair, whistling to himself. She shook the claim ticket under his surprised nose. Thank goodness she'd taken the ticket and slipped it into her clutch, certain Sean would lose it if he stuffed it in his pocket like a child.

Now she could get home on her own.

As for Sean? She had no doubt he'd land on his feet and find his own way home. Guys like him always managed to find free rides.

At first, Nadine thought she'd go straight back to her own apartment. There was no reason to sleep at Caitlin's house tonight. The fish were fed, and they didn't exactly need babysitting. She parked the farm truck in its usual spot and put the keys back on their hook in Caitlin's office. Then she paced down the empty barn aisle. With all the horses outside, the stalls were like dark, blank faces.

Nadine stood at the bottom of her staircase for a moment. A barn cat sat at the top, blinking down at her. She wondered which one it was—Sunny, Gray Thomas, Knightly? In the gloom, there was no telling. After a while, she turned and walked back out the open barn doors. She climbed into her own car.

And sat there, too exhausted and miserable to actually put her foot down and drive away. Where would she go?

The crickets were piping away; the stars were burning brightly overhead; a slightly bored half-moon was slipping up in the eastern sky sky without much fanfare. There was nothing particularly special about this night. And yet it felt like there should be something more. She'd just left behind her boyfriend at an elegant formal party; she'd just given up the best relationship she'd ever had; she'd just wiped away her dreams of the future, all because the guy wasn't who she'd hoped he would be. There should be something momentous in the air, some sign to tell her she'd done the right thing, and a new start was coming.

But there was nothing.

She'd never felt so alone.

Nadine pulled out her phone and clicked through the addresses of people she knew here who might be awake—the list was short, unhelpful. Rosemary was an early riser; Nadine wouldn't set off the woman's anxiety by showing up at her door after ten o'clock at night. Nikki—ditto, getting up early to work at her bakery before heading to the Blue Plate. She flicked through a few others with short shakes of her head—no, no, no.

The last address she landed on, the least likely to offer her comfort, was the house on Wonder Avenue.

She looked at the screen for a long moment.

After a long, last look back at the barn where Sean would come home later that night—assuming he got a ride without strings attached—Nadine turned the car on and headed back into the night.

Her mother was awake, of course. The kitchen was at the back of the house, but the light was shining through the front windows, casting an unhelpful square of yellow on the scruffy front yard. Nadine knocked gently on the front door. She had a key, but she never used it. She didn't want to feel like she could live here.

And then there was Kelly, her arms opening to give Nadine a longed-for hug, and for just a few moments, Nadine felt safe in her mother's arms.

They sat at the kitchen table and drank tea sweetened with honey from a squeezy bear.

"Where is Reg?" Nadine asked eventually.

"Out foolin' around." Kelly rolled her eyes. "A lot of that lately. In and out at all hours. I got used to quiet while he was gone, you know? Quiet and . . . less worry. I think I might kick him out for good."

Nadine looked at her mother and found that for once, she felt nothing but sympathy. Not impatience, not disappointment—just an understanding that love was blind, and often stupid, and the death of it was like a twisting knife. "Oh, Mom."

Her mother shrugged. "You were right about him. I should take your advice about men more often. Or, at all."

"Probably not." Nadine looked back at her mug of tea. She tugged at the string of the bag, took it out and laid it sopping across the saucer. "I left my boyfriend at a fancy party in a mansion out near Union Bridge."

Kelly lifted her eyebrows. "I was wondering about that pretty dress you're wearing. So the boyfriend . . . you left him with or without a ride back?"

"He'll have to find his own way, let's say that."

Her mother's smile was genuine. "That's my girl. Don't let them hurt you. I used to tell you that. My only advice. I'm gratified to see it stuck."

"It was too late. He already hurt me. And probably abandoning him will come back to haunt me. It was basically giving him permission to do something I didn't want him to do in the first place."

"If he does it, he was never worth your time." Kelly's sigh was real. "But you find you're willing to wait for the ones who are worth it. So wait and see, that's my new advice to you. Wait and see."

"Who are you waiting for?" Nadine asked.

"Your father."

The silence that followed was so thick, Nadine felt as if she'd been swallowed up. Finally, she managed to say the words. "My *father?*"

Kelly sipped at her tea nonchalantly, as if she hadn't just dropped a bombshell into the quiet kitchen. "Twenty-seven years ago, we had a fight. I told him to leave. He left. And he hasn't come back. But . . . I hope he will. Maybe he will. I shouldn't have even let Reg through the door, but I didn't know I was still waiting."

Nadine stared at her mother. Kelly didn't *look* lovelorn. She didn't look heartbroken. She looked just as she had always looked: tired, lined, puffy-eyed, sunken-cheeked. A woman who smoked too much and loved too little. A woman who Nadine had never envied and never wanted to emulate. A woman who broke glasses and cried after fights with men who belonged in jail, or at the very least shouldn't be in relationships.

And all of this time, deep down, a woman who was waiting on the one she'd let get away.

Nadine could be like her mother, after all.

The idea was haunting. And suddenly she made up her mind. She wasn't going to do this. Wasn't going to waste her life on a man who didn't really want her. Sean wanted the horse show life. He wanted the big job with his name in lights. He wanted the hunt balls, and the women in ball gowns. "I don't want him back," she said. "He's not worth it."

The words hurt to say aloud. But maybe saying them was the magic.

Maybe that would make the lie come true.

Chapter Twenty-Four

Sean

Sean watched Nadine walk away through the chattering party crowd with a shiver of premonition. She meant it, he knew. If she decided she was done with him, this minute, because he was being a big baby about Simone seeing him here, well then he was as good as dead to her.

He looked at the dark, coffered ceiling, back down at his polished brown shoes, and then rolled back his shoulders, just as she had done outside. He wouldn't make a scene. Wouldn't insist she talk to him. He'd let her cool off, and in the meantime, he'd do what he came here to do. He'd sell Elmwood's hunter pace.

Starting with Simone.

Partially to prove that he could talk to her, and partially to get her out of the way for the night. If Nadine came back to find him later, he'd better not be standing there chit-chatting with Simone. Instead, he'd be able to shrug and say he'd given her a card and moved on with his night.

He looked around the room, and saw her, draped in ivory, golden curls falling around her bare shoulders, looking almost ridiculously like a Greek goddess. Sean absorbed her artificial perfection and wondered why he'd spent his teenage years, not to mention his early twenties, pining over this doll of a woman. Now all he wanted was Nadine—in her lavender gown, in her most torn-up jeans. It didn't matter. Just Nadine.

He fought the temptation to rake the room with his gaze until he found her. Soon enough, he told himself. Get this over with, then find Nadine. Stick to the plan.

Simone's face lit up gratifyingly when she saw him crossing the room. "Sean Casey! What on earth are you doing here? You never said you were involved with the Catoctin Hunt!"

"You know I can't resist any chance to slip into a suit and talk horses," he said with a grin. "But I'm a little shocked you didn't mention it to me. You know I'm living nearby, and I've never heard you mention a visit to Maryland."

"Oh." She batted him playfully on the shoulder. "As if I can remember what rustic little town you live in. I'm sorry, Sean. It's just been like, so busy. I was staying with a friend in Potomac and she said this was always a good party. And you! You missed all the fuss in Wellington. Dauntless bruised his hoof after the Palm Beach Grand Prix and I left him down there with Whitney for some recovery time and a little turn-out. But I need to ship him up to Virginia to prep for the summer circuit. And *work*. Don't get me started on *work*. They're all fussing at me about taking off for the summer. As if I didn't make that perfectly clear."

"I told you getting a real job would be a mistake."

"You were the only one! You knew." Simone laughed, throwing back her head to show off her perfect teeth. "Only Sean knew. How ironic."

"That's an odd choice of words." He snagged champagne from a passing waiter. "Why ironic?"

"Because you're the one who *had* to get a job. Isn't that funny?"

He tipped bubbles past his teeth, drowning out the sarcastic replies he longed to fling at her. *Very funny, when my family committed fraud and left me behind to sink or swim. Ha. Ha.*

"Oh Sean, don't make that face at me."

"There's no face." He gave her a gleaming smile to prove it. "It's very funny. But you went out and got that master's degree, and now you have to prove to everyone what a genius you are."

"I'm really not." Simone sighed dramatically. "I just want to ride horses. I'm so glad we're getting the group back together for Saugerties. I told you, right?" She cast a glance over her shoulder, as if she was looking for someone. "I told you, Toby and Maddie and Alison are all coming, right? We're going to get an even bigger house. Forget the one I mentioned before. I'm going huge. This summer is going to be insane. And they all want you to come, obviously. Everyone has been so worried sick about you, since you disappeared last year."

That explains all the worried sick texts and phone calls I didn't get, Sean thought. He pushed the bitterness away. His friends didn't spend their time worrying about one another's misfortunes. You were winning and you were on top and everyone wanted a piece of you, or you weren't winning and you were best advised to go home and lick your wounds—and fix your riding or your horse—before you brought everyone else down. That was their social contract. It was how parties like this stayed so upbeat. Balls and black-tie affairs were events for the lucky and the successful, not bummers trying to figure out where it all went wrong.

Sean would not make that mistake. "Well, maybe I'll surprise them and show up," he said, a little too much heartiness in his voice.

Simone looked over her shoulder again.

"Are you waiting for someone?" Sean asked. "Don't let me keep you."

"No, don't be silly." Simone waved a careless hand at him. "You just never know who will show up at these things. If I can introduce you to anyone who could put you back on a horse, that would be great, wouldn't it? We need to get you out of Maryland, pronto."

She talked on and on, slipping into her champagne voice as the waiters kept passing, their trays heavy with long-stemmed glasses. All about herself—Simone had only the most passing interest in what Sean was up to. He was starting to realize it had always been like this.

He felt the frown arriving, a crease between his eyes that he couldn't quite flatten out. Simone noticed, too. She cocked her head at him, concern sparking in her hazel eyes. "Everything okay?"

"Oh, yes. Just a little headache. I need more champagne."

She tinkled with laughter. "That solves everything, right up until the moment it doesn't. Come outside and get some fresh air," she suggested, tugging at his arm. "It's a little warm in here. That could be doing it."

Sean let himself be escorted through the crowded room, snatching another glass of champagne as he went. His third, in half an hour. That seemed about right, he thought.

The terrace was quiet, with the buzz of conversation and the music fading behind them as they walked away from the French doors. Sean looked out at the starry night over the dark landscape and remembered spring evenings back at home. Sitting on the wide front porch with a glass of mint tea, his lap full of a fluffy cat or a panting dog. His horses grazing in their paddocks, his mother in the living room, drinking a martini and laughing with friends. His father a quiet presence moving like a ghost through the house, always around, always distracted. He wanted those lamplit evenings back so much, the sensation was like a tight fist in his chest.

He wanted to go home, but home was gone. Maybe homes didn't really exist; he'd been fooled into believing in them, but maybe what lasted was people.

Or maybe people didn't last, either.

He looked around, his gaze skimming the crowd back in the house, but he didn't see Nadine.

Simone tugged him back to her, and they leaned against the railing. Lanterns hung in the trees below, floating balls of light. "Beautiful out here," he murmured, still caught up in his thoughts.

Simone nodded, untouched by the scene. She hadn't *had* to leave, Sean reminded himself. She'd gone to college and grad school, but she hadn't lost any of this, or learned about the hard angles and unlit corners of the outside world, the way he had. "It's very pretty," she said disinterestedly. "I suppose Maryland is nice. The Livingstons always liked it up here. You remember Elliot Livingston? Rode with us until our last junior year? He's an attorney in Rockville now. Hates it. Wants to buy a farm." Simone laughed. "Everyone who leaves horses regrets it."

"It's really nice here," Sean said, with real feeling in his voice. "I like Maryland."

She glanced at him, surprised by the force of his words. "Are you going to stay here?"

"I might." He turned again, skimming the patio, the house, the dark gardens. No Nadine.

"But you're just teaching riding lessons to little kids! What could possibly keep you here? We need to get you back to showing, Sean."

He shook his head. "Come on, Simone. It's not that bad. Have I ever told you about my job? Like, really told you?"

"I don't want to hear about it." Simone leaned her willowy arms against the terrace's stone balustrade and gazed out at the lanterns in the garden. "You're living my nightmare, teaching a lot of kids. I want to *ride,* Sean. I'm not interested in anyone else's riding. Just my own."

He knew she was telling him the truth. Her own deepest truth: Simone didn't really care about anyone else. She never had.

"But I'm having a nice time teaching," he told her, suddenly annoyed she wouldn't at least listen to him. "It's been like a long vacation from all the stress of the circuit. When I come back, I'll be so relaxed, I'll be doing the meter thirty classes with loops in my reins."

Simone laughed uncertainly. "But Sean, be serious—you're not going to stay there forever. The woman with the money—what happened with her?"

"She's tricky." Sean nearly laughed, thinking of Martha's conniving. *Tricky* was one way of putting it. "She wanted to be in control of everything. I had to tell her to back off."

"That was a mistake. Those horses sold. Where are you going to be all summer? Teaching summer camp? *Really*, Sean? What a waste of your talents. And time. We could be having a blast on the circuit. Tell me you'll call this woman back and get something moving again. *Please.*"

"It's not that simple."

"You don't *want* to teach summer camp instead of showing with me..."

"No, of course not." He paused, considering his answer. It had been hasty, given without thought. "Or maybe I do. I don't know. It's not ideal, it's not what I thought I'd be doing, but I'm getting good at it. I think I am, anyway."

A moment of silence stretched between them. Inside, the music soared, a glass broke, someone shouted with laughter. A whole party in there going on without them, and he didn't know where Nadine was.

"You're not going to come to New York at all, are you," Simone said flatly. "You're going to stay here."

"I guess I probably am. Yeah."

She sighed and straightened, and Sean realized she was done with him. He didn't serve any purpose to her anymore. Friendship over? At least, until she had some reason to call him—maybe she needed a horse sold and thought he'd have a contact, or her car broke down somewhere in Maryland and she thought he might come and pick her up.

He watched his oldest friend cast a distracted eye across the terrace, looking for someone better than him.

"Well, I need to go and find Edwin Marlborough," she said at last. "He has a horse I want to try and he said to catch him tonight to talk more about it. Are you staying out here?"

"I think I'm going to go," Sean said. "I just have to find my—friend." He'd almost said *date*. He let the word go for the moment, because he wasn't sure what Nadine thought of him just now, and he was pretty sure he was going to have to work to get that status back.

But Simone saw right through him. She always had. Her lovely mouth twisted in a smirk. "If you mean your *date*, she just ran past us a few minutes ago. I have a feeling she's already gone."

Sean gasped. "But we came in the same car."

Simone, laughing, left him on the terrace.

A few minutes later, the valet was shaking his head at him. "That ticket was turned in, sir. A woman in a purple dress took it. I saw her come in with you, so I didn't think there was a problem." The valet's face was carefully blank. Sean knew he was used to bickering couples, abandoned halves left at the party after indiscretions or obvious flirting.

"It's fine," Sean said, saving face even though he had no idea how he'd get home. "Thank you."

He turned around and Simone was standing there, a shawl draped over her shoulders, clutch in hand. She looked ready to leave, and he wondered what had happened with Edwin Marlborough. Had she made him up? "So, she abandoned you."

"So it would seem."

"I don't blame her. I thought—never mind what I thought." Suddenly Simone's expression became the one he remembered, the friendly playmate of his childhood. "Don't worry about it, Sean. I'll give you a ride home."

Sean's eyes flicked to the champagne flute in her hand.

Her laughter tinkled again. "Oh, Sean. How long have you been out in the wild? Of *course*, I have a driver."

Simone insisted on being taken home before him, sending the driver on with Sean in the backseat, nursing a headache that was more stress-related than anything else.

On a whim, Sean asked the driver to turn left instead of right at the top of the barn drive. He got out of the car and listened to it purr away, heading back to more civilized regions of the state. Before him, Caitlin's house stood imposingly beautiful, floodlit as it was every night of the year . . . and yet all the windows were dark from within.

Sean stood on the dark front porch and leaned his head against the flaking white paint of the cottage. He'd really screwed up tonight. And now he didn't even know where Nadine was. Could she have gone back to the barn? No, there was no chance of that. She wasn't going to be looking for him, waiting for him, after what she must think of him.

He walked around the house, peering in the windows but seeing nothing inside but the purple light of the fish tank. The April night was cool, but not cold. In the round pond behind the farmhouse, frogs were singing a high-pitched tune. Moonlight picked out the hunched forms of flowers in the garden. Sean returned to the front porch. It was wide and welcoming, like the one from his childhood. A wicker patio loveseat beckoned, a plaid throw blanket tossed over one arm. With a sigh, Sean sat down and took off his shoes. It wouldn't be a comfortable night on the porch. But it was the penance he deserved.

He'd wait here until Nadine came back, and he could properly apologize.

Chapter Twenty-Five

Nadine

The horses were already inside by the time Nadine drove up the barn lane, shifting uncomfortably in some high-school era clothes left in her childhood bedroom. She was a little surprised to see the grazing horses—Richie and Rose were efficient, but they weren't generally *that* quick. Then she walked into the barn and saw him, energetically raking out a stall from around a horse, and her spirits sank. Of course, he was going to be a perfect barn helper today. Of course he had taken the entirely wrong message from her abandonment last night, and was going to try to make things up to her, instead of understanding that whatever they'd had just wasn't meant to last.

Of course he was so completely unperceptive.

Nadine chose to stalk past him without saying anything, instead heading directly for her office where she could sit down and go over the day's lessons, make sure all the bills were paid up for the week, and check on entries for the hunter pace. She was hoping her email would be full of entries from the people she'd talked to last night. That would give her plenty to do, finalizing the scheduling for the hunter pace. Getting down to work and keeping her head down: those were going to be her strategies for surviving this day, and all the future days, with Sean Casey in the barn.

And then he'd leave, he'd go off with Martha or Simone and leave her. And that would be fine, too.

Nadine swallowed back the lump in her throat and poured herself a cup of coffee from the lounge.

Mistake. There he was, coming in the door, his face wide open. She should have stayed locked up in her office.

"Not now, Sean," Nadine told him. "I've got so much to do."

"I think we need to talk."

She shook her head. "We can't now. I have to go through the entries, and rework the ride times, and you've got lessons starting at nine..."

Sean sat down and put his elbows on his knees, leaning forward. His face was so intense, she felt a surge of emotion—but she wasn't sure what emotion it was. Regret? Fear? Love? It could have been any of them, and Nadine would have understood where they came from. They were all wrapped up together in her mind.

"Sean," she said softly, "I think we let things go too far."

A crease showed in the skin of his forehead. "Come on, Nadine, don't say that."

"Caitlin said no dating in the staff," she went on, more resolutely now. Her back was up, her shoulders were stiff. She could do this. "I can't lose this job. I've told you that a hundred times—"

"—And you've never really told me why—"

"Because I'll never get another job this good, for one thing. And because I have to watch my mother, for another!" Nadine almost shouted the last words. "That's why I came back to Catoctin Creek in the first place. Not because anyone wants me here. Not because I have great memories from childhood and I wanted to relive them in my hometown. I have to keep an eye on my mother, because she won't do it for herself. She sits there and gets herself into bad situations with people like Reg and I need to be here in case something happens. I need to protect her from herself."

Nadine took a breath, trying to steady her thudding heart. She knew she'd been heard out in the barn aisle; she only hoped no one was close enough to understand her words. "Let me go. I have to get to work."

"Nadine, please stop and talk to me."

"We're done talking." She swallowed a sob on the last word and turned, pushing blindly through the lounge door and down the two steps to the aisle floor. Across from her, in the feed room, Richie stood with a bucket in his hand, looking at her blankly. Nadine shook her head and went into her office, closing the door behind her.

She sat behind her desk and switched on her computer, thinking she could bury herself in her spreadsheets. But running a barn from behind a desk wasn't like mucking out; there was no way to take out her unhappiness on a dirty stall when she was just clicking through different tabs, typing in fiddly little boxes. There was no relief to be found here. Even when she saw that, judging by the state of her inbox, they'd completed their task of filling up the hunter pace.

She took Finn out for a ride after lunch, while Sean was stuck in the indoor teaching kids. After just a month, the horse was going beautifully now—almost good enough, she suspected, to go into a few lessons and find an owner. That was a problem, and one she'd created for herself by training him. She should have taught him to rear and buck. If someone bought Finn, she didn't know what she'd do. Especially now—Finn felt like the last good thing she had in her life.

"You don't want to be sold, anyway," she told him as they trotted easily along a wooded rise, hidden from view by a thicket of budding maples. The world had turned from tentative green to a rich emerald over the past week: brilliant new grass rising across the pastures, curling new leaves on the trees, long tapered green shoots from the lilies along the creek bends. Robins hopped across the warming ground, and a flock of crows were noisily building nests in a stand of trees in the lower pasture. As she turned Finn along a trail which had been liberally dotted with small log obstacles for the hunter pace, a cottontail bunny raced ahead of them, bounding from side to side of the path as if the poor thing couldn't figure out how to push through the shrubbery to find safety.

"The bunny has a white butt, like you," she laughed as Finn lifted his head and snorted at the fleeing cottontail. "Maybe that's what we should have called you. Bunny. My big old Bunny."

They coursed over the jumps as each obstacle rose from the trail, Finn leaping easily out of his flowing stride. Nadine loved the natural feeling of cantering down a wooded lane and hopping the easy fences. She wouldn't have ridden him so quickly over poles in the arenas—he was still green and didn't quite know where his feet landed when he moved—but out in the fields and forests, he didn't need technical know-how to get over the low log jumps.

"I have to ride you in the hunter pace," Nadine told him. "Caitlin wants us to win every division? Well, she better be ready for you." She didn't know how she'd explain to Caitlin that she was the one riding Finn instead of Sean. She had to trust she'd figure that out later.

Nadine checked her watch and realized she needed to get back to the barn. She turned Finn out of the woods and set off across the open fields between them and the buildings of home.

Finn snorted and shied as they came over the last rise, and Nadine nearly tipped over his neck before she realized what he'd spotted.

"Son of a gun," she muttered. "He actually brought them out to jump."

Chapter Twenty-Six

Sean

Sean started the morning lessons in the indoor arena. There was some grousing from a few students who had liked the change to the outdoor arena, but he was adamant: he didn't feel like he could adequately oversee their rides this morning, so they'd stay inside, where four walls and a roof could shut out the distractions which might make their horses fresh and spooky.

But the lack of distractions made him stir-crazy. Hour after hour, the students bouncing around him; the ground flattening beneath his boots as he turned in slow circles, calling out instructions. The up-down students rode early in the day: the little kids and a handful of adults who were still struggling to master the trot and canter without tumbling from the saddle. By the one o'clock session, he was hungry and annoyed at his life. By the two o'clock, he was running on empty and didn't think he could take another moment.

That's when he looked around at the students and realized they belonged out in the open.

Every single one of them was entered in the hunter pace, and this week he had planned to take them out to the pasture to ride. Instead, he'd stayed inside and moped. With a flash of uncomfortable insight, Sean felt terrible for the way he was treating these nice, earnest people. They just wanted to learn to ride horses. The same as he had when he'd been a little boy. And he'd been so busy scheming for a way out, for six whole months he hadn't even given them the courtesy of proper lessons. He'd just watched them bounce around the indoor, getting their legs and their balance on their own, shouting out occasional words of encouragement.

Then Nadine had helped him become a real instructor. And that changed things. He knew, with a burst of enthusiasm which nearly lifted him off his feet, that he wasn't going to leave these people behind. He wasn't going straight back to goofing around with his friends at the in-gate, lounging around while someone else did his fetching and heavy lifting and put his number in with the steward and all those other horse show chores.

He was going to be the trainer. He was going to help these riders reach their potential and actually feel things because of it. Things like satisfaction and pride in the work he'd done.

He was going to earn his own way in life, and stop asking someone else to bankroll him.

He was going to put in the work.

If this was his life now, he'd better enjoy it, and what was more, he'd better be good at it. The hunter pace was coming, and every single one of these students deserved a better shot at preparation than what he was giving them today.

Time for a change.

"Everyone, walk your horses and follow me," he'd called. Four pairs of excited eyes landed on him, and he carried those gazes right out of the indoor, through the barn's side door, and down the path between the paddocks to the north pasture.

Everyone pulled up their horses and looked around in delight as the landscape opened up around them. The hills, the trees, the zig-zag of the creek bubbling through the middle of it all—and the jumps!

Sean decided they'd start with the low log they'd taken Finn over on his first day out there. The worst that would happen was a horse might not pick up his forelegs enough on the first go around, causing him to trip. But he'd figure it out the second time around. Horses were smart, especially about learning where to put their feet.

He looked at his students, who were gazing back at him with wide, excited eyes. Fifteen, sixteen, forty-five and fifty-six: they were an interesting little group, the ones starting their equestrian lives before college threatened to drown all their childhood interests, and the ones reclaiming their lost love of horses after life and career were finally under control. There wasn't much space in horse sports for people like him, people in their twenties, who were supposed to be figuring themselves out. Not without family money, anyway...

But that was okay. The money didn't matter. He'd landed on his feet. He'd just taken a little while to realize it.

"Are we going to jump?" a teenager—Kim—asked, shaking him out of his reverie.

"We're going to trot over this log," Sean announced. "It requires almost no thinking on your part. Just make a big circle—Kim, you can go in front, then everyone follow behind her, plenty of distance between you, and as you come up to the log, drop your heels, go into two-point, and let the horse trot over it."

There were big smiles as Kim took the lead, trotting around on her quiet Quarter Horse gelding, followed by the others on their assortment of personal mounts and school horses. When Kim's horse stepped quietly over the log, Sean figured all of them would, but Chocolate Kiss surprised him by offering a little jump, and the oldest rider's horse, Delegate, actually paused first to snort at the log before going over it.

"Really nice work, everyone," Sean told them. "A few more times around until every horse is convinced the log won't eat them."

They had progressed to the smallest coop, and Kim was leading the field over it when Sean spotted movement off to his right. He turned, missing a shriek as Delegate paused in front of the coop before giving it a deer-jump that nearly unseated his rider. He saw Finn trotting over the hill towards them.

For a single breathless moment he didn't even spot Nadine, and he had a fluttering pulse until he realized she was mounted, not sprawled in a ditch somewhere. Then he had to sit down, as his legs were feeling wobbly, so he settled onto the log and tried to pretend it was all planned. The horses in the lesson spotted Finn and wanted to stand and stare, so he called out to Kim to bring them down to a walk. It was helpful; with them taking a break from jumping, he could try to reclaim his heartbeat. He'd been so afraid, for a moment, that something had happened to Nadine.

It was always going to be like this now. He was going to sit off to one side and worry about Nadine, and she was going to live her life, right in front of him, but without him.

Sean wasn't sure how he would bear it.

Back in the barn, he moved from rider to rider as they untacked and hosed down their horses. The warm day had gotten everyone sweaty, their winter coats shedding out but not quickly enough for the rapid rise in temperatures, and they needed baths before grazing out in the sun. Sean had a break before his next lesson, but he tried to spend it with the students, talking to them about the hunter pace and the things they could practice on their own between lessons.

"It's only, like, three weeks away," Kim was saying as she ran the sweat scraper down her horse's neck. "I was honestly wondering when we were going to start schooling the jumps."

"I wanted to make sure everyone was ready to ride in the field," Sean said, knowing it was only a half-lie. "And see? We had a really good first day. Next week we'll go out and practice some of the fences that have water, different elevations, that kind of thing. I'll have to take a horse to ride or I won't be able to keep up with everyone." It would be a good way to make sure the horses all jumped the fences the first time around, too. Just as they'd taught Finn to follow Calypso, horses often enjoyed playing follow-the-leader. If he took a horse who knew all the fences, there was much less chance of any refusals that could turn into stubborn wars of will.

He wondered who knew the jumps best. Calypso knew most of them, but he was also a bit of a wild card. You never quite knew what mood Calypso would wake up in.

"Today was really great," Kim told him. "Thanks for taking us out there, seriously."

"You're welcome," Sean replied, and he meant it. The students had all had fun, and they'd come into the barn better riders than the ones who had ridden out. Wasn't that what it was all about?

Maybe he *was* doing something with his life.

Sean glanced down the aisle and saw Nadine walking in Finn from his grazing session. His stomach seemed to do a slow roll at the sight of her, and he shook his head at his own reaction. Was this going to be his life now? Just spotting his coworker constantly, all day long, and feeling overcome with need for her?

While she ignored him?

"Sean."

Martha's voice.

He tensed immediately. Down the aisle, Nadine disappeared into Finn's stall. Behind him, Martha waited. He turned slowly. "Hey, Martha," he said weakly. "You're riding today?"

No flowing casual wear for Martha Lane today. She looked impeccable, turned out in good breeches, her best boots, and a tailored riding top that showed off her figure. Martha always dressed well for riding, but she'd clearly gone shopping. She was doing it for him—or rather, *to* him. Martha wanted him to know what sort of level she was operating at. Heads and tails above the kids here, she seemed to be reminding him; that's what he could expect if he gave up Elmwood and went to work for her.

"I joined the four o'clock this week," she told him, a little smile mincing across her face. "I just felt like I needed the extra time in the saddle."

"Oh, what a great idea." Sean tried to infuse a little false enthusiasm into his voice, while he wondered when she'd put her name into the lesson. He hadn't seen her in the book.

"Who am I riding today?"

Nadine always wrote the horse assignments on a white board near the tack room on busy weekends. Sean looked it over, hoping Martha's name wouldn't be there—as if that would give him some kind of out. But no, there it was, scrawled in a different color marker than the rest, but still in Nadine's handwriting.

"Ozzie," he read. Actually, not a bad choice. Ozzie had already gone out once today, and he'd be in a shuffling kind of mood for Martha. "You'll like him. Perfect for today's lesson."

Martha's eyes narrowed. "Why Ozzie? I'd like to choose the horse I ride."

"And who would you like to ride?" Sean asked wearily.

"I'd like to ride Finn," she declared. "The sales horse."

Sean's eyes widened a little. What game was this?

Well, he wasn't going to play it.

"Finn's not in the school program, Martha, and he was already ridden today. As your instructor, it's still my call what horse you should ride, and I think you'll do very well on Ozzie."

He waited for her to get mad, but instead Martha just tipped her head, a sly smile crossing her lips. "Oh, we're getting bossy now, aren't we? Okay then, Sean. I'll do what you tell me."

Sean bit back a groan. Glancing behind him to be sure Kim was walking her horse away, he lowered his voice and hissed, "Please don't make things weird, Martha."

"Weird? I'm just following orders. You're the boss, after all." Martha smirked.

"Well, Ozzie's stuff is marked. Do you need help grooming and tacking?"

"I should be able to manage. But come check on me, Sean. Just to be sure."

She waltzed off.

Sean wanted to bang his head against the wall. But that would just waste time, and anyway, he already had a headache. It had started the moment Martha entered the barn. For a moment, he stood still in the aisle, letting the bustle of the weekend barn spin around him. Horses, children, parents, adult riders, cats, Nadine—

He saw her rushing past, her chin in the air, determined not to look at him, and tried to lunge after her, but a girl leading a pony was suddenly in front of him, asking questions about trimming manes, and Sean managed to choke out, "Never use scissors, promise me you'll wait and I'll show you—" before he darted after Nadine.

He tried to catch up with Nadine before she disappeared back into her office, but she was too quick for him. He stood outside the door for a moment, wishing he had the courage to knock, but after a while, he realized it wasn't going to happen. Not now, on a bustling Sunday.

He'd hurt her feelings, and until the barn was empty of onlookers, he wasn't going to get a chance to win her back.

Chapter Twenty-Seven

Nadine

Avoiding Sean when they lived and worked in the same barn was a feat, but Nadine knew how to sneak around. Her work history had set her up for this perfectly. Escape him in the middle of the barn aisle by telling a little girl to harass him about pony hairdos? Done. Dart from her office back to her apartment without even letting Sean spot her? Done and done. He was still in the arena when she locked up her office for the night and bolted. Now she was home free until night-check.

She just wished she had some food.

Nadine looked at her bare cabinets and realized she was going to have to sleep at Caitlin's again tonight, if only so that she could eat something besides out-of-date Triscuits for dinner. She was supposed to be there, anyway. The fish probably needed fed again, and she'd left some clothes in the guest room, which she'd need to clear out before Caitlin came home tomorrow afternoon.

She wished she had gone over earlier. Now she had to get out of the barn without being heard. And that wasn't a simple task when

Sean could hear every footfall she made as she walked around the apartment.

Ugh. She'd really screwed up by getting involved with Sean. It was one thing to mess around with a mere coworker, slightly worse to escalate things with a neighbor, but they literally shared a wall! She couldn't hide from him forever; her creaking floorboards had probably already given her away.

She knew he was next door already—she could hear him over there, making slow rounds between the living room, bedroom, and kitchen. She wondered what he was making for supper. Probably something that didn't take much effort, ramen or the little tubs of mac and cheese that the barn kids liked so much. Not enough for a man who worked as hard as he did, between teaching and riding and the barn work he'd done this morning, besides. She'd known what he was doing out there. He was trying to make things up to her.

There was food in Caitlin's kitchen. Good stuff. Meat, bread, veggies. She could make him a proper meal.

But why should she?

Nadine slipped on her oldest, softest sneakers and tried to creep out her front door, but the floorboards beneath her gave every step away. She sighed, opened her door, and went out.

The barn was dim and quiet; a barn cat flitted through shadows at the end of the aisle, hunting in the empty stalls for mice scavenging fallen oats. With all the horses outside for the night, the place was almost unbearably silent. She was used to the scuffling and chewing of horses, who were awake and eating twenty-three hours out of the day. Each tread of the staircase groaned beneath her, the sound ricocheting through the empty space.

On the other side of the barn, she heard Sean's door open and close. Then, his footsteps, as slow and cautious as hers. She felt hunted. It might have been upsetting, if, deep down, she didn't want to be caught.

Nadine had to suppress the urge to run down the rest of the stairs, whip around the corner, and wrap her arms around him. What kind of point would she be making then?

Because, she realized, this *was* all just a point she was trying to make. Sean didn't get to make her feel small; Sean didn't get to make Elmwood and her work seem unworthy of his time. And as soon as he recognized that and offered his apology, she'd forgive him.

The realization brought a timid smile to her face.

It was still there when Sean came around the corner and saw her, dawdling on the last step, one foot held just above the aisle floor.

He stepped forward, hands out in supplication, and made his case.

"I was an idiot."

Her smile broadened; she put the hovering foot on the floor. "Good start," she told him. "Go on."

"I should have taken you right into the center of that party and told everyone to turn around and meet my amazing girlfriend, this incredible horsewoman who I was lucky enough to work with. I should have shown you off to Simone and told her the truth: that you're making me a better riding instructor and a better trainer, and I've progressed more in a few weeks of working with you than in ten years working with our old so-called trainers."

She put the other foot on the floor, with her hands, she clutched the stair-rail; she wasn't going to walk to meet him until he had finished his speech.

No getting off easy now.

Sean's face worked; he was emotional now, and her heart was thumping as he went in for the big finish. "I don't want to go anywhere else. I don't want to *be* anyone else. I want to be where you are. I'm so sorry, Nadine. I didn't mean to make you feel like you weren't important. I love you, and you deserve better than that."

Nadine's smile pulled at her cheeks as it spread from ear to ear. She felt a lightness in her chest, in her shoulders, in her arms as she finally opened them up to him. "Come here, Seany-boy," she whispered. "I love you, you big mess."

She made him dinner, after all.

Nothing gourmet, of course. She cooked burgers in a pan and made fries in the oven. She pulled together a salad with the last of the greens in Caitlin's fridge. There was a carton of cookie dough ice cream in the freezer. It was a good supper for a late spring evening, the temperatures still warm and a breeze playing over the back porch, where they sat and ate by the light spilling from the kitchen window.

They talked about the difference between living in a barn apartment with windows that overlooked stalls and aisle, and living in a farmhouse which gave a view of hills and fields and distant mountains. "I feel more light out here," Sean admitted. "I don't want to complain about our living space, but it's kind of a drag living inside the way we do."

"It really is. A place like this would be the dream," Nadine said, looking at the stars over the dark humps of the Catoctin Mountains. "I'd like to live closer to the mountains. I've always felt connected to them, somehow."

"Maybe we could," Sean said lightly. "Maybe there's some farm out there we could lease and run ourselves."

Nadine looked over at him, slightly alarmed. "You're thinking we should go into business ourselves? We don't have any money, Sean."

"Other people might," Sean said, shrugging.

"Not Martha," Nadine warned him, but she was only half-serious. Obviously not Martha. It didn't have to be said.

But Sean gave her a sideways look, one which made her pause and wonder if something was still going on there. "You *know* we can't do business with Martha, right? She's bad news."

"Oh, I know."

Nadine gave a sigh of relief.

"But I don't think she's through with us, here."

"What's that supposed to mean?"

Sean rubbed at his hair, making it stand on end, then flattening it again. "I mean—I didn't want to say anything, but she got really pushy about Finn tonight."

"About *Finn?*" Nadine stared at him. "What about Finn?"

"About trying him out . . . maybe buying him."

"But that's ridiculous. She doesn't know a thing about Finn. No one does."

"Except for you. And I know we've been quiet about who is riding him, but you're still pretty affectionate with him."

She looked down at her feet. "Oh. Are you saying—"

"Yeah. This is about getting back at me . . . through you."

"This is about getting back at me, too. She knows you're turning her down because of me, you said that already."

"True." Sean gave her a sideways smile. "Are you up for an archenemy in the barn?"

"Not really." Nadine sighed. "But it shouldn't matter. She can't buy him. She can't even *ride* him."

"We're going to find out. She's riding him on her Tuesday lesson."

Nadine was aghast. "Sean! Absolutely not! What are you thinking?"

"I'm thinking she's one of Caitlin's clients and she has to buy a horse to keep Caitlin happy." Sean shook his head. "If she goes to Caitlin and complains we won't let her ride the barn's number-one priority sales horse, we're both in trouble. Look, she'll ride him, she'll fall off, she'll get over this idea, and everything will be fine."

"And what if she doesn't?"

"Doesn't—what? Get over it?"

"Doesn't fall off, Sean!" Nadine stood up and took a few steps into the backyard. The grass was cool and damp beneath her bare feet. "He's a good horse—he'll work to keep her in the saddle. I know he will. And then she'll buy him and then I'll—" Her voice trailed off. There was nothing else to say.

She'd what? She'd get over it. Eventually.

Just like she'd gotten over every other horse she'd fallen in love with over the years. She was a pro. She knew how this game worked. Falling in love was a mistake, every time, and when it happened—as it inevitably did—you just had to swallow the hurt and watch the horse leave. They were business.

But Finn had seemed different from the start. Finn had seemed special.

And maybe she'd allowed herself to dream that she could keep this one.

As if her feelings mattered in some way, beyond the everyday transactions of dollars and cents. A ridiculous thought, she knew. But Nadine had started having ridiculous thoughts, hopes and dreams which went beyond just the base level of "stay employed, stay safe." She'd started dreaming bigger.

Probably a mistake, but it was too late to fix things now.

Sean followed her, his footsteps light on the grass, and she felt his presence at her back before he wrapped his arms around her, before he rested his chin on her shoulder. He was a warm comfort, and she crossed her hands over his arms, pressing against him. But Sean couldn't fix this problem for her.

She had to figure it out on her own.

Caitlin returned to daily operations on Tuesday, sweeping into the barn like a hurricane. Richie and Rose were bringing in horses two by two, while Nadine was throwing hay into the stalls. The radio was softly singing some seventies rock, which reminded Nadine of her mother.

"Is it true?" Caitlin demanded, her face appearing around a stall door.

Nadine took a moment to compose herself. "Is what true?"

"Is it true you called Martha and told her that she couldn't ride Finn in her lesson?"

"Oh, that." Nadine took a deep breath. Perhaps not her best-ever decision, but it had felt really good at the time. "Yes, I did tell her. I've been doing horse assignments for a really long time and I don't think Sean realized—"

"If she wants to ride the horse, that's between her and Sean," Caitlin said firmly. "More to the point, it's between her and *her*. Nadine! I think it was made pretty clear that Finn is for quick sale. What do you even know about it? Sean rides the horse, not you."

"Well, I—" Nadine stopped. There was nothing she could say which wouldn't involve giving away the truth about who was riding Finn. And she wouldn't throw Sean under the bus. "I was just looking out for Martha," she said finally, squeezing out the lie from beneath her most earnest expression.

Caitlin laughed at that. "I don't believe you. I think this is about Sean. I know he was up to something with Martha, and you didn't like it, so now you're getting in the way every time she wants to do something—"

"He's not up to something with Martha," Nadine interrupted. Her face was flaming hot. "That was all Martha's scheming, not Sean."

"You're very defensive of him! I thought you couldn't stand Sean."

Nadine wanted to hide from Caitlin's knowing gaze. "We're on better terms now," she muttered.

"Are you? Well, that's perfect news. Here's what you're going to do: stay out of Martha's business. And if you really think she can't ride that horse, I'll humor you—this time. But I want to see what he can do. Sean said he's jumping out in the fields." Caitlin thought for a moment. Nadine held her breath. "Tell you what, you and

Sean do a team in the hunter pace. He can compete Finn, you can pick another horse. Whoever you like. But preferably Calypso. I don't think anyone else wants to ride him."

"You want us to *compete* together?"

"Yes. You can fit in a ride time. Actually, even better, you guys can go first. Set the optimum time. I was going to use the averages, but this will give us another level of measurement."

"You know I'm going to be incredibly busy that day running entries and keeping on top of times, right?"

Caitlin waved away such practical concerns as actually administrating the hunter pace. "Relax. You've got everything scheduled out to perfection, and I can step in and manage admin while you ride. Or I'll get a volunteer. We'll have Richie and Rose around to grab the horses when you two are done. But you guys can go out first, show everyone how it's done. And give everyone a good look at those horses, too. I'm going to make it really clear they're for sale, you know? Time to get some sales in."

Nadine felt a painful pricking in her palms and realized she was clenching her fingers so tightly, her fingernails were cutting into her skin. She carefully unwound the tight fists. There was money in her savings account, she thought desperately. She could make an offer this instant.

And then what? She'd have no savings, no escape route if anything went wrong here. And she'd have a horse to pay board on, possibly pay vet bills on; she'd definitely have to pay for shoeing, for the dentist . . . the list went on and on.

Nadine remembered something Reg had said to her when she was still a teenager and had just started working up at the sales barn. She'd come home excited from a few minutes' worth of riding lesson she'd earned by mucking out the stalls. "I'm going to be a rider," she'd told her mother, unguarded for once, her happiness outpacing her caution. "It's really happening! I'm going to be a professional trainer, and ride horses my whole life, and—"

And of course Reg had been there, skulking in the kitchen. She remembered the gleeful malice in his tone when he said, "Riding isn't for poor people like you, Nadine. I wouldn't get used to it."

She'd had plenty of arguments, all bitten back in her throat. She didn't know any rich people, but she knew plenty of children of land-poor farmers, and some of them had horses. But it wasn't a very good defense, and she knew it, because they did have land, and barns, and fields, and she had nothing but her own tiny bedroom in this stupid townhouse on Wonder Avenue.

Then, she'd thought that she could change the future. But now here she was, more than ten years later, with all of this experience and the best job she'd ever had . . . and she still had no land, no barn, no fields, nothing but an apartment overlooking a barn aisle.

Maybe there was no rising above the place where a person was born. Maybe the American Dream was a big American con, a story people told themselves when they got up to work at the jobs which would make someone else money and when they paid the rent on a house which was making someone else's mortgage payment. Maybe Reg had been right all along, and she had always wanted too much, more than she had any right to have. Maybe the Simones of the world would always have the good stuff, and she'd always have to work her tail off just to get a peek.

"So you're good with this plan, right, Nadine?" Caitlin was glancing at her phone, skimming through messages, moving on with her day.

"I'm good, sure," Nadine agreed, as she had been going to do the entire time. "I'll put our ride time in first."

"And practice with Sean," Caitlin reminded her, turning away, already lost to her next appointment. "Get out there and do those fences. Practice your pace. I expect the two of you to impress everyone."

Chapter Twenty-Eight

Sean

Sean came downstairs late, dressed for riding. He peeked in Nadine's office and saw her sitting with a cup of coffee, going over the lesson book. She was wearing shorts. The cut-offs he remembered from last October. Appreciated, he thought, but the wrong attire for his plans.

"Hey, silly, go upstairs and get into breeches! We have time for a ride this morning."

"Caitlin's back and she's been buzzing around the barn all morning," Nadine said, hardly bothering to look up from her work. "I don't think now will work, unless you want her to find out I've been riding Finn. Or you want to ride him. I should probably stop putting off the inevitable and give my horse back."

"Oh, maybe we should just come out with it." Sean threw himself into the chair opposite her desk and waited to see how his suggestion would fall. But Nadine still didn't look at him. "What's going on? Are we in trouble? Did we leave the house in a mess or something?"

"No, everything was fine with the house-sitting. We got away with it," she added, putting down her pen and giving him a rueful smile. "But this whole Finn thing has really blown up."

"I told you not to call Martha." When she'd said she was just going to give Martha a little nudge in the right direction, Sean had suggested she was actually making a very bad decision. So she just did it while he was teaching a lesson and couldn't try to stop her.

"Yes, you did warn me. Congrats, you were right."

"I didn't mean it like that. What happened?"

"It's like Caitlin just remembered he's in the barn. Now she wants us to form a hunter pace team and ride first, sort of show the way for the students and set the optimum time. And show off how great Finn is, so someone buys him right away. With half of Catoctin Hunt there, I'm completely out of luck. Someone's going to snap him right up."

Sean didn't know what to say. "Oh no," he managed, finally. "I'm so sorry."

"Don't be." Nadine picked the pen back up and drew an emphatic line through one of her old assignments. Sean wondered if she was redoing the entire afternoon, just to take her mind off Finn. "I shouldn't have let myself get my hopes up. I can't buy a horse. Where would I keep it? My job doesn't come with board, and Caitlin would never discount a stall for me. She's already constantly on my tail about improving profits. I feel like I work at a department store sometimes. It's all bottom line with her."

Sean lifted his eyebrows, surprised to hear Nadine complain about Caitlin so effusively. Usually she was the soul of a grateful worker. "Maybe wintering with me in Florida doesn't sound so bad, huh?"

She looked at him from beneath her eyebrows. "Let's not mention that again. You're not taking Martha's money, and anyway, she already said she won't have me."

"Makes that decision easy," Sean proclaimed. He was still hoping to lighten the mood. "I won't go anywhere without you."

She smiled at that. "And I won't go anywhere. So you're stuck."

Sean glanced around, then leaned back and shut the door. "Let me ask you a question. Are you really that dedicated to staying here forever? What does Caitlin have on you that keeps you here?"

"I'm not staying here *forever*, Sean, obviously, but nothing better is going to come along anytime soon. And I already told you why I'm staying in Catoctin Creek. That makes it double-unlikely I ever get another job offer."

"Okay, but what if you did? Would you consider leaving Elmwood?"

"Who have you been talking to?" Nadine tipped her head at him. "Please tell me you're not chasing rich divorcees again."

"No, literally no one. It's just talk. But I'd like to know . . . if something came up . . . what your answer would be."

Nadine put down her pen again. She leaned back in her chair and rubbed her face, as if that would help her see the answers. "It would have be to a step up from this," she said eventually. "An apartment with windows that face outdoors, for starters."

Sean nodded. "So, not a huge ask. Just a normal way to live."

She laughed at him, shaking her head. "Have you ever tried looking for a barn management job, Sean? Or any job, besides your current one? You got lucky, getting hired here. It's a jungle out there, and the horse business is worse than most. Maybe you should be content with what you've got. At least for a little while."

"No, you're right."

"And why would you want to leave? You're doing well all of a sudden."

"I'm not saying I want to leave. I'm just—"

What? What was he doing?

She looked at him carefully. "Let's not rock the boat, Sean."

Sean subsided, letting her get back to her work. He didn't have any ideas. He wasn't even sure why he'd brought it up. He just didn't feel like they could stay at Elmwood forever. He hated watching her struggle with the Finn issue, watching her give in to Caitlin again and again. Maybe this had been a good next step for Nadine, but he thought she was ready for the next one. They both were, in fact. They needed their freedom, a place where they could ride the horses that were best for them, and be in a relationship without worrying about what the boss would think.

He was going to be on the lookout for it.

Rosemary Beckett was standing outside of Trout's Market, a paper bag of groceries tucked under one arm, when Sean parked his car on Main Street and headed to the store to pick up some lunch.

She shielded her eyes against the brilliant sunshine and squinted at him. "Seany-boy! Have you seen my husband anywhere about town?"

"I've just driven in. Sorry, Rosemary."

"Ugh." She put the bag down at her feet. A baguette and the green heads of several carrots poked out. "That weighs a ton. He was supposed to just run and get gas while I was picking up groceries, and now I don't see the car anywhere."

"That's weird." Sean looked up and down Main Street as if Stephen's car would magically appear. But the road was pretty empty, with just an old farm truck rattling past their spot on the sidewalk. A coffee-colored dog watched them from the truck bed, tail wagging gently. Cute dog. No Stephen. "He wouldn't usually just drive off, would he?"

"Oh, Sean." Rosemary rolled her eyes. "If he got a call and someone wanted something quickly, and he thought he could sneak away and manage it without me noticing, absolutely. I don't know how long he thinks buying a few groceries takes, but this isn't the first time he's driven to someone's office or house at the drop of a hat. I'll just have to wait. I'll go over to the Blue Plate and bother Nikki or Lauren."

"Do you just want a ride home?"

She lifted her eyebrows. "Seriously? But you're getting lunch."

"I'll run in and let them know what I want. It'll be done when I get back. You want the ride?"

"I get to go straight home, and it will confuse Stephen," Rosemary mused. "Yes, I like this plan. Thanks, Sean."

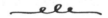

Sean had been to Notch Gap Farm before, when he'd attended Rosemary's horsemanship seminar at Caitlin's request. Just a few minutes outside of town, the graceful farmhouse stood over a green lawn bisected by the noisy waters of Notch Gap Run, with a beautiful stone and lumber bank barn as its companion. The foothills of the Catoctins rose up behind the house, and woods ringed the property, giving it a hidden quality Sean found incredibly endearing.

"You're so lucky to have this place," Sean said as his car rumbled across the bridge over the creek. "I used to live on a huge property, but I think a little farm like this would be perfect."

"Hard to come by, these days," Rosemary agreed. "Everyone wants a little piece of Catoctin Creek now. I still shudder to think what it would be like if Stephen's original plan for Long Pond Farm had gone through. Can you believe he wanted to build a subdivision over there? And I still liked him enough to marry him." Rosemary laughed and sighed. "Well, to be fair, he didn't know the area at all when he decided it would be better as houses."

"And he didn't stick to his guns," Sean pointed out. He parked in front of the house. "It's important to let yourself grow when you get additional information. Here, let me get that bag for you."

"Oh, it's nothing," Rosemary demurred, but she still handed him the grocery bag when he reached for it. She climbed out of his car and headed up the porch steps to unlock the front door.

Sean lingered by the car, looking across the property. Spring was kind to Notch Gap Farm. Day lilies were blooming with orange audacity along the lower section of the barn and in the grassy knolls along the creek. The vegetable garden along one side of the house was coming in with a vengeance, green plants waving above the rows of brown soil. On the hillside beyond the house, Rosemary's little herd of rescue horses grazed on the lush spring grass.

The farm was perfect. He wished he could find a place like this where he and Nadine could train horses and live in peace, without a boss like Caitlin policing their every move.

"Sean? Are you coming?"

He nodded and went up the front steps, handing her the bag as she went into the front hall. At the door, he paused, looking back through the thickening spring foliage that separated the farm from Long Pond. He could just see the twinkling of water through the trees. "What's going on with the school project?" he asked, finally following Rosemary into the cool, dark hallway.

"You mean next door? It's going forward. They're restoring the house right now, and building the school dorms and classrooms in a new building that's on the other side of the hill." Rosemary started putting away groceries in the old-fashioned kitchen. "I'm glad; I'm all for the school, but I didn't really want to look at it. It should open for the first class in the fall, they say."

"You're teaching at it, aren't you?"

"Just horsemanship. Nothing too strenuous." She glanced at Sean suddenly. "They haven't hired a riding instructor yet."

"You wouldn't happen to know anything about that process, would you, Rosemary?"

She gave him a level look. "I might. Why do you want to know?"

The front door opened behind them, and Stephen was calling, "Rosemary? Did you con poor Sean into giving you a ride?"

Rosemary smiled at him. "Let me see what I can find out, and I'll be in touch," she said. Then she turned and looked down the hall. "Down here," she called. "You can't just abandon me like that, Stephen! Sean will turn my head and steal me away!"

Chapter Twenty-Nine

Nadine

Nadine knew she ought to ride Finn, but now her heart wasn't in it. And anyway, Caitlin kept buzzing in and out of the barn, taking notes and making calls. She couldn't get on Finn with Caitlin around, but usually that wasn't an issue. Her boss rarely spent more than a few hours at the farm before she sped off into town to make her deals.

Nadine was beginning to feel nervous every time she saw Caitlin, as if some awful piece of news was about to drop. Everything Caitlin had ever said about running low on money and downsizing programs suddenly rang in her ears. What if Caitlin had finally made a real estate buy so big, she was willing to give up Elmwood for it?

What she really needed was for Sean to come back and tell her she was being silly, but of course today was the day he took forever to come back with lunch. Nadine wandered up the aisle and stared down the barn drive, as if she could will his car to show up. She was surprised to see an old truck driving up the lane. Surprised—then disappointed, because it was definitely Reg. Back on another assignment for Caitlin—was it possible he was being perfectly above-board and just doing odd jobs? Maybe getting the boot from Wonder Avenue had done him some good.

But somehow Nadine doubted it. She watched the truck suspiciously as it turned towards the house, then disappeared behind the thicket of trees which blocked Caitlin's house from the barn area.

Nadine only took a few minutes to decide. Then she went running up the drive herself. She didn't know how she was going to eavesdrop or figure out what Reg was doing, but she had to make an attempt. Something was going on around here, and if her mother's now-ex was involved, it couldn't be good.

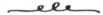

"He said he'll take all of them," Reg was saying. "No problem. Just call when you're ready and I'll arrange transportation."

Nadine pressed herself close to the house. The living room window above her head had been opened to let in the breeze, a fact she was grateful for right now. Also grateful for the thick hedges that ran around the base of the house, giving her a very secure hiding place. She had crept behind their full branches the moment she'd reached the house, then scuffled along as quietly as she could until she heard voices. Pretty lucky, that Caitlin had decided to entertain Reg in the living room and not the kitchen at the back of the house. Nadine's knees were scuffed up enough as it was. She was thankful to stop and listen.

Caitlin's voice filtered through the window, sounding skeptical. "I need your word on this one. There can't be any funny business with auctions or cheap sales lots. You know that, right? These are quality horses and I have a name to uphold. The ponies are all going to Sam Tilden's sales barn in Virginia, you know, and Sam can't get mixed up with any slaughter sob stories, either. The horses have to go to real homes."

"Look, I promised you everything would stay above-board. The Remsens—"

"The Remsens! Mike and Joe? That's who we're talking about? But they're right up the road. I need some distance. Think PA. Think South Carolina. Kentucky, even. Come on, Reg. Be real here. I called you on this job because I thought you had contacts all over the place."

"They've got people in all those places. They're dealers. They'll get you your distance."

Nadine heard Caitlin sigh. "If I'd wanted to deal with the Remsens, I'd have called them. I didn't. I called *you*. I thought you'd do better than this, to be honest."

"Look, I'm your buffer between Elmwood and the Remsens. You don't have to get mixed up with them. And the horses will never go to their place. I'm just using them for contacts."

"Fine. I have to get to a meeting in Frederick. Just—make sure it's taken care of. I'm not waiting on news anymore, so you can give them a date. June thirtieth. I'll know how many a few days out. Hopefully I can sell a bunch in the meantime."

"I've got you. Trust me on this."

Caitlin's low laugh told Nadine that her boss didn't really trust Reg not to screw this up. Neither did Nadine.

She stayed pressed against the cool bricks of the farmhouse long after Reg had driven away and Caitlin had locked up, the sound of her BMW purring along the farm drive. Heading into Frederick for yet another business meeting, something else which didn't involve Elmwood. Clearly, she'd found something bigger and better. Nadine couldn't understand it. How could Caitlin turn her back on this place? On her horses?

And now what did this mean for her job?

"Nadine!" Sean was happy to see her. So happy she could barely bring herself to look at him. She was hurting all the way through, and his cheer couldn't do anything but make her feel worse. "Good news! Caitlin left, and my three o'clock cancelled, so we can fit in a ride."

"Great," she said woodenly. Sean tipped his head at her curiously, and he wrapped an arm around her shoulders, tugging her close. She leaned into his strength, wishing the security she felt with him was real, and not a placebo, a very excellent facsimile of the real thing.

There was no security in life. No one knew that as well as she did.

"What's going on, baby?" he asked tenderly.

It was the first time he'd ever called her *baby*. The endearment made her eyes well up with tears, and she swiped at them quickly, afraid he'd see them and mistake their meaning. She wasn't the kind of girl who got all crybaby over a sweet word.

Was she?

"I think Caitlin's going to sell the farm," she said finally.

Sean's arm stiffened. "What makes you think that?"

"Well, for starters, I know what Reg is up to now. He showed up again, and I followed him to the house."

He turned her around, staring into her eyes. "Is this a conversation for outside the barn?"

"Definitely." Richie and Rose were omnipresent. Richie, in particular, managed to overhear everything.

"Let's tack up the horses," Sean said. "We can talk it over in the field."

They sat by the stream and went over the details forwards, backwards, and around—over and over. Until even Sean had to admit that things looked bleak.

"I'm just really shocked," he said over and over.

Nadine tipped one toe against Finn's nose as the horse grazed close to her boots. "I'm not," she admitted. "This is what happens with horse farms. With people like Caitlin. She's gotten a taste of making money and now she wants to pursue that. She can say that she gave her mom's legacy a fair shot, but in the end, it wasn't enough. And it wasn't for her. We both know she's no horsewoman."

"You shouldn't just shrug this off," Sean argued. "This is a betrayal."

"Yeah, it is." Nadine shrugged, then laughed at herself for being so literal. "What can I do about it, though? All we can do is figure out where we're going next. I didn't want to leave Catoctin Creek, Sean!" Her voice rose, but it didn't matter—no one out here would hear her besides the birds and the horses. "I wanted to stay and find a way to belong here, for *real*. But it's not going to happen. I guess it wasn't meant to be."

"About that . . ."

She looked at him, her heart suddenly seized with worry. He wasn't about to say he was leaving, was he? That was bad news on top of bad news that she just couldn't take right now. At this point, he could lie about staying, and she'd appreciate the deception.

Sean's eyes seemed to study her face, as if he was trying to read her expression before he said anything else.

"Tell me what you're thinking, Sean."

"It's probably nothing."

"Now you have to tell me. For heaven's sake!"

"I was talking to Rosemary a little while ago."

"And?"

"I might have . . . suggested . . . that I be considered for riding instructor at Long Pond. When the school opens in the fall."

Nadine stared at him. "You're joking."

"No, I'm serious."

"You—*want*—*wa*it—so now you want to be a riding instructor, after all?" Nadine stared at him, feeling exhausted. He wanted to be a horse show boy. Then he wanted to be a trainer. Then he wanted to get better at teaching just so he could keep his job. Now, suddenly, he was thinking about making a career move as a coach?

Men could be really exhausting, Nadine thought. Surely she was never this hard to track.

He shrugged, looking endearingly sheepish. "You helped me see its value. You changed things for me."

She didn't know how to take it in. She reached out a hand and ran it through Finn's dark mane, hoping the feel of the horse would help her. Horses had always given her strength when nothing else seemed good enough. "I don't know what to say," she admitted finally. "I'm not saying it's a bad idea. I'm just surprised. And a little overwhelmed by everything. In general."

"Don't say anything," Sean said, shrugging. "Let's wait and see where it goes. And in the meantime..."

"Yeah?"

"We have a hunter pace to wow everyone at." Sean nodded at Finn. "And that's the horse you're doing it on."

"No, Sean. You have to take him. If I ride him, Caitlin—"

"Will know you're an incredible rider?" Sean grinned. "And Rosemary will know what an amazing job you've done with her horse? And you'll receive a little more street cred in this crazy little town? This is exactly what you need, I think. Catoctin Creek doesn't know what a gem they've got in you."

"And Finn will sell."

Sean fell quiet.

"I mean, I know he has to," Nadine said. "I know Rosemary bought him to raise money for the sanctuary. I have to put in a good showing on him and sell him. Or you do. Someone has to. Finn has to bring in the big bucks."

"So, now you have to make everyone else's money. Just like Caitlin has you running the hunter pace to save the therapeutic riding program," Sean pointed out. "Which she must be canceling, if she's selling the horses. Maybe it's time you started thinking about yourself. Your good deeds aren't really paying you back."

Nadine shook her head. She still couldn't believe it. June thirtieth. All the farm-owned horses. Leaving. "Well, Sean, make it make sense. Because I sure can't."

"Maybe whatever opportunity arose was really sudden." Sean shrugged. "Maybe back in April she thought the farm was still her primary business. Things can change really fast in business."

"But what about us? Don't we deserve any consideration, here? I put together the hunter pace. I filled it up! You and I both did! We did everything we were asked. And we're still going to lose the program? The lesson horses? Everything!" Nadine was almost shouting again. She lowered her voice as Finn lifted his head and gazed at her with pricked ears. "Sorry, buddy. But things are confusing right now. I thought yelling would help."

Sean rubbed his chin, thinking. "You know, I did everything my father asked, too. I made the farm money, seriously! But he still kept things from me. And then when he sold everything and left town, I was the one who had been kept hanging. Until the very last day, I thought he was working to save the farm. But he didn't care at all. The farm had always been going. I just hadn't seen it."

Nadine swallowed hard. "So you think it's really ending, no matter what?"

"I don't think it's expanding. I can tell you that much. Maybe we hang on a while longer, but eventually . . ." Sean looked into the distance. "I just don't see Elmwood lasting, not like it is now."

Nadine dug her fingers deeper into Finn's mane, but he was pulling away from her, heading for lusher grass, and she had to let go. She glanced around and saw Sean's hand out, waiting for her. She put her hand there.

Maybe she couldn't put all her faith in a horse, or a job, or a boss who had given her a chance. Maybe there were no answers, and she just had to carry on as if nothing was wrong.

But she had Sean.

That was something. Something big.

"Good morning, hunter pace," Nadine whispered.

The final weeks before the event had gone by in a flash, a flurry of last-minute bookings and appointments. Meeting vendors and contractors as they arrived to set up their tents and trucks and generators. Slowly driving the farm truck over the course with a mallet and a bed full of flagged stakes to hammer into the ground at the side of each obstacle, making the long course clear and easy to follow.

Now, on this gorgeous May morning, it was all real. The north pasture and north paddocks had been transformed into a long, winding course of coops, rustic rails, logs, and water splashes. The paddock just behind the barn had been sacrificed for trailer parking. A mobile office for checking in, picking up numbers, and signing releases had been established beneath a white tent in front of the scattering of food trucks and mobile tack shops who had set up in the next paddock over. That tent would be Nadine's office all day, or at least until the last team came back from their course. And that last round was currently scheduled for three-thirty that afternoon.

So, the tent was all day.

The little horse show she'd helped create—indeed, that she'd done most of the work on, despite lip service assistance from Caitlin and the recruitment help from Sean—was almost enchanting in the predawn coolness. A pink sunrise was gathering itself behind the low hills to the east, and the ponies and horses who had gone out all night were clustered at the gates, eager to come inside for breakfast. For just a moment, Nadine could look upon her works and feel mighty, feel proud. Maybe this land and these fields and this barn weren't actually hers, but this accomplishment and these responsibilities were, and she was living up to the challenge.

At least she could be proud of that.

Caitlin had found someone else to sit and watch the admin table for the first hour. That someone was Nikki Mercer, and she was fiercely protective of the paperwork and laptop set up on the card table in front of her. Nadine showed her how to check everyone's signed forms and issue numbers. Other than that, there wasn't much to it. Nikki was of the opinion she could handle things just fine, and since she ran a restaurant and was opening a bakery, Nadine didn't see any reason not to trust her. Also, Nikki brought her blueberry muffins. Fortified with sugar and berries, Nadine went back into the barn to get Finn ready.

Sean was already saddling Calypso. The Thoroughbred moved restlessly in the cross-ties, tugging and pawing. "So much fussiness," Sean grunted as she walked Finn past them. "I'm pretty sure this horse has never shown before."

"I don't think he has, now that you mention it." Nadine paused to hold the horse's halter, hoping to still him while Sean got the girth tightened. "You ought to go give him a spin around the indoor while I get Finn ready. Knock some of that excitement down a peg."

"Hopefully Finn's no problem," Sean said, stepping back from Calypso's side and surveying his tack. "You don't know his history, either."

That was true. But Nadine was used to riding horses with issues. If Finn decided today was too scary for him, they'd find a way to work through it.

And, she thought rather blithely as she pulled a grooming box out of the tack room, if he acted the fool, no one would want to buy him. So they'd have *that* going for them.

Finn was pretty hyped up by the activity outside the barn, too. Nadine decided he could use a few minutes of schooling in the indoor as well. She checked her watch as she led the tacked horse out of the cross-ties—they had about half an hour before they needed to head out on course. Not long at all.

Calypso was already whirling around the arena at a brisk canter, his head and tail both up. Nadine stopped in the aisle, dismayed. When Sean saw her waiting to enter the indoor, he pulled up, but the move wasn't without a struggle.

"What are you doing?" she demanded, as Sean brought Calypso to a snorting, prancing walk in front of her. "You're going to wear him out and then we'll never set the right time! We'll be too slow."

"Oh, you couldn't wear this horse out," Sean said grimly. "Believe me, I've tried."

Calypso danced beneath him, snorting and ducking his head against the bit. He was already sweating, despite the cool spring morning. Nadine shook her head as Finn tugged backwards against her, feeding off Calypso's nervous energy. "Easy, big boy," she told him. To Sean, she asked, "Could we be making a huge mistake?"

Sean loosened the reins and let Calypso spring away, bounding back through the indoor. He didn't bother to answer her, but Nadine figured his answer was pretty clear. Mistake or not, they were going to head out on that course. It was their job.

It took an effort to get Finn to stand long enough to let her mount, and he was already walking away, yanking his head against the reins, before she even got her feet into the stirrups. Nervous at his attitude, she took the horse into the center of the ring, trying to stay out of Sean's way, and let him break into a high-stepping trot.

They were barely warmed up before her phone alarm pinged, letting her know they were out of time.

"Sean, we have five minutes to our start. We have to get out there."

Sean had been walking Calypso for the past few minutes, and the Thoroughbred seemed to have gotten the worst of his jollies out of his system. But Nadine was still worried he'd worn the horse out.

Finn felt a little better as they walked out to the starting area at the top of the north pasture. He looked hard at the assorted horse trailers which were springing up like mushrooms in the back paddock, and the admin tent made him threaten to spin in place. But he settled and went forward when she asked him firmly. Her shoulders relaxed as he flicked his ears back to her, clearly listening.

Finn was a good horse. And Nadine had a good feeling about their ride. "You ready for this, Sean?"

"As ready as I'm going to be." Calypso was still prancing; Sean tossed her a grimace as he sat deep in the saddle. She thought he already looked more capable of riding a tough horse today than he had a month ago, but she kept the thought to herself. Now wasn't the time to crow about how she'd helped improve his seat with the lessons she'd given him on Finn.

"You look really good," she told him, deciding a simple compliment was in order.

Sean winked at her. "Let's go run around this course and try not to die."

Nadine wished he wouldn't say things like that right before their ride. "I wasn't planning on dying," she said, trying to keep any emotion out of her voice, but she was afraid she just sounded prim. "Let's just be careful and have a nice ride."

"Here's hoping," Sean replied. But he didn't look too confident.

Chapter Thirty

Sean

Sean was really feeling the pressure, and he knew that was reflecting in Calypso's antsy behavior. But he couldn't settle his own racing heart. They were about to go out in front of everyone with their horse swap revealed, and Caitlin might just lose it on him. But worse than that, Finn's performance could track in either direction—and both would be bad for Nadine. If he went like a pro, she'd look great, and the horse would sell like a flash. With that color pattern? The only way to keep him from selling would be to hide him. Yes, he knew Finn had to sell, but he wished they could get some more time to look for an answer which let Nadine keep the horse.

And then, of course, if he went badly, Nadine would take the blame.

His mind raced as Sean tried to think of something—anything —he could do to fix this.

Calypso wasn't helping his thinking process, though. The horse *was* full of beans—Sean hadn't been kidding when he'd said he couldn't tire the horse out. Calypso was some kind of marathon horse. Sean figured he'd only been unsuccessful on the racetrack because American races were too short for the horse to hit his stride. He should have been a timber horse. In fact, he'd probably make a great field hunter. Maybe he should have thrown his photo around at the hunt ball. At least Caitlin would be happy with him for selling a horse.

They rode up to the starting box, just a few dozen feet beyond the admin tent. Both horses spooked at the tent, its white fabric catching the morning sunlight. He saw Nikki stand up from behind her card table and wave hello. Beside him, Finn lifted his head and stared, ears pricked and forelock flying up like a black unicorn's horn. Sean turned away before he caught sight of Nadine's face, and instead he saw the bystanders and other competitors staring at Finn.

Finn and his flashy Appaloosa coloring...

He wished Nadine could have fallen in love with a plain bay Thoroughbred like Calypso. A horse easy to hide, a horse who could have been a thousand other horses. But no, it had to be an eye-catching black beast with a dappled blanket of white spots. A horse who could never be forgotten.

There was a crunch of tires as a car entered the parking lot and pulled through to the paddock behind them. Something made Sean turn around in the saddle, and his eyes widened as he saw the hunter pace's newest arrival.

"Let's get to the starting box and get going," he hissed to Nadine. "Quick, don't pause another second."

She glanced at him, startled. "We're going, Sean. It's right there. What are you so worked up about?"

"I just want to get rolling before Calypso starts up again," he lied, and gave the horse a little thump with his left leg—the one Nadine couldn't see—so that the horse tugged at the bit again.

This is all about me . . . this has nothing to do with Martha's car pulling in right behind us . . .

"You'll manage," Nadine was saying, nodding at the three-sided starting box ahead. Just a couple of posts and rails, large enough for them to walk in, turn, and ride out of when the starter said go. "Here we are."

Calypso jigged his way into the starting box, turning sideways and insisting that was a better way to walk. *Fine, we'll crab-step all the way across the course.* Sean gave up trying to settle him. Calypso would do what he wanted—the horse always did. Sean was literally just along for the ride once Calypso opened up for a gallop, anyway.

He looked over his shoulder; Martha had gotten out of her car and was walking across the short grass to the admin tent. She was looking around the grounds—she was staring at them. And hustling to the tent. Caitlin wasn't there at the moment—Nikki wouldn't stand for any nonsense—but this chance wouldn't last. He didn't know what she had planned, but he figured they had a minute to get out of here before Martha caused them any trouble. Maybe less.

"Let's go," Sean said to the starter. "Come on, man."

The starter, a disinterested local dad whose main qualification was the possession of a stopwatch, shrugged. "Head out, then."

Nadine looked at him, confused. "But we have another minute—"

"Just start," the man said wearily. "It's a minute, lady."

Nadine, who admittedly had done all the scheduling, opened her mouth, prepared to argue.

He heard Martha's voice. "Are you in charge? I want to talk to someone about that *horse—*"

"Let's go," he told Calypso, shaking out the reins, and the Thoroughbred plunged past Finn with a squeal of delight—or maybe rage, who could say with this horse—and they were off.

―――⁂―――

The course seemed to vanish beneath their horses' drumming hooves.

Five miles, winding through the north pasture's varying landscape, splashing through the stream, jumping logs, winging over coops, cutting across the neighboring farm—there were so many twists and curves, the course had looked like tangled-up snake on the maps Nadine had drawn up and distributed in the welcome packets. They didn't need the maps while riding, of course—small signs pointed out the route, flags marked the turns and fences, and it was almost always possible to see the next jump and get an idea of where to go.

Sean knew they were going too fast and Caitlin would be annoyed at their time. The optimum time would be determined as an average once everyone had ridden the course, and if they kept on galloping at this pace, they would be outliers, somewhere near the top of the chart. She'd wanted them in the middle, to show the way at a sensible pace. Fox hunts were not all go-go-go; there were plenty of quiet moments: pauses for the hounds to pick up a scent, or walks through thick undergrowth and forest, or trotting from one likely spot to the next. The hunter pace was expected to go at roughly the same sort of pace, up and down, with breathers and calm between bursts of speed and energy.

So as they cantered down a gentle slope towards the creek, Sean stood in his stirrups and slowed Calypso to a trot. The horse shook his head, but finally gave in. Ahead of him, Finn checked his speed of his own accord, his ears flicking back to keep track of his friend. Nadine looked back, saw him slowing, and sat in the saddle.

"Did we get away too fast?" she asked once they were walking side by side. "Finn just wanted to get away from that crowd once we were rolling. And I have to admit it was pleasant to let him move."

"Calypso just wanted to roll all the way to the finish line." Sean grinned, patting the Thoroughbred on his hot neck. "He's been out here a dozen times and still doesn't understand that it's a long ride, not a sprint."

"I feel that metaphor in my soul," Nadine said.

"Let me ask you a question." Sean reined back Calypso, halting in the shade of an oak tree, and Nadine circled Finn around him until the big horse decided he could stand still. "Do you want to win this? Come in right down the middle? Or do you want to throw it and make Finn look green? Because I'll follow your lead. We can race this thing like it's the Kentucky Derby and make it look like two crazy horses just went to town without arena railing to keep them inside."

Nadine laughed and sighed at once, a sad sound which tore at his heart. He wanted to fix this for her so, so badly. But just as he'd been powerless when his father sold Simone's horse, he was powerless now. The people with the money held all the power in this game. They were pawns.

Pawns on horseback.

"I want to win this," Nadine said suddenly. "Finn deserves it."

"You deserve it, too," Sean reminded her. "Credit for the win, credit for the training."

She shook her head. "Caitlin didn't even see us ride out. She doesn't know I'm on Finn. It's still possible she'll never even know."

"You don't think she'll be waiting for us on the finish line?"

Nadine shrugged. "Who could say what she'll do next?"

She was waiting for them at the finish line.

Sean saw her first; he was cantering slightly ahead of Finn, who had eventually tired and was striding out purely as an attempt to stay with his friend. He turned back to say something to Nadine. But she didn't need the warning—her face was already hardening.

In the end, though, nothing much was made of it. Caitlin made a wry comment to Nadine which he couldn't quite hear as they slipped from their saddles. Then Nadine was handing off Finn to Richie so that she could drink some water and take over her admin duties as quickly as possible. Sean saw the catch in her movement as she relinquished the reins, saw the quick pat she tried to give Finn as he was whisked away. He gave her one last glance as he led Calypso after the big horse, but Caitlin was already talking her ear off about the hunter pace, and the teams which were readying to go out, their order staggered by a few minutes so that no one overtook one another out on the course.

He didn't see Martha anywhere.

Inside the barn, the students buzzed as they groomed their horses, already armed with questions which they started to throw at Sean the moment he arrived. He fielded their requests for information as best he could, telling them everything he could about pacing and fences and footing. But in the end, he just kept saying, "Have fun out there. Have fun out there. Just have fun out there."

The younger students swallowed this advice and went on grooming and tacking up. The older ones, the teens who knew about Sean's grinding ambition to get back on the show circuit, eyeballed him uncertainly. He'd been making a big deal about their giving him winning rides. Now, this morning, was when he chose to ease up on them? Something wasn't right.

It was Kim who finally decided to ask him. "What happened to win, win, win? Did you change your mind about all that?"

Sean trained the hose on Calypso's neck, the sweat sliding away in white-rimmed sheets of water. He shook his head at Kim. "I guess I'm just learning that it doesn't matter if all you do is win, Kim. The bigger picture things don't change."

She lifted her eyebrows at him.

He shrugged. "What can I tell you? Hard truths out on course today."

Kim chose to roll her eyes at him, which Sean found oddly comforting.

At least he was old and out of touch to the young riders now. That meant his changing opinions must actually mean something.

By the end of the day, gray clouds were thickening across the formerly pristinely blue sky, and there was a definite smell of rain in the air. Sean helped his last students shower off their horses and put them away for the evening, grateful any heavy weather had held off. The Maryland hills grew slick in the rain, their clay bases treacherous when wet.

He was impatient to see the final numbers averaged out. The optimum time was never given ahead of time, so no one knew how they'd done until all the riders had gone. Hitting optimum time dead-on was a feat usually performed only by the most experienced riders. Sean hadn't realized that until fairly late in their prep, and it was another reason Caitlin's demand that her students sweep their divisions was absurd. But Sean felt like he was beginning to expect absurd demands from Caitlin. He also suspected the entire thing was a set-up, so she could fire him no matter what.

If he was gone, with no replacement, the lesson program would die a natural death. No one would blame her for selling off the lesson horses in a hurry.

Was he just a scapegoat for Caitlin's unpopular next move?

He looked up as he closed the last stall door and saw Caitlin herself stalking down the aisle, her gaze sweeping along the stalls like a hawk seeking prey. When she saw him, her gait quickened. That meant *he* was the prey. Sean hung up the horse's halter and steeled himself for the ticking off she'd probably been planning all day long.

"You did well today," she said. "Looks like a couple of the barn teams will finish in the top six."

"Oh," was all he could manage. What did a person say when he was getting fired? "Thanks? I mean, that's good."

"I'm guessing Nadine told you that this was a big test for you."

"Nadine?"

"Oh, don't play coy with me. I see the way you two look at each other. You weren't fooling anyone. And that's what set off Martha, in case you're wondering. That's why she was out there this morning trying to stuff money down my throat for that horse. The one you were supposed to be training?" Caitlin cocked an eyebrow.

"Yes. Well. Nadine and Finn just hit it off really well—"

"It's fine." Caitlin brushed aside his concerns like a gnat hovering around her face. "Look, it's not all bad news, is what I wanted to say. The event did really well, and I'm pleased with everyone involved—yeah, you, included! But it doesn't change a few things. I've been working on a lot of projects off the farm—"

As if he hadn't noticed. As if they all hadn't noticed.

"—And I'm scaling things back. I admit, I expanded the business too quickly. I didn't have the right model to make money with a full barn, and now these stalls are costing me. Big. I need free cash for some other investments around town."

Caitlin kept talking, the business-speak Sean knew from talking to his father, the only language that man had ever really spoken fluently. He half-listened, but he was really waiting for her to get to the parts that mattered: the students, the horses, Nadine's job. And yeah, his job, too.

"The therapy program is funded for another six months, thanks to the hunter pace. But it's moving to Meadow Farm, which is closer to Veronica's base, anyway. I'm leasing them the ponies they want. The others are selling. The lesson program can keep going for boarders, but the sales horses are heading out to brokers with more reach," Caitlin continued, finally capturing his interest. "And that's where your job changes a little. It won't be full time anymore. When we're down to just boarders, I foresee you working part time. So, we might want to work out a freelance contract that works better for you."

"Oh," Sean said again. That was fine. He would be fine. "And what about Nadine's job?"

"There will be fewer horses. Less work. But someone still has to run the barn. So it's still hers if she wants it," Caitlin said, shrugging. "I haven't talked to her yet." She looked him over. "Do you want to tell her?"

"I'll give her a head's up," Sean decided. "But it's your dirty work, boss."

Caitlin laughed. "Yeah. It is. Shoot me a text when she's ready."

Sean watched her walk off down the aisle, head high and phone out, already moving on to the next order of business. She'd just explained the end of Elmwood Equestrian Center as they all knew it, but she wasn't bothered about the changes at all.

Just like his father hadn't been bothered when their home was about to become a memory.

Sean wondered how he'd ended up working for someone so similar to his father. It must have been a psychological thing—he could probably work it out with a therapist; he'd probably *have* to, at some point, or he'd just keep sabotaging himself.

Although, there weren't two people much more different from Caitlin or his father than Rosemary and Stephen Beckett.

He wondered if she'd asked about the riding instructor job. He wondered if she had any news.

Sean pulled out his phone. First, he'd text Nadine. Warn her, as he'd told Caitlin he would. But then he was going to check in with Rosemary.

Chapter Thirty-One

Nadine

Nadine sat perched on her folding chair and watched the hunter pace take itself down around her. Trailers were pulling out; horses were neighing; canvas tents were flapping in the rising wind. It would rain soon; a heavy, drenching rain, according to the forecasts, and that was just what Nadine's mood was crying for.

Caitlin had already left. She'd gone back to her house and left the rental companies and caterers and vendors to remove themselves from the farm at their own pace. Richie had carted in the tent and card table that had served as Nadine's office. Soon, all that would be left of the hunter pace would be this folding chair, and Nadine, sitting in an empty field beneath a darkening sky.

It felt appropriate.

She couldn't believe Caitlin was turning her back on all her plans for Elmwood. Even though she'd known, even though she'd heard the plans with Reg to move the sales horses out. And when she'd blurted it out, Caitlin had been so startled she couldn't defend herself.

"How did you know about that?" Caitlin asked, astonished.

"I followed Reg when I saw his truck coming," Nadine admitted. "And then I hid under your living room window."

"For crying out loud. This isn't a spy novel, Nadine."

"He's not trustworthy. I don't know what he was doing in your house before, while you were out at the Eastern Shore, but you can't—"

"You knew he was in my *house?*"

"Yeah. I'd taken my stuff over early, so it would be done before evening lessons," Nadine lied. "And I ran into him there, moving boxes."

"The boxes were nothing," Caitlin said. "Files, business records. To my new office."

"Your new office?"

"Above the ice cream parlor. In my new building in Catoctin Creek. Listen, I'm not scaling back Elmwood because the place is bad, or doesn't deserve my attention. I just need to do more in Catoctin Creek as a whole. I've finally figured out what I'm good at: it's helping other people grow their businesses. I can do this for the town, but only if I'm not worried about Elmwood twenty-four-seven. This was my mother's place, Nadine. I've tried to make it work because I wanted to honor her wishes, but sometimes you just have to follow your own heart."

"I get that," Nadine said softly. "I really do. And I support you if that's what you want. But Reg? Caitlin, come on. You know he's bad news. I don't care what he promised you while he was doing odd jobs for you, he will *not* place those horses carefully."

Caitlin looked at her for a long moment. "You might be right. And maybe I needed to hear that from someone who knows him better than me."

"I know him too well," Nadine said. "Trust me."

"Okay. I'll place the horses with brokers myself. It'll cost me more, but, if you're sure—"

"Positive," Nadine said, relieved.

"And what will you do? Are you staying? There will still be some boarders, and the lesson horses . . . but that leaves the place half-empty. If I keep Richie and Rose on, it won't be a full-time job."

"I'll have to think about it," Nadine said.

And that's exactly what she had been doing for the past hour. Thinking.

Sean came out as the first raindrops began to fall. "Hey you," he said, holding out a hand to her. "It's time to come inside."

She got up grudgingly, noticing the sudden chill in the wind. It brought goosebumps to her bare arms. Sean slipped off his jacket and put it over her shoulders, then picked up her folding chair. "In we go."

They were quiet all the way to her office, Nadine observing that Richie and Rose had done evening feed without her and were now trying to decide if they should turn out the horses. "Not if it's going to rain heavily," she told them. "If it lightens up, Sean and I will put them out later."

"Thanks," Richie told her. "We'll just throw extra hay."

"Volunteering me for late-night turn-out duty?" Sean smiled as he ushered her into the office, where a cup of coffee was already waiting on her desk. "You're very generous with my time."

"I know exactly how much of it you waste," she replied, flashing him a weary grin. "Thanks for the coffee. And the jacket. It turned cold quick, didn't it?"

"That's spring for you." Sean sat across from her and they looked at each other for a moment. Sitting in their old spots, but aware of the changes between them. Tonight, nothing was the same.

"Caitlin said my job is going to be part time," she blurted, just as Sean said, "I talked to Rosemary."

"Oh." Nadine blinked. "What did Rosemary say?"

"She found the right buyer for Finn," Sean said. "It's the school. She had a conversation with their board and she'll be taking over the program administration while it's getting up and running. So, she's selling them Finn. He'll move to Long Pond when the new stable is ready."

Nadine's eyes welled up, and she brushed at the tears. "Oh. That's good. I don't know why I'm crying."

"Stop. I'm not done yet. Rosemary wants us to come work there, too."

Her gaze lifted again. She didn't understand. "Work—at the school?"

"They want to get the riding program in gear this summer. We'd have to prepare the barn, buy horses, tack, everything. We'd be a duo. Property manager, riding coach package deal. No one else is living there right now, but they're going to put the teachers and administration in the new building. It's not done yet, so Rosemary said we can have the farmhouse."

Nadine's jaw dropped. She couldn't think of what to say. How had—when had—*what?*

"I told her we'd think about it."

"*Sean!*" Nadine reached for her phone, fumbling with cold fingers.

"Relax. You know Rosemary isn't going to offer this to anyone else." Sean was grinning, pleased with himself.

As well he should be, Nadine thought. She leaned back in her chair and stared at him. "I'm in shock," she said. "I think I might be dead."

"Not dead." Sean shook his head. "I don't believe in ghosts."

"Thank goodness," Nadine said, starting to laugh. "Because I hear Long Pond is full of them, and I'll need someone to protect me."

Chapter Thirty-Two

Sean & Nadine

Darkness fell as they sat side-by-side on Caitlin's porch, listening to the rain pelting down on the metal roof. Every so often, a distant flash illuminated the countryside, and Nadine would nestle a little closer to him, sometimes uttering a little *oh* if the lightning bolt was visible.

Nadine was a little afraid of storms! This was new and delightful information to Sean. Finally, something which caused the infinitely strong Nadine to ask for a little help. He hugged her tight each time the sky flickered, silently promising to protect her from all storms.

Caitlin brought out a tray of drinks and set them on the low table in front of the wicker loveseat—the same one Sean had slept on a few weeks ago, hoping to talk to Nadine the moment she came downstairs, not knowing she was at her mother's house. "A little celebratory drink," she announced. "I hope no one objects to bourbon. I was out of champagne."

"Out of champagne," Nadine murmured. "The horror."

"There's been a lot to celebrate lately," Caitlin went on, ignoring her. "Even without the hunter pace going so well. We've got Nikki's bakery opening in two weeks, and Connie found the ice cream parlor's original tiles under some old drywall . . . I really feel like since I started on this real estate journey, things have gone right for me. I hope you guys can manage to feel the same. The school sounds like an amazing opportunity."

"As long as the horses here are taken care of. I just don't want to worry."

"With you helping out some this summer, and Sean still teaching a few afternoons a week, and Richie and Rose moving the travel trailer up here, I think we'll be perfectly happy. Maybe I'll hire some teenagers to help out. Sean, I'm sure some of the students would love a part-time job."

"Absolutely," Sean agreed. "I can give you at least four who would be a big help this summer."

"There you go. See? Everything works out. And Nadine, I called Reg and told him he's off the deal. He bellyached for a little bit and then said it was better. He's going to go join his brother on some job in Tennessee. So he's out of your life for a little while."

"Oh my gosh," Nadine breathed. "That's amazing news. *Thank you.*"

"My pleasure." Caitlin laughed. "My good deed for the day, sending your arch-enemy packing. Or was your arch-enemy Martha?"

"It's hard to say. Reg has been a problem since I was a teenager. I just feel like my mom never gets her life going when he's in town," Nadine explained. "Maybe now she has a chance. She was talking to her friend Rochelle about picking up some hostess shifts at her restaurant."

"Rochelle?" Sean thought the name was familiar. "Why do I know that name?"

"No idea," Nadine said. "Are there any women in town you *don't* know?"

"Ha. Ha." He gave her a little pinch, and she squealed and slapped him.

"Enough of that, you two." Caitlin picked up her glass and regarded them with amusement. "I should have known this would happen."

"What?" Nadine asked, feigning ignorance.

Caitlin toasted them both and raised the glass to her lips. "A happy ending," she said, and drank.

Nadine looked around the sprawling front field of Long Pond with delight. The farm's namesake pond shimmered in the dawn's pink glow. A long-legged blue heron stood like a statue on the near shore, eyes pinned on the waters. In the mist swirling through the trees along the property line with Notch Gap Farm, she saw a herd of deer taking careful, mincing steps through the underbrush.

She was still taking it all in when Sean came up beside her, and she tugged him close. "Is this a dream? Are we really doing this?"

"We're really doing this," he told her, his voice husky with sleep. "And I'm really tired. Do you get up this early every morning?"

"Yes," she replied, giving him a kiss on the cheek. "And now, so do you."

"Lovely," Sean sighed, but she could tell he wasn't really moping about an earlier wake-up call. After all, with this view to wake up to, and a barn of their own to take care of, who could really complain?

"Come on," she said. "I'll make you coffee and then we have to get out and take care of our horses."

"We have exactly two horses," Sean laughed. "How long do you think it will take?"

"And then we have to go teach at Elmwood, and I have to help with evening chores." Richie and Rose took over mornings entirely; she was handling the farm with the help of a teenager on Saturdays, to give them a day off, and working evening feeding time as well as a few office hours every week. Along with everything she had to do at Long Pond, her schedule was busy—but Nadine had never felt so energized by her work.

Or so supported. She leaned against Sean, utterly content.

"We don't have to go anywhere until late afternoon," Sean countered. "We have the whole day to settle in here."

"I'm sure there's plenty to do here," Nadine laughed. She turned and went back into the house, holding the screen door open for him. "Are you coming?"

Sean looked back at her. For a moment, he was silhouetted against the brilliant morning: against the shimmering waters of Long Pond, against the yellow sun gleaming over the treetops that protected the farm from the road and the world beyond.

They were a step closer to home, and to roots which would grow deep in Catoctin Creek.

Nadine was so grateful, she hardly knew where to begin.

"Coffee?" Sean reminded her, moving out of the sunlight.

"Oh yes," she laughed. "We need coffee for sure."

The End

Christmas at Catoctin Creek

Join Rosemary and Stephen, Nikki and Kevin, and Nadine and Sean for a holiday season with heart in Catoctin Creek!

The crisp months of autumn are flying by and Catoctin Creek is booming, thanks to new businesses and the support of Caitlin Tuttle, human whirlwind and real estate investor. The new girl's school has opened at Long Pond, bringing an influx of visitors and shoppers on weekends. Nikki's bakery is thriving, Rosemary's horse education classes are keeping her busy, and Nadine and Sean are settling into a rhythm running the school riding program.

But when Rosemary's equine sanctuary is asked to take in twelve horses who need homes, she has to turn to her friends for help. As they're trying to find a way to fund an expansion of Rosemary's farm, a newcomer arrives in town. Kelly O'Connell is reporting on a missing woman in the Catoctin Mountains . . . and catching the eye of William Cunningham, the town prodigal son, who has just returned after a lengthy disappearance.

Christmas at Catoctin Creek features all of your friends from the first three Catoctin Creek novels, plus a few newcomers, a mystery or two, and a love story you won't want to miss.

Read the first chapter now!

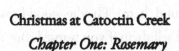

Christmas at Catoctin Creek
Chapter One: Rosemary

"Twelve horses!" Rosemary stared at Ethel Hauffmann in dismay. "You're sure there are *twelve?*"

"D'you think I miscounted?" The older woman gave Rosemary a sharp look. Then she shrugged her bony shoulders and glanced back at the dilapidated barn behind her. As if the inhabitants knew they were being watched, a thin whinny floated from the open door. "You don't want 'em?"

Rosemary felt her heart twist at that hungry neigh. Of course she wanted them—Rosemary had never seen a horse she didn't want. That was one reason she'd started an equine sanctuary at her family farm in the first place. And these twelve horses were in need, with no one to stand up for them. She couldn't say no, but . . .

How?

Shivering in the wind blowing off the gray-green Catoctin Mountains, Rosemary ticked over the facts. Notch Gap Farm was full. Her permanent horses, the ones who needed lifetime homes after years of trauma, occupied every single stall. Over the sunny Maryland summer, when she could let some horses live outside day and night, she'd accepted some horses who were suitable for adoption. But now winter was coming on, and the first snowflakes could fall any day now. Or worse, freezing rain. Sleet. The sort of elements she couldn't possibly let horses try to endure without shelter.

"I don't have a single stall," Rosemary said, spreading her hands helplessly. "I don't know what to say."

"Well, I don't know who else'll take 'em," Ethel went on, her tone matter-of-fact. "I figured you was the one to call, being the horse rescuer around here. They're good-looking horses, too. Reckon you could sell them if you wanted. But they're all hungry. Dunno when's they last ate anything besides hay."

Sell them! Ethel really had no idea what Rosemary did. She swallowed back her anger; sharp words wouldn't help her with this woman. Ethel Hauffmann had lived in Catoctin Creek for all of her fifty-six years, and she had been popular for exactly none of them. This leopard would not change her spots now.

Rosemary looked around, as if she might spot a way out of this mess in the jungle of overgrowth surrounding the tumbledown barn, or maybe in the dark fir trees ringing the dilapidated brick farmhouse a short distance away. Wan Christmas lights gleamed bravely through the pearly gray daylight; Mrs. Wayne had decorated early this year. What were the chances of that, Rosemary wondered, when the old Wayne couple wouldn't make it to Thanksgiving?

No one had really known the Waynes very well; they kept to themselves. Like their cousin Ethel, they'd lived in the rolling farmland around the small town of Catoctin Creek for their entire lives. But while Ethel and her quiet husband presided over a fairly prosperous and modern hog and soybean operation, the Waynes continued to rely on feed corn and dairy cattle, as Mr. Wayne's father and grandfather had done before him. This had never been more than a hardscrabble homestead; it was even more desolate than Rosemary remembered on this dark November day.

Of course, Rosemary had only been here once or twice, anyway; as a child, her mother and Mrs. Wayne had shared some duties on various church committees. Even then, the childless Waynes had been secretive and wary of visitors getting in their business. Her mother had warned her that even in a big-hearted farming community like Catoctin Creek, there would be a few loners who wanted to be left alone. Best to just respect them, she'd advised her wide-eyed daughter. Don't ask too many questions.

So she hadn't, for most of her life . . . but now Rosemary wished she'd asked a few more questions before she'd answered Ethel's request to meet her at the old Wayne farm. This wasn't the way she'd expected her day to go.

She'd been planning on going into Frederick and doing a little Christmas shopping, maybe picking up some new twinkle lights for the barn and front porch. With November blowing in so gray and gloomy, she thought it was time to cheer the place up a bit. She'd hummed a little holiday tune as she brushed her wavy dark hair and picked out a silly pair of candy cane earrings her friend Nikki had given her as a gag gift the year before. *Sleigh Ride.* That was everyone's favorite, wasn't it?

"Babe, I'm heading into town," she'd called, and her husband, Stephen, replied from his upstairs office that he hoped she'd have a nice time.

Then her phone rang, and Rosemary's Christmas shopping plans were derailed.

On the phone, Ethel hadn't said how many horses they were dealing with, just that she was handling the Wayne estate and they'd left behind some livestock, and she figured Rosemary was the person to call about the horses.

"Of course," Rosemary assured her, because horses always came first.

So Rosemary had taken off her nice black wool peacoat, bought on a weekend in Manhattan with Stephen, who thought even self-described country mice like his wife deserved to be pampered in the city (he hadn't been wrong—she'd had a marvelous time) and threw on a heavy old canvas barn coat, pulled on rubber muck boots over her jeans, and then drove through the wet countryside towards the old Wayne farm, waving to friends who were out hanging their own Christmas lights and setting up their plastic snowmen on their lawns. It seemed like everyone was bound and determined to cheer up this gray month with extra holiday cheer.

Rosemary hadn't known what to expect. She'd heard about the Waynes' passing, of course. It had been a surprising case. The elderly couple had passed away as quietly as they had lived, and the town of Catoctin Creek hadn't realized they were gone until Dennis Wayne failed to pay his feed store bill on time. Luckily—if there could be luck in such a situation—they had a hired farmhand to care for the animals. But when no one refilled the feed bins, he hadn't bothered to alert anyone. He'd just thrown the animals hay and gone on with his day. And when his last paycheck didn't arrive, he'd gotten into his battered old truck and headed for greener pastures.

That was the story going around, anyway. No one really knew where he'd gone. Just that Elaine from the feed store sent out her son Joe to find out why the Waynes hadn't paid their bill and why they weren't answering their phone, and he'd reported back that he'd climbed onto the porch roof, looked into the front bedroom window, and seen the two of them asleep.

" *Very* asleep?' I asks him," Elaine explained to a court of eager listeners at the Blue Plate Diner, and Rosemary had felt a prickle of horror run up the back of her neck. "And sure enough, he jimmies up that winder and he says, 'Ma, they're stone-cold.' I says, 'Joe, you get outta that house and you call the police.' And of course you all know the police took them to the hospital and checked it out and said they died of natural cause."

Joe had also checked the barns and found the horses in the stalls, hungry and thirsty. He watered them and threw everyone hay. And now it was a day later, and Ethel was telling her the horses should be her problem.

She tugged her coat a little tighter; the wind out here on the flat valley floor was sharper than back in her protected cove, her farmstead carved into the foothills. Time to get a plan in motion before everyone froze. "Well, I'll manage feeding them," she assured Ethel. "The rescue has a line of credit at the feed store, so I can tap into that. I'll make sure they're fed and watered, but can they stay here? Like I said, I don't have room for them at my farm. At least we could keep their stalls clean and turn them out here."

Ethel merely shrugged again. She was an annoying woman, Rosemary thought. No heart to speak of. She was Dennis Wayne's second cousin by marriage, but according to Nikki, who got all the gossip first from her privileged positions as proprietress of both the Blue Plate Diner and the Catoctin Cafe & Bakery, Ethel had no interest in administering the estate a second longer than was required of her. There were already rumors swirling that she'd take the first offer on the property, whether it was from a farmer or a developer.

She definitely didn't plan to take care of twelve half-starved horses. If Rosemary didn't handle the horses, Ethel would have them shipped straight to auction, and with no history or information on what they could do, they'd go for meat prices. The exact scenario which Rosemary's rescue was supposed to prevent.

"I mean, I'll find a place for them eventually," Rosemary continued, trying to keep her voice neutral. "But at first—"

"No, I don't see any good keeping them here," Ethel interrupted, swiping crossly at a strand of hair blowing in her face. "The outbuildings are falling down. Dennis didn't take care of nothing, as you can see. And if the real estate man I talk to wants the barn taken down, the barn's going down." Ethel shrugged. "I can't say for sure how long it'll even be there. Let's just get the animals gone."

"Give me a few days. I'll find somewhere for them soon, I promise," Rosemary assured her, then turned away, already tired of the woman's callousness. Sure, horses had no place on a dairy farm. Sure, they were an added stress on Ethel. But there was no reason to shrug off their misery when something went wrong. For whatever reason, the Waynes had seen fit to acquire a dozen horses. Now they needed to be fed and housed. It was a simple matter of morality for Rosemary. She couldn't understand why more people didn't see things that way.

Putting a few feet between Ethel and herself, her rubber boots squishing into the late-autumn mud, Rosemary called her husband to tell him why she'd be home late. Stephen was quiet for a moment, absorbing the news. She bit her lip as she waited; Stephen was a very good sport, but he often worried about people taking advantage of her kindness. Would he raise any objections to her taking in the horses?

Well, he'd just have to get over it, Rosemary decided. It wasn't like she had a choice in the matter. Horses in need were her job. They were her calling. And she'd been thinking about expanding the rescue's capacity for a while now. This would just speed things up.

The silence stretched out for several seconds. Then, Stephen asked in a quiet, thoughtful voice, "Would you say there's enough money in the rescue bank account to handle this many horses?"

"For a couple of weeks," Rosemary guessed, hoping it was true. "There's the account at the feed store. And I still have something left from selling Goliath to the school." The large Belgian horse had appeared like a gift over the summer, offered cheaply at an auction where Rosemary sometimes picked up former Amish workhorses. Rosemary bought him and brought him home, then immediately called Sean at Long Pond, where he was putting together the riding school program at the girl's school before the September opening. Rosemary was the head advisor on the program, but she left the horse decisions with Sean and his girlfriend, Nadine. Sean tried him out, and Goliath turned out to be saddle-broken and steady, an excellent addition to the program.

When the school opened for its first semester, both Goliath and Finn, another of Rosemary's rescues, were instant favorites with the boarding school girls. Sean said they'd never seen anything like them. That did not surprise Rosemary. Goliath was a full-blooded draft horse; Finn was half-draft, half Appaloosa. They were nothing like the expensive, lighter-boned warmbloods favored by the horse show set. She was delighted to introduce some new experiences into the girls' lives.

"Can the school use any of them?" Stephen asked now.

Rosemary didn't want to explain how awkward she felt about using her clout in the riding program to place her rescue horses. "I couldn't say off hand," she hedged. "I don't know if any of them ride. Look, maybe we can place some at other rescues. I'll have to call around, see if anyone has openings. But in the meantime, I'm it. I'll have to stay a little later here and make sure they're comfortable. The barn here is . . . not the best."

"Do what you have to do," Stephen replied, as she'd known he would, eventually. "I'll feed our guys tonight."

"Thanks, love." Rosemary was endlessly grateful for his steady temper. If Stephen had freaked out about the horses, she might have, too.

But, knowing his quiet support was waiting in the background, she could handle this challenge.

Before Rosemary went back to Ethel, she called the feed store and spoke with Tricia, the high school girl who propped up the counter on weekends. She confirmed the rescue's credit limit, then ordered feed and hay for delivery. Tricia spoke with the guys in the warehouse and promised she'd have it in an hour. "Special rush delivery for the rescue," she promised.

"Thanks, Tricia." Rosemary pocketed her phone and looked back at Ethel. The older woman was still gazing angrily across the land, looking as if she wished she could give the abandoned farm a kick in the rear. And maybe her dead cousin, too. Rosemary sighed, pushing out another wave of frustration with her breath before walking over to join her. Time for this grump to get out of here.

She said, "The feed store's sending me a delivery. They'll be here in an hour. I can handle things from here, if you want to go."

"Thanks," Ethel said, jingling her keys in her coat pocket. "Oh, by the way, did you hear the latest about the lost hiker?"

"There's an update?" Rosemary had been trying not to think too much about the story. The local news stations had reported a hiker's disappearance a few days ago, and a slow trickle of reporters from the D.C. area had made their way through Catoctin Creek, looking for background information. But the hiker wasn't from their town, and no one had anything to say other than to offer their best wishes. The journalists had scampered off to other towns in the region. "Did they find her?"

"No, but there's a person of interest," Ethel said. "The boyfriend." Her grin flashed, inappropriate and unwanted, and Rosemary felt the same sick feeling she'd gotten when she first saw the news, and again when the news vans pulled into town. Her old brush with agoraphobia rose up when she thought about being lost in the woods, and all she wanted to do was drive back behind the gate of Notch Gap Farm and stay there, safe and sound, forever.

It was a terrible impulse, one she had to fight with disappointing regularity.

"It's awful," Rosemary replied absently, looking towards the Catoctins. The mountains rose up several miles to their west, low Appalachian ridges thickly forested with drab, past-peak fall color. Even though the calendar page insisted they were in early November, many of the trees still clung to their dried old leaves.

Their matted crowns of brown and burnt orange looked forbidding against the gray sky. Rosemary hated to imagine being lost up there—and yet at the same time, she found it odd. The Catoctin Mountains were hardly uncharted wilderness. Farmland surrounded the long mountain chain on both sides. Civilization was always nearby. This implied something else was going on with this missing woman; something more than simply wandering in the forest.

That was another thing which bothered Rosemary. If she wasn't lost, where was she?

"Well, I'd better go." Ethel clearly sensed Rosemary wasn't interested in gossiping with her. "Call me if you need anything, but you don't need to give me any updates. Whatever you do with them is fine. I'll let you know if anything changes with the barn."

Rosemary watched Ethel walk across the rutted driveway and climb into her truck. The woman drove away without so much as a wave goodbye.

"What a witch," Rosemary muttered, then turned back towards the rotting barn. The sight wasn't a cheerful one. Gray boards with wide black gaps, a shingled roof peeling back at the corners, an overhang over the barnyard that was slowly sinking towards the muddy ground. The opposite of her own cozy farm, and she hated to think that horses had been locked up in there for what, a week? More? And she couldn't even let them out now. With the threat of chilly rain on the wind, and the sucking mud of the barnyard, and the tumbledown fences surrounding the farm, they'd be in even worse shape before the next morning if they were allowed out. They might even end up on the road.

But if she couldn't move them to greener pastures, at least she could cheer them up with a good grooming and some warming food. For that, though, she could use a little help. Rosemary picked up her phone again and called the barn office at Long Pond. "Hey, Nadine? I know you're busy with the school, but . . . could I borrow you?"

Read Christmas at Catoctin Creek in paperback or ebook from your favorite retailer!

Acknowledgments

It's been a pleasure taking you to Catoctin Creek over the past three books! I hope it's been a pleasant journey. While I'm saying goodbye for a little while, I can't rule out a few more visits to my little Maryland village in the future.

The writing of *Prospect* overshadowed this book a little bit, and I had to dig deep to make it happen. One thing which kept me going? The preorders! If you preordered this book, this thanks is for you. When you preorder a book, you're telling the author to keep going—someone is waiting for this story. I knew people were waiting for *Springtime*, so even though I wasn't always sure I had the story right, I pushed through the process, deleted a lot (an entire complete manuscript, actually!) and worked until Nadine and Sean had the romance and happy ending they deserved.

Many thanks as always to my Patrons, who make my work possible. Without their support, I simply wouldn't be able to invest as much time in writing my own fiction—I'd be busy writing someone else's work to pay the bills! Thank you, thank you, thank you! This list includes Heather Voltz, Cindy Sperry,

Rhonda Lane, Princess Jenny, Emily Nolan, Lindsay Moore, Brinn Dimler, Tricia Jordan, Megan Devine, Sarah Seavey, Cheryl Bavister, Zoe Bills, Liz Greene, Diana Aitch, Orpu, Mary Vargas, Kathi Hines, Kaylee Amons, Heather Walker, Ann H. Brown, Dana Probert, Claus Giloi, Jennifer, Di Hannel, Risa Ryland, Silvana Ricapito, Emma Gooden, Karen Carrubba, Thoma Jolette Parker, Annika Kostrubala, Christine Komis, Peggy Dvorsky, Katy McFarland, Amelia Heath, Andrea Parker, Kathleen Angie-Buss, Alyssa, Harry Burgh, Mel Policicchio, Leslie Yazurlo, Jean Miller, Maureen VanDerStad, Libby Henderson, Renee Knowles, and Elizabeth Espinosa.

It is such a pleasure talking with you through the writing process, working on your books with you, and collaborating every day! Thank you for being there for me!

And thanks to all of you for spending your reading time with me.

About the Author

I currently live in Central Florida, where I write fiction and freelance for a variety of publications. I mostly write about theme parks, travel, and horses! I've been writing professionally for more than a decade, and yes...I prefer writing fiction to anything else. In the past I've worked professionally in many aspects of the equestrian world, including grooming for top eventers, training off-track Thoroughbreds, galloping racehorses, working in mounted law enforcement, on breeding farms, and more!

Visit my website at nataliekreinert.com to keep up with the latest news and read occasional blog posts and book reviews. For installments of upcoming fiction and exclusive stories, visit my Patreon page and learn how you can become a subscriber!

For more:

- Facebook: facebook.com/nataliekellerreinert
- Group: facebook.com/groups/societyofweirdhorsegirls
- Bookbub: bookbub.com/profile/natalie-keller-reinert
- Twitter: twitter.com/nataliegallops

- Instagram: instagram.com/nataliekreinert
- Email: natalie@nataliekreinert.com